OUT FOR BLOOD

One of the two ranch hands with Charlie retched when they saw the burned bodies. The other cowpokes' faces paled.

All of the outbuildings had been burned to the ground. The rock walls of the ranch house remained standing, but the roof had caved in. Tendrils of smoke still rose from the charred timbers. Leland Pickett lay in the ruins of the porch. His wife and child were on the bed, two blackened lumps. Three ranch hands lay on the hardpan surrounding the house.

A cold fury seized him. He turned his eyes toward Albert Barnett's Triple B and laid his hand on the worn grip of his Frontier Colt. His face taut with rage, Charlie fought back the urge to ride over to Barnett's and call him out. He regretted his promise to Ben, but a promise was a promise. He would do nothing until Ben returned, but once he did, that sonofabitch Barnett was going to pay. . . .

Other *Leisure* books by Kent Conwell:

THE BLOODY TEXANS
THE LAST WAY STATION
CHIMNEY OF GOLD

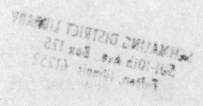

DAYS OF
VENGEANCE

Kent
Conwell

LEISURE BOOKS NEW YORK CITY

*To my Grandfather, Papa Conwell, who first showed me the
wide-open freedom of the Texas prairies.*

A LEISURE BOOK®

August 2009

Dorchester Publishing Co., Inc.
200 Madison Avenue
New York, NY 10016

ISBN 10: 0-8439-6226-7
ISBN 13: 978-0-8439-6226-0
E-ISBN: 978-1-4285-0715-9

The name "Leisure Books" and the stylized "L" with design are
trademarks of Dorchester Publishing Co., Inc.

Printed in the United States of America.

10 9 8 7 6 5 4 3 2 1

Visit us online at www.dorchesterpub.com.

DAYS OF
VENGEANCE

Chapter One

Ben Elliott clutched the wound in his shoulder, gritting his teeth against the searing pain. He could feel the warm blood seeping between his fingers. He lay motionless, gasping for breath and peering through a tangle of brittlebush and scrub mesquite at the big man wearing a Union blue uniform. A thick black beard covered the hombre's face. His kepi was pulled low over his forehead, and a black eye patch covered his left eye.

A cruel grin twisted the renegade's lips when he spotted Ben. He raised the muzzle of his six-gun and settled the sights on Ben's forehead.

The wounded Confederate tried to crawl away, but his muscles refused to move. Without warning, the six-gun roared and an orange plume burst from the muzzle.

The blast of gunfire yanked Ben Elliott from a sound sleep. He stared groggily into the darkness above, reliving the same dream that had haunted him since the war; only this time, it was even more vivid.

Another sharp spatter of gunfire followed by the

frightened bawling of cattle jerked him out of his bunk. The rumble of thundering hooves shook the ground.

This was no dream.

Clad only in his red long johns, he grabbed his .44 Colt and raced outside, anger and frustration washing over him. Shadows filled the valley below, flowing across the lighter background of the meadows—thick, dark shadows punctuated by yellow muzzle blasts. He started to throw off a couple slugs, then realized that some of his own nighthawks might be down there trying to turn the stampede.

Charlie Little stumbled to a halt by Ben's side. "How in the hell they get past our hawks, Ben?" His words formed a frosty question in the chilly night air.

Ignoring Charlie's question, Ben spun and raced for the barn. "Who in the hell knows," he shouted over his shoulder.

The rumble of the stampede grew fainter.

Moments later, the two men, bareback astride their ponies, cut across the broad meadows and down into the valley. The pale starlight barely illumined the ground at their feet, but they had no trouble following the thundering herd.

Ben felt an icy hand squeeze his chest when he realized the direction the rustlers had pushed the herd. Suddenly, he knew the answer to one of the questions that had puzzled him since the rustling began some months earlier.

Charlie pulled his roan up beside Ben and yelled over the pounding of the hooves. "The bluff. They're driving the cattle to the bluff."

Ben leaned over his pony's neck and the strong animal bunched his muscles and leaped forward.

Abruptly, the gunfire ceased, but the thunder of

the stampeding herd continued to shake the ground and stir up smothering clouds of choking dust. Ben grimaced and dug his bare heels into his dun's flanks, driving the large stallion hard, trying to force his will on the laboring animal. He leaned forward, laying his hand against the dun's lathered neck in an effort to extract every last bit of speed from the gallant pony.

Less than two miles ahead, the meadow ended at the edge of a six-hundred-foot drop to a rocky canyon below.

The dust thickened. The thundering grew louder. The two cowpokes were closing the gap, but as they swept past an ancient, twisted bristle cone pine near the end of the valley, Ben knew they could never reach the herd in time.

Even in the shade of the front porch of the Slash Bar, the early afternoon breeze was scorching, the chill of the autumn night burned away by the blazing sun. John Wills chewed furiously on the wad of tobacco. He glared at the three men before him, then focused his fiery eyes on Hank Ford, a middle-aged rancher whose body had gone to fat. That Hank had come to prefer good food to hard work was no secret.

The gray whiskers on Wills's jaw bristled as he shifted the chaw of tobacco into one cheek so he could speak. "There ain't no way I'm selling the Slash Bar, Hank Ford. You got cockleburs for brains if you think I'm giving up ever'thing I worked for."

Hank Ford hitched his gun belt up over his belly and glared back at John Wills. "Reckon that's up to you, John. That band of rustling Comancheros is going to rob us blind." He looked at Chester Lewis who was squatting next to the front door staring at the plank porch beneath his feet. "What about you, Ches?"

Chester Lewis, a lanky, dried-up Rebel who came to Arizona Territory to start anew after the War of Secession, shifted his squat from one foot to the other and shrugged. "I . . . I don't reckon I can say. I ain't really thought that much about it."

J. Albert Barnett, a giant of a man dressed in a hand-tailored suit, was as out of place with the other three ranchers as a crib-girl in a church choir. His polished shoes reflected the sun, and his plate-size hands held his Western hat, a solid white Stetson, his one concession to the blistering Arizona sun.

Barnett had listened patiently to the discussion, his face a mask of amused tolerance. "That's smart, Ches. A man shouldn't make hasty decisions he might later regret."

Jowls flopping, Hank Ford shook his head adamantly, and his belly popped back over his gun belt. "Ches, you and John there is askin' for trouble. We all been hit two, three times by them rustlers. If Pickett and Weems was here, they'd tell you the same thing. We're crazier than popcorn on a hot stove to try and hang on." He paused and looked to the south across the grassy pastures and tall pines. "Where's Ben? I thought he said he'd be here. After all, he's been hit harder than any of us. How much has he lost, a hundred, two hundred head?"

John Wills grunted. "Thereabouts."

"And you, Ches. At least seventy-five or so. Ain't that right?" Before Ches could reply, Hank continued, pointing a fat finger at John Wills. "John, you probably lost about as much as Ben. Leland Pickett says he's lost sixty or seventy. Colly Weems says about the same."

He pulled off his wide-brimmed hat and wiped his forehead with his bandanna. "All I'm gettin' at, boys, is that unless we do something soon we gonna have nothin' thanks to them Comancheros, and then the bank'll take our places." He jammed the bandanna in his hip pocket for emphasis.

Wills spoke up. "Dammit it, we don't know them rustlers is Comancheros, Hank. That's just the talk. Nobody's ever cornered one of them."

Ford grunted and nodded to Barnett. "Maybe so." He poked his finger in his own chest. "Me, I'm at the little end of the horn . . . up to my neck in mortgages at the bank." He looked around at Barnett. "I can't hold on, and I sure ain't ashamed to take Albert's offer of two dollars a head and two fifty an acre."

John Wills snorted. "It ain't a fair price. That's what I paid for this spread eight years ago, Hank. What about the time and effort I put in. You're loco to even consider an offer like that." The crusty old rancher glared up at Barnett. "No offense intended, Albert, but your price ain't nowhere near fair, all things considered."

The well-dressed rancher nodded. When he spoke, his voice was smooth as oil. "You're right, John. It isn't a fair price, but you got to remember the risk I'm taking. Two dollars might not be much for stock, but if I buy your beef and those rustlers hit my place, I lose not only the cattle but I'm out whatever I paid for them."

Hank Ford grunted. "Well, I'm taking Albert's offer. I want something for all the work I done." He looked at Ches Lewis. "What about you, Ches? You decide anything?"

Ches unfolded his lanky frame from his squat next to the front door of John Wills's ranch house. He cleared his throat. "I . . . I don't know, Hank. I got ever' cent and eight years in the place. I don't really know. Don't seem right to chuck everything."

Hank grinned sadly. "At least you'd have something, Ches. We keep on going like this and every last one of us will be busted flat. I ain't stupid. I'm selling out, and if you fellers was smart, you'd get rid of your spreads as fast as you can."

Pushing himself away from the porch post against which he had been leaning, John Wills growled. "Not me. Not while I'm alive." Tobacco dribbled down the sides of his lips and stained his gray beard. He spread his legs and doubled his fists. "And you, Ches Lewis. You don't have nothing under your hat but hair if you listen to this hogwash falderal Hank is passing out."

Hank Ford snorted. "Now, dammit, John, what I say makes sense. If you wasn't so hardheaded, then . . ."

John spun on the large bellied rancher. "You go straight to hell, you fat—"

The drumming of hooves interrupted the argument. As one, all four ranchers turned to see Ben Elliott emerge from a forest of golden aspens and into the lush meadow of bluestem, a quarter of a mile below the ranch house.

"There," snorted John Wills. "Now, we'll see what Ben has to say. He ain't no quitter like you two."

Hank Ford rolled his eyes and remained silent.

Ben hitched his lineback dun to the rail.

John Wills waved. "Howdy, Ben. Coffee? We done had some," said the old rancher. He glanced at the others, remembering his manners. "We got plenty if you boys want some more."

They declined the offer.

Ben stepped into the shade of the porch, removed

his hat, and wiped the sweat from his broad forehead. "None for me, John. Thanks."

"Glad you made it, Ben," said Hank, taking a step forward.

"Almost didn't," Ben replied, his dark eyes blazing from his sun-bronzed face, and his jaw rock hard.

A cold silence settled over the porch. "More trouble?" John Wills finally asked.

Ben tugged his sweat-stained hat back on his head and eyed the four men carefully. "Night riders run forty head of my prime breeding stock off the bluff. Killed every last one of them."

"Damn." John Wills leaned back against the porch post like the wind had been knocked out of him. "Comancheros?"

Ben shrugged. "Got no idea. All the boys saw was shadows."

Hank looked at Ches and John as if to say I told you so. "That's what I been saying. If we don't sell out now, soon we ain't going to have nothing left."

For a moment, Ben studied the fat rancher before him. He glanced at John Wills suspiciously. "Is that what this get-together is all about? You old boys selling out?"

The old rancher squirted a stream of tobacco across the porch. "Not me." He nodded to Hank and Ches. "Them two is. Colly and Leland ain't here. Colly's in Prescott, and Leland's wife is ailing."

"That's right, Ben," Hank Ford whined. "These rustlers is going to bust us all. Mr. Barnett is agreeable to buy our stock for two dollars a head, and—"

John Wills interrupted, his gray eyes boring into Hank Ford. "Which is too damned cheap." The fiery rancher looked at Ben. "Ain't that right, Ben?"

Ben stood hipshot, his wide shoulders relaxed, his arms loose at his side, the fingers on his right hand caressing the smooth walnut handle on his worn Colt. A bone-handled knife rode on his other hip. He shook his head slowly. "If I'd known this was what this whole kit and caboodle was going to be, I'd have saved myself a two-hour ride. I'm staying right where I am. I started the Key eight years back, and I don't plan on leaving."

Hank Ford blubbered. "But, Ben. What about the rustlers? What about—"

"Hank, shut up," snapped Ben. "To begin with, we got more than rustling going on here. Last night, forty head was run over a bluff. Rustlers don't steal just to kill the stock. They steal because they're too damned lazy to get out and work for their money. They can't sell dead beef."

Ben paused, studying the effect his words had on the others. Up until now, their trouble had looked like the work of rustlers, but last night put the whole problem in a different light. No, Ben felt certain there was more than rustling taking place beneath the Mogollon.

Hank shook his head. "It coulda been just a mistake on their part last night, Ben." He cast a quick glance at Barnett. "Maybe they just wasn't that familiar with your spread. You know that drop-off of yours is the only one like it in the valley."

"I thought about that, Hank. And that could be, but I don't think so." He jabbed his finger at them. "I'll tell each and every mother's son of you that starting from the time I bought that place from old John here, I've worked day and night to build me a ranch. If I lose it, I'll lose it fighting whoever I got to, rustlers, owlhoots, or the bank. But I don't plan to give it away."

A frown wrinkled J. Albert Barnett's forehead, but he quickly erased it. He cleared his throat. "And I don't blame you, Ben. Not a whit."

Ben looked at the well-dressed man, remembering the first time they had met eight years earlier. Then, Ben could have sworn he and Albert Barnett had met at some time in the past, but he later decided that it was Barnett's ingratiating manner that had struck the chord of familiarity.

J. Albert Barnett was tall, almost six-six, had a barrel chest and tree-stump arms. His physique belonged on a working man, not a wealthy cattle baron. His square face was solemn. "I feel just like you boys. Now, I know what I'm offering don't seem fair, but that's what they're worth. Same as my beeves. Sure, at the railhead, you'll get a better price. But that's the best I can do. I'm not chomping at the bit to buy you out. Truth is, I'd just as soon not, but all of us here have been friends these last six, eight years, and I've been a tad luckier, so—"

John Wills cut him off. "We ain't friends, Albert. You know better'n that. I respect you, but we ain't friends."

Albert Barnett nodded, a tolerant grin on his face. "The war's over, John. Eight years. Let it lie. We all have."

The old rancher shook his head. His gray eyes hurled daggers at the big man. "I'll never let it lie, Albert. You Yankees whupped us, and that was one thing. But when you all come in here and ride roughshod over us is another matter."

"Now, John," replied Albert Barnett patiently. "Did I ever try to take advantage of you?" He gestured to the others. "Or any of my neighbors here? I never tried to ride roughshod over anyone."

John Wills glared at Barnett, a bantam rooster standing up to a red-tailed hawk. The anger faded from his eyes. "No. Dammit, to be honest, you never did, but a lot of them Yankees made up for you," he added hastily.

Ben tried to pacify the old rancher. "Albert's right, John. He's always done fair by us. He doesn't deserve to be lumped in with them carpetbaggers and scalawags. We can't hold it against him just because he caught a few breaks we didn't."

Hank Ford nodded eagerly. "Ben's right, John. You're jumpin' to conclusions about Albert here. He's tryin' to do us a good turn."

Stroking his square jaw with his cigar-size fingers, Barnett said, "My offer still goes. I'll buy whatever you got to sell, be it beef or land. And tell you what. You change your mind in the next six months, you can have it back for the same price."

"Well, you got mine, Albert, lock, stock, and barrel," said Hank Ford. He looked at Chester Lewis. "Better take the offer while it stands, Ches."

Ches shook his head. "I got to think on it."

"Not me," barked John Wills. "I got to think on nothing."

Chapter Two

Ben swung through the forests of towering ponderosa pine carpeting the Mogollon Plateau on his ride back to the Key, eighty thousand acres of lush grass, thick forests, and streams of sweet water in the valley below the plateau. A handful of worrisome ideas filled his head.

Despite Hank's protests, Ben still believed his stock had been deliberately driven over the cliff. His past experience with rustlers was they hit one or two ranches in the area and then ran for the timber. In the last few weeks here, they had struck five ranches, not once, but two or three times. It was as if they weren't scared of being caught and hanged.

Almost like they were trying to drive the ranchers out. But why? Who would gain? Who would buy the land? Albert Barnett's words rang out in his mind. *I'll buy whatever you got to sell, beef or land.* Could Albert have something to do with the rustling? Ben shook his head and chided himself. Albert Barnett was rich enough to buy the whole valley, even the damned mesa itself if it was for sale. Besides, his place was already larger than all the other ranches put together.

Ben pulled his dun up at the edge of a sheer escarpment overlooking the lush valley where his ranch was located. No. Yankee or not, Albert had been a good neighbor for the last eight years. A man couldn't be blamed because he knew how to make money, or because he came from the North. Besides, look at the risk Barnett would take if he bought the beef. He could lose twice over if the rustlers hit him again.

Reining the lineback dun around, Ben wound his way down the narrow trail to the valley. From now on, he'd double the guards every night, and every day he'd scour the hills for sign of the rustlers. The way he read the hand he'd been dealt, his only chance to survive was to hunt the rustlers down and introduce them to a hemp party.

An hour later, Ben reined up in front of the chuck house. Charlie Little, his foreman and wartime compadre, was breaking horses in the small corral. Ben waved him in and ambled inside for a mug of thick coffee.

Old Foss Collier, the cookie, always kept a wide-bottomed pot of six-shooter coffee boiling. Ben poured two tins of coffee and plopped down at the table as Charlie, thin as a snake on stilts, limped in, a broad grin on his freckled face.

"Hiya, boss. What's up? What'd you fellers gossip about over to John Wills's?" He threw his good leg over the back of the straight-back chair and sat, reaching for his coffee in the same motion. He sipped it, puckered his lips, and arched his eyebrows at Old Foss who was busy mixing pie dough for supper. Small puffs of flour dust filled the air. "Whew. You can float two six-shooters in this concoction. What'd you do, Foss? Double the recipe?"

Without taking his eyes from his business, Foss replied in his usual wry drawl, "Same as always. One handful of Arbuckle's to one cup of water. You don't like it, don't drink it. Now, leave me be. I'm a'fixin' red bean pie for supper." Grabbing an empty whiskey bottle and dusting the dough with flour, Foss started rolling out piecrusts.

Charlie winked at Ben and grinned. A likable, easygoing jasper, Charlie always got a kick out of baiting Old Foss.

Ben grinned back at him. "You oughta stop fussing at Foss, Charlie. He just might up and decide to ride out of here one day." He watched Foss out of the corner of his eye.

Charlie's grin grew wider, running his freckles together in one big blotch. "Naw, not old Foss. Why, this here place is home to him. Besides, where else could he go and find all the fine company and genteel folks like he's got here on the Key?"

Foss never said a word, never gave a sign he heard them. He just kept rolling and folding that dough. Suddenly, Ben sneezed.

Charlie's grin vanished. He opened his eyes wide. "What day is this?"

"Monday. Why?"

He shook his head, his grinning face serious. "That's bad. Sneeze on a Monday, you sneeze for danger."

Ben shook his head in exasperation. "You and your crazy idiot superstitions, Charlie. One of these days, you're going to end up in a kettle of hot water because of them."

"Don't make light of them, Ben. You remember that time I had that wart?"

Ben arched an eyebrow, but Charlie ignored it.

"I rubbed that wart with a piece of meat and buried the meat. And you know yourself, by the time that chunk of beef had rotted away, my wart was gone."

"It would've been gone anyway. Warts ain't permanentlike."

Charlie shook his head adamantly and leaned forward, his tone low and guarded. "Oh, no. There's a lot going on that folk like you and me don't know about; couldn't understand even if we knowed about it."

Blowing through pursed lips, Ben shook his head. He knew exactly where this nonsensical argument about superstitions was headed, so he changed the subject. "The only thing you and me got to worry about is who in the hell is trying to run us off our land."

Charlie paused in the middle of a swallow of coffee. He coughed, choked it on down, and stared at Ben with unbelieving eyes. "Run us off? What are you talking about? I know we've got some rustling on our hands, but . . . run us off? I don't follow you."

Ben saw the confusion in his friend's face. Briefly, he told Charlie the gist of the meeting on John Wills's porch. "Hank Ford is selling out for sure. Chester Lewis will probably follow Hank's play. That leaves Pickett, Weems, John, and us."

"What about Barnett?"

"I'm talking about small ranchers. With the backing Albert Barnett has, he could restock his place a dozen times over. It's the four of us we got to worry about."

Old Foss had paused in his work and turned his attention to the conversation. Charlie shoved his hat to the back of his head. Wrinkles cut worried lines in the pale skin of his forehead and ran down past the sun-browned line. "You certain someone is trying to run us off, Ben?"

Ben drained his coffee and stared across the table at his old friend. "You remember back during the war when we was escorting the wagon of gold through the Mohawk Mountains back east of Yuma?"

Charlie patted his game leg. "How could I forget? Them Yankees gave me this gimp for life."

For a moment, each man was lost in his own recollection of the ambush in the Mohawks. Even after all of these years, Ben still clung to the hope of finding the butcher who killed the entire company of soldiers except for Charlie and him. He shook his head, jerking his thoughts back to the present.

"I got that same itchy feeling now. You know yourself, if the lieutenant had listened to me then, you wouldn't have that limp, and the others would still be alive. I tried to tell him things wasn't right."

"I remember," Charlie replied, his own eyes taking on a glassy look as he relived the ambush once again. "I always reckoned he was always suspicious of you 'cause you'd lived a spell with the Injuns."

Ben steepled his fingers and pressed them against his lips. He stared at Charlie. "Injun or not, I don't believe last night was an accident. I figure those night riders deliberately run our stock over the bluff. You think back, Charlie. What rustling we've seen in this valley the last eight years has been a one-shot affair. Not like this, not regular, not four or five places about the same time."

Charlie frowned. "You mean, some others got hit last night besides us?"

"No. Not last night. But remember last week? And

two weeks before that. Three or four of us been hit since then."

For several seconds, Charlie pondered the thought. "You got any idea who's behind it?"

"Not a glimmer."

Old Foss broke his silence. "If you was to ask me, I'd figure that damned rich J. Albert Barnett was behind it. Them rich folks ain't never satisfied. Always wanting more."

Ben and Charlie grinned at each other. Foss hated well-heeled ranchers. Claimed they cheated their hired hands to get ahead. Ben cleared his throat. "I don't think so, Foss. The rustlers been hitting Albert along with the rest of us. Why, he could buy us out easy enough if he wanted the spreads."

The old cookie grunted and turned back to his dough. "That don't make no never mind."

Charlie had grown serious. "You just tell me what you want to do, Ben, and by gum, I'll see it's done."

Leaning forward on his elbows, Ben said, "Two guards every night in shifts. One at the creek between us and the Slash Bar, the other at South Pass between us and Pickett. Tomorrow, you and me will try to pick up some sign." Ben paused; his black eyes grew cold and hard. The muscles in his jaws twitched. "Whatever yahoo started all this might not know it, but he has just bought into a poker game with the highest stakes he's ever seen. The only way anyone will get me off this land is feet first."

Charlie Little set his jaw and nodded.

Chapter Three

The autumn sun highlighted the distant snowcapped summits of the Juniper Peaks back to the northeast, bathing them with a golden glow, but down in the valley, night came early. The temperature dropped quickly, bringing a bracing chill to the ranch. Cowpokes pulled closer around the potbellied stove, savoring the luxury of a full stomach, a warm fire, and a batch of tall tales.

After supper, Charlie stationed the nighthawks. "Call out if you spot riders. Could be neighbors. If they ain't, fire three shots and stay hid. We'll come a-running. A couple boys will relieve you in four hours."

The night passed without incident. Come morning, the early morning nighthawks rode in just minutes ahead of John Wills.

Ben stood in the chuck house door watching his old friend ride up. He was always glad to see the older man, but he couldn't help wondering the purpose of this surprise visit. Had John Wills changed his mind? Had he decided to sell out like Hank Ford?

He stepped from the door and held up his hand.

"Howdy, John. Light and come on in. Old Foss mixed up a bowlful of saddle blankets. And we got plenty honey and venison."

Inside, Ben and John Wills sat at the table with the ranch hands. Ben was not one to keep secrets, believing the more a man knew, the better his judgment. Very little went on at the Key that every last cowpoke didn't know about, for much of Ben's business was conducted wherever Ben happened to be at the time, and usually that was in the presence of his ranch hands.

Over a plate heaped with sourdough flapjacks and soaked with sweet wildflower and white clover honey, John came right to the point. "Hank Ford went ahead and signed his place over to Barnett after you left yesterday." To punctuate his statement, he stabbed his venison with his fork.

Ben cut a chunk of venison and dipped it in the honey. "Figured he would. Hank's been looking for a way to bail out of here. But, I was surprised about Ches hedging like he did. He's always been a contrary old Reb. Hope Colly and Leland hold on." He studied the old rancher across the table from him. John Wills, head down, elbows spread, poked food down his gullet with both fork and knife.

An unbidden grin came to Ben's lips. He knew the old man had never understood how Ben could talk and eat at the same time. To John Wills, grub time was for eating, not talking. "You're not having second thoughts, are you, John?"

Wiping the honey from his lips with the back of a gnarled hand, John Wills snorted. "Not me. That's why I come over here. To lay out some plans with you."

Suddenly wary, Ben asked, "What kind of plans?"

He always went his own way, made his own plans. That lesson he had learned early on when Tin Man was killed. And his years with the Coyotero Apache reinforced that philosophy.

"About my place," John replied.

Ben relaxed as John Wills continued. "To be honest, I got me a bad feeling about what's going on. I reckon we might see some trouble from all this."

"Hell, John. I'd say we got us some trouble right now."

The old rancher shrugged off Ben's remark. "I know that. I mean, more trouble. The killin' kind."

Ben arched an eyebrow. "Hope not."

The old rancher stroked the gray stubble on his craggy face. "You and me have knowed each other since the war. If I had a son, I'd been right pleased if he'd been like you. So I figure I can ask you a favor . . . if something happens to me."

The ranch hands around the table paused momentarily, glanced at each other, then returned to their grub.

With a crooked grin, Ben replied, "Now, John. You know as well as me that the only cowpokes that are in danger of getting hurt around here are them rustlers."

"Maybe so," the old rancher replied, returning to his flapjacks. "But you know my daughter, Mary Catheryn?"

"You showed me her tintype. I never met her."

John frowned. "That's right, I forgot. Yeah, I sent her to Baltimore before you got here." He paused and shook his head. "Damn, has it been that long since she was back home?"

Ben remained silent.

John shrugged and gave Ben a sheepish grin. "I reckon

it's about time I get her back here. I guess I just got used to the once-a-year trip to Baltimore to see her. Never really thought about bringing her back home."

Ben arched an eyebrow. "She finished her schooling?"

"Yep, and then some. She went back there for her letters and numbers. When she done them, she told me about what they call 'finishing schools.' Well, what with her ma being dead all those years, I figured the child needed something like that. Me, I don't know nothing about 'finishing schools.' Hell, I don't even know what a finishing school finishes."

Suddenly realizing how he was prattling on, John Wills grinned and poked the last of his flapjacks in his mouth. While he chewed, he grew serious. "You and me been friends a long time, Ben. I don't reckon anything will happen, but if it does, look after my spread until my girl gets back, you hear? She's a levelheaded, no-nonsense woman. She can handle it then without help from no one."

Ben brushed aside John's concern. "Nothing's going to happen."

"I know, but promise me."

"Hells bells, John. You bet. I promise."

Nodding, the old rancher drained his coffee. "You got time one of these days, I got a couple green broncs I want you to see. One of 'em might make a dandy pony for my little girl."

Charlie Little cut his eyes toward Ben, who shook his head. "Can't this morning, John. Charlie and me have got us a little tracking to do."

"Tracking?"

"Yep. We're going to see if we can pick up sign of those night riders who drove my stock over the bluff."

The old rancher's face grew hard. "I hope you find them. You do, run them off a damned cliff."

Picking up the rustlers' trail at the bluff, Ben and Charlie followed it across the valley and up a rocky trail to the rim of the Mogollon Plateau over which the beef plunged. The rustlers' trail led southeast along the rim, and then abruptly cut east and vanished.

Charlie Little pulled his blue roan to a halt and stared in disbelief at the edge of the cliff overlooking the sprawling valley far below. "What the hell is going on here?"

Ben pulled up beside him, his dark eyes studying the tracks they had been following, tracks that led through the pine and aspen, right up to the rim of the plateau and then disappeared. A wry grin tugged at the corners of his lips.

Charlie snorted. "I don't see nothing to grin at, Ben. We've been hoodwinked."

Ben nodded. "And a damned good job too, Charlie. Damned good." He turned the dun in a small circle, his eyes fixed on the ground. "Whoever's behind this has been down the river more than once," he added, climbing down from his dun and studying the tracks.

"Well, what happened? They sure as hell didn't fly."

Near the edge of the bluff, Ben brushed aside the layer of aspen leaves and pine needles. "Here's your answer."

Charlie looked at the faint impressions. He shoved his hat to the back of his head and scratched his sandy hair. "What am I looking at? I can't make nothing out of it."

Without replying, Ben knelt and stared along the edge of the bluff. His theory concerning the rustling was holding up. He shook his head and knelt on the ground. He picked up a broken branch several inches long. Picking it up, he said, "They split up here. Some rode north and the rest south along the bluff."

The wrinkles in Charlie's forehead deepened. "How can you tell. I don't see no sign."

"You won't," said Ben, turning his dun back to the Key. "There's only one explanation. They can't fly. Only birds fly. These hombres stopped here and wrapped their horse's hooves, but even wrapped hooves can snap branches like this. Then they split up." Brushing the dust from his denims, he swung back into his double-fire rig. "We're not going to find them rannies this time."

With a curse, Charlie Little kneed his roan up beside Ben's pony. "So, now what?"

"So now, I'm riding over to John's. I want to see those broncs he was bragging about." It was a half-truth. The other half was that he wanted to test his theory on John Wills. He wanted to persuade the old rancher that the rustling was not why someone was stealing the cattle, but because that someone wanted the land bad enough to exterminate forty or four hundred or four thousand head of beef.

Maybe the two of them could come up with a notion on who was behind it all.

Chapter Four

John Wills was forking a wild-eyed, bawling piebald when Ben rode up. Sticking to the saddle like mud on a hog, the burly rancher gave Ben a broad grin and dug his spurs into the squealing piebald's flanks. Dust exploded from around the sun-fishing animal's feet as they drove stiff-legged into the ground.

Nodding to a young wrangler perched on the opera rail, Ben remained in the saddle, one leg crooked around the saddle horn, watching and measuring the animal under John Wills. He fished a bag of Bull Durham from his pocket and rolled a cigarette, as always, impressed with the older man's riding skills.

Finally, the piebald had enough. The lathered animal staggered to a halt and stood spraddle-legged in the middle of the corral, his head drooping between stiff legs.

John climbed down and tossed the reins to the young wrangler. "Walk him around, Joe, if he's got anything left." He grinned up at Ben. "Howdy, Ben. Glad you came over." He nodded to the piebald. "What do you think of him?"

"Don't give that one to your daughter." He grinned.

"Hellfire, I know that. But what do you think?"

Ben studied the animal, assessing its conformation, its carriage. He took another drag on his cigarette and flipped it in the dirt. "Might be a good one if he has staying power."

"He has that," replied John Wills, shifting his tobacco to the other cheek. "Come on. I want you to see the other one, a mare."

Nodding, Ben swung down from his saddle and followed after his old friend. "The mare the one you picked for your daughter?"

"Yep," said John over his shoulder. "Ain't no way I'd turn any female loose with that piebald."

"Don't blame you."

The mare was a gentle sorrel, a perfect animal for a young woman whose riding skills had grown rusty. Breaking her to saddle would be easy. The old rancher beamed when Ben nodded and complimented his choice of horses for his daughter.

"Yep. Figured I'd have time to gentle her down good and proper, but that was before I got Mary Catheryn's letter. It come this morning." With a broad grin, he pulled a folded letter from his vest pocket and held it up for Ben. "She's coming out here. Next week, she says here," he said, waving the letter.

Shoving the letter back in his pocket, he nodded to the door. "Let's go get a cup of coffee. It's been on the stove three or four hours now. It oughta be just about right." He laughed. "All the boys except Joe there is out working cattle."

Later, seated at a scarred table in the chuck house and sipping the thick, black coffee, Ben told his old friend about the trail ending on the edge of the Mogollon rim. "As sure as I'm sitting here, John, we aren't dealing with plain rustlers. I don't know who, but I'd bet you a double eagle someone wants to get rid of us."

Arching an eyebrow, John Wills grunted. "I don't need no boulder to fall on me to know who that 'someone' is. Albert Barnett, that's who."

Ben shook his head. "What proof you got, John? Even a rich man's got rights. You got any evidence that Albert is behind all this?"

"Hell, no, but that don't make no nevermind. Look what he's got to gain. Right now, he owns half the territory and has got his eyes on the other half. I figure the others is going to sell, and our two places would be a feather in his cap. We got cool, sweet water and thick grass. Hell, that grass is so rich that you can grow a two-year-old calf in six months. Besides, why you taking up for Albert? You don't owe him nothing."

A grin played over Ben's features. "No, but I'd take up for you or anyone else who was accused without evidence, John. I've seen it happen too often where someone points a finger at a jasper and ten minutes later, the poor, damned soul was dangling on the end of rope." He shook his head. "You know yourself. We don't have the right to up and accuse someone, even Albert, without good cause. Besides, he's been hit just like us."

John Wills cursed and squirted a stream of tobacco on the hard-packed floor of the chuck house. Before he could speak, a clatter of hooves broke the silence. Stepping into the doorway and shielding his eyes against the bright sun, the crusty rancher watched the rider approach. "Speak of the devil, it looks like one of Albert's boys." He hesitated, then added, "Wonder what in the hell he wants."

The rider yanked his pony to a stiff-legged halt.

"Mr. Wills, Mr. Wills. Mr. Barnett sent me over for you. He wants you to come right over."

"What the hell for?" John Wills snorted.

The young cowpuncher's reply chilled Ben Elliott. "Mr. Barnett, he killed a rider trying to run off some of his stock. He thinks this might be one of the rustlers you been looking for."

John Wills looked around at Ben in disbelief. "Well, I'll be damned."

Ben shrugged. "What'd I tell you, John? It could prove downright embarrassing jumping to conclusions."

"Who's jumping to conclusions? Not me. Now, stop arguing and let's get over to Albert's and see just what that yahoo was. I'll get my pony."

A wry grin curled Ben Elliott's lips as he watched his old friend disappear into the barn. He removed his wide-brimmed hat and dragged his arm across his sweaty forehead. His life had been checkered with fortune and misfortune, but one lesson "Tin Man" Elliott had pounded into his skull was to always be certain you had the right facts, the right truth, before taking that first step.

Tin Man was a peddler who found Ben wandering among the spiny ocotillo and giant yucca deep in the Chihuahuan Desert east of the Dragoon Mountains.

Ben was about four. The peddler stuck him in the wagon and backtracked, searching for the boy's parents, but never found any sign of them, only a burned-out wagon. Two days later, he passed Ben off as his own kin to the Apaches who wanted to buy the boy and raise him as their own.

An articulate and educated man, Tin Man named the boy Benjamin Franklin after his favorite American, then tacked on his own surname, Elliott. He taught Ben to read and write using worn and battered copies of Ben Franklin's *Poor Richard's Almanack*.

Though Ben was still only a child, he knew that Tin Man was one of those rare men who fit in with any crowd, with any race, from dusky Apaches to pale-faced Easterners. Ben tagged along after him as he traded with various Indian tribes, over the years coming to feel more comfortable around the Apaches than the white man.

Like all men, Tin Man made mistakes, but when Ben was nine, the peddler made a fatal one when he climbed between his blankets only to discover a rattlesnake had claimed them first. A friendly band of white Mountain Apaches, the Coyoteros, found Ben sitting by Tin Man's body. After burying the old man, they took Ben to live with them where he remained for the next several years. To the Coyoteros, he became known as Little Tin Man.

Then came the war. Ben joined up, looking more for adventure than duty. During the war, he met Charlie Little, a Texan with a fast gun who was running from the Texas Rangers. He and Charlie became close friends, and from Charlie, Ben learned and then refined the techniques of the fast draw and accurate shot. While he never quite surpassed his mentor's skill with the six-gun, Ben could dust Ms. Liberty's nose on the double eagle two out of three times. Of course, Charlie did it three out of three.

But, he always kept in mind Tin Man's words: have the right facts, the right truth, then take the first step.

Neither Ben nor John Wills recognized the rustler. He was laid out in the barn, his clothes caked with blood and dirt. His sightless eyes gaped open. Ben noticed the exit wounds. They were in front, one in the throat and two in the chest.

Albert Barnett shook his large head. "I hoped you boys might know him."

"Nope. Never seen him before," replied Ben, looking up at the big man towering over him. "What happened?"

Barnett nodded to his foreman, a silent, sullen man with a perennial sneer on his face. "Borke and me were checking the stock back south. We ran across this hombre pushing half a dozen beeves into that box canyon near Sweetwater Creek. We called to him, but he threw a couple shots at us and then hightailed it. Borke here nailed him when he topped out on the bluff."

"He the only one?"

"The only one we spotted," replied Barnett. "Didn't hear any other horses either." He nodded to his foreman. "Hitch up a rig and carry this jasper to town. Tell the sheriff what happened."

Borke grunted and left.

Barnett ushered them from the barn. "How about a glass of ice-cold lemonade. The China boy just made some."

Both men declined and climbed into their saddles. With a cursory wave, John Wills wheeled his pony around and urged him into a walking trot. When they were some distance from the ranch, he slowed his pony, allowing Ben to pull alongside. "Looks like I was wrong about Barnett. Of all of us, he's the only one who's got his hands on one of the rustlers."

Ben nodded. "Looks that way." But he wondered. He still had the feeling he had met Barnett years earlier, but try as he might, he could not remember an occasion when he had run across the cattle baron with Tin Man, or the Coyotero Apaches, or during the War of Secession.

Chapter Five

An uneasy silence lay over the valley the next several days. The night riders seemed to have dropped from sight, but Ben continued to put out extra nighthawks every night, and each day, he and Charlie combed the valley and the mesa for sign.

"Maybe they decided pickings was better somewhere else after Barnett got one of them," drawled Charlie Little over his coffee one morning. "They probably figured we'd catch up to them sooner or later and lit a shuck out of the country."

Ben arched an eyebrow. "Maybe. Maybe not." But, in the back of his mind, he wondered. After all, just because a chicken had wings didn't mean it could fly.

The distant pounding of hoofbeats caused both men to look around. Ben squinted through the open door. In a billowing cloud of dust, a rider was racing toward them. "Looks like one of John's boys." They went out to meet him.

The young cowpoke jerked his pony to a sliding halt. "Mr. Elliott, Mr. Elliott. Come quick. Mr. Wills is bad hurt. Horse stomped him."

* * *

John Wills died before noon, and the next day, he was laid to rest beside his wife in the family cemetery a short piece from the main house. Ben and Charlie walked back to the ranch house with P. H. Hall, John Wills's foreman, an old cowpoke whose sun-darkened face was carved with forty years of well-earned wrinkles.

Behind them, Albert Barnett and his foreman, Borke, watched silently. Chester Lewis helped his wife into their rig and headed back up the valley to his spread. Colly Weems and Leland Pickett did the same.

"Damned shame about Mr. Wills," said the foreman. "He was getting too old to bust them broncs. That piebald especially." He gestured to the chuck house. "Coffee's ready."

Ben rolled a cigarette and touched a match to it. The story didn't make any sense to him. John was too good a horseman to get killed by a horse, but for the time being, he kept his opinion to himself as he stomped into the chuck house behind the foreman. "You see it happen, P.H.?"

"Nope. We was all out working the stock. Mr. Wills, he was here by hisself. We found him in the corral with the piebald." He handed Ben and Charlie their coffee.

"Thanks." Ben slipped in at the sawbuck table. He sipped the coffee, then took a long drag on his cigarette. Exhaling, he stared thoughtfully through the rising smoke. "Well, it is a damned shame, especially since his daughter is coming out here."

The foreman looked at him in surprise. "Ms. Mary Catheryn? She's coming home? Mr. Wills didn't say nothing to me about it."

Ben shrugged. "That's what he told me. Had a letter."

"A letter? We found one in his pocket, but none of us old boys could read it." He sat across the table from Ben.

"I reckon that was it."

P.H. grunted and poured his coffee into a saucer. After cooling it, he slurped the saucer empty. "Hope she don't plan on selling out," he said.

"Howdy."

The three men looked around. Albert Barnett's large frame filled the door. Behind him stood his foreman. He sniffed the air. "Any of that coffee left?"

"Sure, Mr. Barnett. Plenty. Help yourself," replied the affable foreman, gesturing to the potbellied stove.

Borke poured two cups. Barnett sat at the table beside Charlie while his own foreman remained standing. "I hope you don't think I'm intruding, Ben, but I couldn't help overhearing your discussion of John's daughter."

Barnett continued, "I know John asked you to look after his place. He couldn't have picked a better man, believe me. I have a great deal of admiration for what you have accomplished."

Ben glanced at Charlie, who rolled his eyes at Barnett's words. Ben replied simply, "John and me were good friends."

"True. And you being such a friend, I know you want to do what's best for his daughter."

"What's your point, Albert?" A straight-from-the-shoulder man, Ben quickly grew impatient with circuitous explanations.

Albert Barnett's cheeks colored. "Just this, Ben. I hope his daughter stays and runs the Slash Bar. But, if she doesn't want to stay in this part of the country, I'll make her a generous offer for this place."

Ben shook his head. "I don't figure this is the time or place for business, Albert."

"Maybe not, but life goes on. I hate it just like you that John got himself killed, but you and I both know he was too old to be busting broncs."

Ben took another drag on his cigarette and flipped it out the open door. His knuckles whitened as he squeezed the coffee cup, struggling to control his anger. Albert Barnett was a businessman first, a human being second. Making a business deal on a man's grave was no more unnatural to him than making one over a poker table. "Save your breath, Albert. John Wills would never have sold this place. I know it, and you know it." He rose from the table and stared down at the taller man. "If I suggest anything to Mary Catheryn, it will be to hold on to this place as long as she can."

Barnett shrugged. "I hoped you'd be on my side, Ben. Life out here is hard. I sure wouldn't want any harm to come to John's daughter. My way, she can go back to Baltimore and live the kind of comfortable, safe life she's grown accustomed to."

Ben ignored Barnett's last remarks. He nodded to Charlie. "Ready?"

"You bet, boss," Charlie replied, unfolding his long legs from under the table.

Ben started around the table when Borke stepped in front of him. "Mr. Barnett ain't finished yet, Elliott." The stench of dried sweat emanated from the big foreman. He wore a crooked grin on his unshaven face.

Ben stared at him, his temper boiling. In a menacing voice, Ben growled over his shoulder. "Albert, tell your sheep-dip sidekick here that in five seconds, I'm going over him or through him. It don't make no difference to me."

Borke's grin broadened, revealing a mouthful of rotted, stinking teeth. "Well, now, Mr. Elliott, why—"

Ben's fist exploded, slashing upward and catching the burly foreman on the point of his chin. Taking two quick steps forward, Ben threw a left cross that almost tore Borke's head from his shoulders. He followed with a straight right that sent the big foreman crashing through the window and left him prostrate on the hardpan outside the chuck house, a trickle of blood running down the side of his mouth. Two decayed teeth lay on the ground beside the unconscious foreman.

For a moment, Ben stood looking down at the man. He jerked around and glared at Barnett, daring the rancher to interfere.

Barnett shook his head, and in a calm voice said, "His play. Not mine. Appears he wasn't man enough to back it up."

Releasing his pent-up breath, Ben turned back to his dun. "Let's go, Charlie," he said, climbing into his saddle.

During the ride back to the Key, Charlie pulled up beside Ben. "I reckon you're feeling purty good about now, huh?" Charlie wore a mischievous grin on his freckled face.

Ben shook his head, wondering just what his foreman had on his mind this time. "What're you talking about? Borke?" He inspected the torn skin on his bony knuckles.

"At least you're talking to me. I was wondering."

Ben frowned. "You get snakebit or something, Charlie? You're not making any sense."

"Well, back there in the chuck house. Albert Barnett came right out and said how he admired you. I figured those words coming from such a genteel man like Mr. Barnett, you might get the big head and never talk to common people like me." His grin broadened.

Ben shook his head. "Between your far-fetched superstitions and your wisecracks, I don't know how you ever get any of your work done."

"I manage, boss."

Both men laughed.

They rode along the shores of the pristine stream winding through the valley below the Mogollon, enjoying the sprawling beauty of northern Arizona Territory. "What do you think she's like, Ben?"

"Who?"

Charlie looked at him in surprise. "Who? Why, Mary Catheryn."

Ben shrugged. "Who knows? Those jaspers back east live in a whole different world than out here. If she's got the common sense of her daddy, she'll work out fine. If not . . ."

"She'll have problems," Charlie added.

Overhead, a red-tailed hawk was pinned to the deep blue sky, his four-foot wings spread, hanging on the breeze that blew through the cloud-free day. Rocking in the saddle to the beat of his dun's gait, Ben watched as the great predator pulled in his wings and dropped, honing in on its prey.

"That's when we'll have to be there to help, Charlie. John only asked me to look after the place until his daughter got home. He never asked us to help her, but we will."

A few minutes passed in silence, too long for Charlie. "Hard to believe John got hisself kilt by a horse," he muttered, his words spoken more in wonder than question. "He was a damned good buster, even for his age."

"Too good," Ben replied over his shoulder.

Charlie frowned at Ben's back. "What're you saying, Ben?"

Ben pulled up and pointed out across his own valley, lush with thick bluestem and Indian grass accented by colorful slashes of scaly-barked pine and white aspen with crowns of autumn gold. "Look at that picture out there. You ever seen anything prettier?"

"Nope."

"I'm telling you, Charlie," Ben said, scooting around in his saddle and facing his old friend. "There's people who'll kill for something like this." Charlie frowned. Ben continued. "I'm not saying someone killed John, but like you said, he was too good a buster to get stomped to death. Last week, I watched him fork that piebald they claim killed him. He rode that animal to a standstill."

Pursing his lips, Ben stared at the mountains far to the west. "There's too many loose ends, Charlie," he said. "The piebald didn't kill John. Someone knocked John on the head. Then that same someone stomped him with his own animal and left the piebald in the corral."

Charlie's sunburned face wrinkled in a frown. "Barnett! Hell, the way I see it, he's the only one to gain from all this."

Ben urged his dun on down the trail. "Maybe so, but that don't make sense either. He's got enough money to buy everyone out. Truth is, he's offering a fair price, as fair as could be in times like this. And anyone with the brains to make the money the way Albert has is too smart to get involved in a killing."

Charlie shrugged. "Maybe so, but you never can tell

what people might do." He pulled up beside Ben. "You think Ches and the others will sell out now?"

"Hope not." Ben considered the old Rebel. He guessed Ches would stay and fight, not that he wanted to, but because he wouldn't let himself run. No true Southerner would ever run. Colly and Leland were another matter. Ben had no idea what action they might take.

Charlie studied Ben's profile. "What do you figure is gonna happen now?"

Scratching his broad jaw, Ben grinned. "Who the hell knows? Whatever does happen, we got to be ready for it."

Charlie chuckled. "We will be, boss. We always have. Don't worry."

Ben grinned at Charlie, then clucked his tongue, putting his dun into a running walk back to the ranch. Though the two men were the same age, Ben had always looked upon Charlie as a younger brother, but he didn't worry about him. They had lived through hell together, forging a bond only death could break.

Chapter Six

That bond began when the two cowpokes enlisted in the Confederate Army on March 17, 1861, in Mesilla, New Mexico Territory, into a company formed by self-appointed brevet General Lorenzo Wilder, who, caught up in the euphoria of war, marched them to join Confederate captain John Baylor, the unwitting beneficiary of the frightened retreat of the Union troops at Fort Fillmore.

After taking Wilder's company, Baylor decreed that all territory in Arizona and New Mexico south of the 34th parallel belonged to the Confederate States of America. His next step was to reduce Wilder's brevet rank from general to lieutenant.

The next two years were nightmares of carnage.

In December 1862, Lieutenant Wilder was killed in a pitched battle between the Federals and Confederates in Van Buren, Arkansas.

In March 1863, Lieutenant Alastair Bunyan, a conceited young man from a wealthy Southern family, assumed command of the company whose first assignment was to escort a gold shipment from Yuma to Tucson.

The first few miles out of Yuma were uneventful, but as the company crossed the barren Mohawk Valley, approaching the mountains by the same name, Ben grew uneasy.

From his years roaming the territory with the Coyotero Apaches, he had learned to trust his instincts. Now, riding point with Ray Boy Collins, a smooth-cheeked farm boy from Mississippi, he studied the desert before him, a thick, low growth of brittlebush and mesquite beneath the candelabra arms of the giant saguaros. Ocotillos waved their spiny branches ominously.

He and a thousand Apaches could have hidden within twenty feet of the patrol, but because of the darting swallows and swooping larks, he knew the trail before them was open. Then he turned his eyes to the forbidding ramparts of the Mohawk Mountains.

"What'cha see out there, Ben?" Young Collins's gaunt face was pale. His Adam's apple bobbed like a perch cork.

Ben forced a grin. "No Apache. But keep your eyes open anyway, you hear?"

The youth nodded, tearing his eyes from Ben and searching the desert before them.

Leaving Ray Boy at point, Ben rode back to the lieutenant with the request that the point push out a couple miles ahead of the patrol as a precaution.

Lieutenant Bunyan shook his head. "Stay at your position." He peered at the mountains, an arrogant jut to his jaw. "Everything looks fine to me."

Ben argued. "All due respect, Lieutenant. I know this country. That's the danger in it, the fact that it does look so peaceful. I . . ."

"That's enough, Sergeant." He glared at Ben. "I've heard about you until I'm sick of it. That's all Lorenzo

Wilder talked about. About how you lived with the savages, how you know this country like the back of your hand. I hear you even carry Injun moccasins in your war bags. Well, I'm in charge here, and I say there's no danger. So you get back where you're supposed to be and do your job. Is that clear?"

Ben's ears burned. He clenched his teeth and yanked his remount around and raced back to the point.

Two hours later, as the main body of the company creaked through a rocky canyon, the crags and peaks exploded with gunfire. A half a mile ahead, Ben and Ray Boy turned back to the patrol, but well-aimed minié balls knocked them from their saddles.

Ben hit the ground. His head bounced off the rocks and stars exploded in his head. Instinctively, he rolled into some nearby underbrush abutting the canyon wall. His eyes squeezed shut, he lay motionless, tensing as the pain from his wound pounded in his head and unconsciousness swept over him.

His eyes popped open when he heard the crunching of sand beneath footsteps. He peered through the drooping branches of the brittlebush and mesquite.

A big man wearing Union blue stood with his back to Ben.

A second man in blue ran up, thin, bearded. "We got 'em, Jake. We got 'em all."

The big man named Jake turned. A thick black beard smothered his square face. A worn kepi was pulled down over his forehead, and a black patch covered one eye. "Anyone still alive?"

"A couple."

"Kill 'em. We don't want no witnesses."

"Whatever you say, Jake."

"What about them two on point?"

The second man grinned. "Them too, I reckon. I told you, Jake. We got them all. The gold is ours."

The big man glared at the smaller man. "Make sure about them two on point. I . . ."

A muffled groan interrupted him. His six-gun leaped into his hand as he jerked his head around, trying to locate the source of the moaning.

Ben froze.

The big man in blue eased toward a cluster of boulders. He peered over one and a cruel grin twisted his face. "Well, well, well. Look here. A Johnny Reb." He cocked his revolver.

A faint cry cut through the hot, still air. "No, no. Please."

Ben tried for his own six-shooter, but two booming explosions filled the air before he could palm it. He dropped his forehead to the sand and bit his lips to keep from crying out.

The bearded giant turned to the smaller outlaw. "Now git out there and make sure that other point rider is dead, or I'll put you in his place. Make no mistake about it."

"Okay, Jake . . . I mean, yes, sir, Mr. Barnes. I will. Don't worry."

Jake Barnes looked around one more time, then started back down the valley.

Ben sneaked a glance over his shoulder. Behind him, a small fissure, covered by mesquite, split the granite wall of the canyon. Ben crawled inside and passed out.

The sun was peering over the granite ridge to the east when Ben awakened the next morning, his shoulder stiff and sore, his head throbbing. He sat up and inspected the wound. Luck had been sitting on his shoulder. The minié ball had struck the deltoid muscle in his shoulder, tearing out a chunk of flesh, but damaging no bones. He had a knot the size of his fist on the back of his head.

Moving cautiously, Ben eased from his hiding place and peered over the boulders. His blood ran cold when he saw the stiff body of the youngster from Mississippi, his face blown away.

Ben set his jaw and slipped back down the canyon, wondering if any of the patrol had survived; but when he rounded a bend and spied the rag doll bodies of his company sprawled all over the canyon floor, his hopes sank, and he had to force down the gorge in his throat. At his approach, buzzards lumbered into the sky, beating their cumbersome wings frantically. He resisted the urge to fire at them. They settled high on the surrounding crags and waited patiently.

A soft moan in the brush to his left caused Ben to jerk around. He pulled his revolver and listened. Then he heard it again. Stealthily, he slipped through the brush in the direction of the sound.

Peering over a boulder, he saw nothing, but then a faint movement caught his attention. He peered through a cluster of undergrowth and spotted a pair of boots sticking out from under a granite shelf. Someone was alive. His hopes rose.

"Who's under there? It's me, Sergeant Elliott."

The boots moved, the heels of one digging into the sand in an effort to pull the body out. A muffled voice called out. "Ben? Ben, it's me, Charlie."

Quickly, Ben clambered over the boulders and grabbed his friend's feet and pulled. Charlie yelped. "Not so hard, Ben. The right leg hurts bad."

Gently, Ben pulled his friend from under the ledge.

Charlie grimaced, his freckled face pale and drawn. Ben helped the wounded man into the shade of a granite slab and inspected his leg. The minié ball had shattered Charlie's right leg below the knee. Ben set the break. "Damn. Wish to hell we had a doctor here. I'm afraid you're going to be limping on that leg from now on, Charlie."

Forcing a grin, Charlie muttered, "I don't reckon that would hurt my fiddle playing, huh?"

Puzzled, Ben frowned. "No. I don't reckon so, but I didn't know you played one."

Charlie grimaced in pain and forced a laugh. "I don't, but it's a comfort to know it won't hurt none if I ever take up fiddle playing."

Shaking his head at Charlie's quip, he made the injured soldier as comfortable as possible; then Ben eased back down the canyon to see if anyone else lived.

They were all dead.

The bushwhackers had taken everything, gold, wagons, horses, weapons, and most importantly, water. Ben closed his eyes and his body shuddered in anger. Slowly, his anger faded, replaced with a cold and deadly resolve. One day, he would find the cold-blooded killers and make them pay.

Hauling Charlie on a travois, Ben followed the trail out of the canyon to the valley. A wry grin curled his cracked lips when he spotted the barrel cactus along the trail, its ribbed sides stretched tight with water.

That night, they quenched their thirst with the pulpy flesh of the cactus and satisfied their hunger with four quail Ben had trapped. After dark, instead of hiding his fire, Ben built it up, hoping to catch the attention of any roaming Apaches.

"I hope you know what you're doing," Charlie muttered between clenched teeth. Sweat beaded his forehead.

Near midnight, a band of Mescalero Apaches found them. Two of the party had once been Coyotero, but, following Apache tradition, they became Mescalero when they had married into the tribe. They remembered Ben.

With the Apaches' aid, Ben and Charlie reached the army post in Tucson three days later.

Ben's wound quickly healed, but the memory of the bloody slaughter back in the canyon festered and grew. Each night in his dreams, he saw the big man with the patch over his eye wheel and palm his six-gun in a lightning-swift move, a move faster than Ben had ever seen, and each night, Ben awakened soaked with sweat. Sooner or later, he would find the butcher and kill him—or be killed.

But the large man with the patch over one eye completely dropped out of sight. Ten years later, the dreams had become less frequent; but Ben, absorbed in building his ranch, from time to time still wondered of the whereabouts of the killer.

Chapter Seven

The young lady in a black riding habit stood on the edge of the porch of the Slash Bar ranch house. She pointed an accusing finger in Ben's face, red blushes of anger coloring her milky white cheeks. "You, Mr. Ben Elliott, I hold responsible for the death of my father. Had you not talked him out of selling the ranch to Mr. Barnett, Father would still be alive." Mary Catheryn Wills paused, her green eyes fierce as the violent thunderstorms that rolled through the valley and battered the mountain peaks. "I don't need your help, and I will never forgive you."

Behind her, a pasty-faced man watched through the window, an eyebrow arched.

Ben stood silent under the tongue-lashing, telling himself that her reaction was simply grief. Once it was out of her system, she would begin to think rationally. Charlie Little, standing by his side, started to refute her words, but Ben nudged him with an elbow.

P. H. Hall, the prune-faced old ranch foreman, spoke up. "Mr. Elliott ain't really to blame, Ms. Mary Catheryn. Some of the ranchers sold out and some didn't."

She shook her head, her fiery red curls bouncing.

"I don't care, P.H. As far as I'm concerned, Mr. Elliott is to blame." She hesitated, tilted her chin, and deliberately turned her back on Ben. "And tell him he is not welcome on the Slash Bar ever again." Her dress billowing out behind her, she stormed into the house, slamming the door behind her.

P.H. shrugged his shoulders. "Sorry, Ben. She's just wrought-up with grief right now."

Distant hoofbeats cut off Ben's reply.

The imposing figure of J. Albert Barnett forked the first pony. Behind him rode his foreman, Rafe Borke. Ben shook his head. Barnett sure didn't waste any time.

Barnett pulled up at the hitching rail. "Morning, Ben, Charlie, P.H." He wore a smug grin. "You boys are out early."

"Morning, Albert. Yep, we heard Ms. Mary Catheryn had come in, so we came over to welcome her," Ben replied.

Barnett climbed from his saddle and wrapped the reins around the rail. Borke remained on his pony, a long-haired mustang with a hammer head. "Well, now. That's the very reason I came by, and to offer her any assistance she might be in need of," he added.

Not one of the three men on the porch believed him. He had come to make Mary Catheryn Wills an offer for her ranch, pure and simple. And the only help J. Albert Barnett would give her was the loan of a buggy to carry her off the ranch.

The front door opened. A comely, though rotund, Mexican señora stepped onto the porch. She glanced uncomfortably at Ben, then spoke to Albert Barnett. *"Buenas tardes,* Señor Bar—"

"Why, you must be Mr. Barnett. How good to meet

you," said Mary Catheryn, sweeping onto the porch and offering her hand to the cattleman. "Let me introduce you to my fiancé," she said, turning to the pasty-faced man who had stepped from the house. "Mr. Zebron Rawlings, of the New York Rawlingses," she added, her tone haughty. Her flashing eyes cut defiantly toward Ben.

Barnett and Rawlings shook hands. For a brief moment, their gaze locked, then Rawlings quickly turned to Ben and Charlie. "Gentlemen." He nodded, but did not extend his hand.

Ben returned the nod. Rawlings was tall and thin, his complexion sallow, the kind most jaspers acquired by long hours spent in a saloon. His fingers were long and thin, made for a deck of cards or the butt of a six-shooter, and the black six-gun on his slender hip looked mighty worn.

Charlie glanced at Ben, who gave a terse shake of his head. "I just rode over to see if you need anything, Ms. Wills," said Albert Barnett. "Your father and I were good friends."

Mary Catheryn's eyes gloated with smug satisfaction at Ben. "I'm glad you're here, Mr. Barnett. You've saved me the trouble of sending for you."

Barnett's grin faded momentarily, then reappeared. "Any way I can be of service."

Tossing her head, she said, "Yes. I want you to make me an offer for the ranch."

For a moment, everyone was silent, stunned by the suddenness of her declaration.

Barnett stepped forward. "Certainly, Ms. Wills." He shot a look at Ben. "But, the porch is no place for business, do you think?"

Chin tilted, she spoke to the housekeeper. "Teresa. Coffee and cookies, please." Mary Catheryn gestured to the door. "Won't you come in, Mr. Barnett."

"Hold on a minute," said Ben, taking a step forward.

Zebron Rawlings stepped in front of Ben. "This, sir, is none of your business."

The hair on the back of Ben's neck bristled, but he suppressed his anger and ignored Rawlings. He looked at Mary Catheryn. "Ms. Wills. Contrary to what you might think, your father never asked me to help you."

The red-haired young woman arched an eyebrow. Ben continued, "What he asked me to do was look after the Slash Bar until you got here. He said you was level-headed enough to run it then. I knew John Wills for eight years, and I never questioned a thing he said. I don't question him now. He thinks you can run the ranch; I believe him. Just don't sell him or this place short."

A frown wrinkled her forehead. "And just what do you mean?"

Zebron Rawlings took her arm and tried to guide her into the ranch house. "Don't pay any attention to him, Mary Catheryn. He . . ."

Eyes flashing, she jerked her elbow from his grasp. "No. I want to hear what Mr. Elliott has to say." Sarcasm edged her voice.

"Just this, Ms. Wills. Albert Barnett here offered your pa two dollars a head for the stock and two fifty an acre for the Slash Bar. Why, in Tucson or Prescott, you can get two, three times that price."

"Mr. Barnett's offer is a fair price, Ms. Wills," said P. H. Hall, her foreman.

Ben glanced at P.H., puzzled. Before he could respond to the question P.H.'s remark raised, Albert Barnett interrupted. "But, she isn't in Tucson or Prescott, Ben," he said, a strained tolerance in his voice.

Ben turned back to Mary Catheryn. "I can't deny that Albert's right, but there are folks there looking for ranches. You won't have any trouble finding a buyer."

For the first time, a hint of indecision knitted her eyebrows. Ben continued, "All I'm saying is that you owe it to your pa to get the best price possible. I'm not trying to take anything away from Albert. He's always done right by us. He wants the place, fine. Let him match the best price."

For several long seconds, Mary Catheryn Wills stared at Ben, her green eyes blazing defiance. Without a word, she spun on her heel. "Come along, Mr. Barnett. Let's talk business."

Giving Ben a smug grin, Albert Barnett followed the young woman into the house.

Disappointed, Ben watched as the door closed behind them. He shook his head. "John is turning over in his grave," he muttered. Charlie Little agreed.

Old Foss whipped up a whopping supper of steak, potatoes, beans, whirlups, and bird's-nest pudding, but Ben had little appetite.

"You did the best you could, boss," said Charlie. "Couldn'ta done no more."

Ben agreed. "I just hate to see everything John worked for be taken over for no more than a handful of silver."

Not even the broad golden strokes of the sunset across the sweeping sky could pull Ben Elliott from his depression. After a last cigarette, he kicked off his boots and crawled into his bunk.

Chapter Eight

The next morning during breakfast, one of Ben's north-line shack hands came boiling across the valley, laying the leather to his pony. "Ain't that Two Bits?" Charlie gestured with his fork at the oncoming rider.

"Looks like it," Ben said, recognizing the bantam-size rider's habit of banging both legs against his pony's belly like a chicken flying for its life.

Two Bits jerked his pony to a halt and hit the ground running. "Rustlers, Ben. They hit last night. Monk's following their sign. I come after you."

The rustlers left a broad sign, one of them riding a pony with a nail missing from a shoe, the right front it appeared. Periodically, Ben pulled up, studying the sign for that particular shoe. Ahead, he spotted Monk squatting, his finger tracing an imprint on the ground.

Monk grinned up at them, revealing a single tooth. "This is them owlhoots' trail, Ben. No doubt about it. Crossing over to the Slash Bar."

"Then, I reckon we best stay on their tail."

As Ben and his hands dropped down off a small

mesa bordering Wills's ranch, the Slash Bar, a handful of riders emerged from a stand of ponderosa pine to intercept them. A woman rode at the head.

Mary Catheryn Wills!

Ben frowned. What in the hell was she doing out here? He figured she'd have already been on her way back to Baltimore with Zebron Rawlings and a suitcase full of money. Quickly scanning the riders behind her, Ben failed to see Barnett or Rawlings. His frown deepened.

She held up her hand, and Ben reined in his men.

Instead of the fancy riding habit, she wore ranch clothes, soft wool pants, linsey-woolsey shirt, and buckskin jacket. A flat-crowned, flat-brimmed black hat sat cocked on her head, snugged down by a lanyard under her chin. He nodded, feeling none too friendly. "I figured you'd be on the way back to town by now, Ms. Wills."

A faint smile curled her lips. "Why is that, Mr. Elliott? Because I'm a woman?"

Ben wasn't quite sure how to answer her question. He just shrugged. "That isn't important." He gestured to the sign before them. "Someone hit my ranch last night. Their trail cuts across the Slash Bar here."

Her faint smile faded into a hard frown. "My place too. Fifty head, P.H. says," she replied, glancing at her foreman.

Her words surprised Ben. "Your place? But, I thought you . . . I mean, you and Albert . . ."

"I am not a helpless female, Mr. Elliott. Regardless of what you might think."

Ben glanced at P.H., then back to her. "You didn't sell out last night?"

"No."

A grin sprang to his face. "You're keeping the Slash Bar?"

"For the time being."

The grin faded.

She continued. "Oh, I'm going to sell it, Mr. Elliott. But, I'm no flighty, foolish schoolgirl. I must admit you were right about the selling price. Mr. Barnett was trying to take advantage of the situation, but that's just business. I've sent word to Tucson and Prescott that the ranch is on the market. Mr. Barnett objects, but if he plans on purchasing the ranch, he will meet my price." She hesitated and dropped her eyes momentarily. "I apologize for being so rude yesterday. I was upset. How well I know my father had a mind of his own. Neither you nor the good Lord himself could have persuaded Father to do anything he didn't want to do."

Ben was speechless. She had fooled him good. Instead of the empty-headed schoolgirl, she appeared to be a hardheaded businesswoman, but then, John Wills had said as much. An unbidden grin came to his face when he remembered his old friend's words.

"Did I say something humorous, Mr. Elliott," Mary Catheryn asked.

His grin broadened. "No, ma'am. I was just remembering what your pa said about you."

Her eyebrows knit in puzzlement. "Oh?"

"Yep. He said you were a levelheaded, no-nonsense lady, and you could handle things without no one's help. I reckon I might have forgotten that little tidbit of information. If so, I hope you'll accept my apology."

Mary Catheryn Wills smiled at Ben. "Only if you accept mine."

The two parties pushed on after the rustlers, moving

north across the eight-mile breadth of the Slash Bar. Midafternoon, they crossed the line between the Slash Bar and Barnett's ranch, the Triple B, eight hundred thousand acres of timber and grass.

The rustler's trail blended in with sign from Barnett's stock.

Ben pulled up, squinting at the trail before him, searching for the shoe with the missing nail. He found it along the edge of the trail. Tracking was much slower now, for the broad sign indicated several head of cattle departing the main trail at various locations. Each time stock veered off, Ben sent riders to follow the sign. He planned on bulldogging the trail of the jasper riding the horse with the missing nail.

Not long before dusk, Ben, Mary Catheryn, Charlie, and the last two hands topped out on a small rise overlooking Barnett's ranch house and outbuildings. The once broad trail had thinned, but the remaining tracks led directly to the ranch.

Charlie pulled up beside Ben. He rested his hand on the butt of his Frontier Colt. "What do you think, boss?"

Ben kept his eyes on the ranch house. "I think we'd damned well better watch—" He hesitated and glanced sheepishly at Mary Catheryn. "I'm sorry, Ms. Wills. I meant we best watch our step from here on in."

Mary Catheryn looked from one man to the other, her brow knit. Slowly, her eyes widened in understanding. "You mean . . . You think Mr. Barnett . . ."

"I don't know," Ben replied, interrupting her. "All I know is the trail leads to his place." He shucked his six-shooter, a Colt Army, only a year old. He spun the cylinder and inserted a .44 cartridge in the empty chamber. "We don't need surprises." He holstered the Colt.

Charlie and the two Slash Bar hands followed suit.

With a cluck of his tongue, Ben urged his dun down the rise and across the meadow to the ranch house. Barnett's burly foreman, Borke, poked his head from one of the bunkhouses as Ben approached.

Borke, his hat shoved to the back of his head and sucking on a stem of grass, sauntered out to meet the oncoming riders. He halted in their path and faced them. A two-day stubble of black whiskers darkened his square jaw. His small eyes flicked to Mary Catheryn, then settled on Ben, blazing with hate.

"Whatta you want, Elliott?"

"Not you, Borke. This time I want to see your boss, Barnett."

Borke rolled his shoulders. He looked at the hands who had followed him from the bunkhouse. A leer split his face, revealing the gap left by the two teeth Ben had knocked out. "He ain't here. Come back tomorrow."

Ben glanced at the ranch house in time to see a curtain fall back into place. A spurt of anger burned his ears. "Then you'll have to do," he said, his eyes fixed on the foreman's. "I come to look at the animals in your barn."

Borke snorted. "Forget it, Elliott. The only place you're going is off this spread." He reached for his six-gun. "Now, git before I . . ."

"No. You git." Ben hissed and spurred the dun at Borke.

"What the . . ." shouted the burly foreman, jumping aside.

Ben yanked his boot from the stirrup and smashed Borke upside the head as the dun shot past. The foreman fell like a tree.

Wheeling the dun in a tight turn, Ben unleathered his Colt and pulled down on the Triple B ranch hands.

"Steady, boys. Just don't you reach for those hog legs. I don't want trouble."

"Well, Ben, it seems you got a funny way of showing it," said a laconic voice from behind. Albert Barnett stood on the porch of his house, his thumbs hooked over his belt. He looked at Mary Catheryn. "Ms. Wills." Then he nodded to his foreman on the ground. "Seems like you already found some trouble, Ben."

A crooked grin curled one side of Ben's lips. "Borke there? He wasn't no trouble, Albert. I hope you aren't either. At least, you came out from behind the curtains," he added, his voice tight with anger.

Remaining cool and implacable, Barnett arched an eyebrow. "Well, Ben, whether it's trouble or not all depends on what you're after."

Ben nodded to the barn. "I want to check the animals in your barn, Albert. Any objections?"

"Not especially. Mind telling me why?"

"Rustlers. Hit me and the Slash Bar. We followed the trail to right here."

For several seconds in the growing dusk, J. Albert Barnett studied Ben. With a sly grin, he grunted. "Help yourself."

Ben started for the barn.

Barnett spoke to Mary Catheryn. "Fresh coffee's in the house, Ms. Wills. You're welcome to come in and relax while Ben does his job." He called to Ben. "Night's coming on. There's lanterns in the barn."

Two dozen jittery horses pranced around the corral. As soon as Ben entered the enclosure, he knew he would not find the one for which he searched. There was no stink of fresh sweat, but just to make sure, he checked them all.

After turning the last pony back into the corral, Ben

shook his head at Charlie. "Well, that's got me buffa-loed. The tracks came right up to the hardpan. I'da bet that cayuse would have been filling its belly in here."

"If it ain't in here, then . . ."

Ben nodded. "Grab a lantern. Let's check outside."

For the next few minutes, they searched the edge of the hardpan to no avail. Finally, Ben called a halt. "Let's come back in the morning. This light's so dim, we could be stomping all over the tracks."

Barnett and Mary Catheryn were waiting on the porch for Ben and Charlie. Borke, holding a rag to the side of his head, stood behind his boss, glowering. "Didn't figure you'd find what you were looking for, Ben," said Barnett pleasantly. "I could have saved you some trouble if you'd asked."

"How's that, Albert?" Ben rested his palms and the saddle horn and leaned forward.

"Rustlers hit us early this morning." He gestured to the hardpan in front of the ranch house and barn. "Nervy jaspers too. They drove the stolen cattle right across the yard out there. That's why you followed them up to my place here."

Ben stared at Albert Barnett, realizing that he had made a fool of himself. The one angle he had not considered. "How many head did you lose, Albert?"

"A hundred or so. Lost the trail on the rim."

While the two men spoke, Mary Catheryn climbed into the saddle.

"We'll come back tomorrow and see about picking up the trail," said Ben. "It's time we stop these yahoos."

To the east, a full moon rose over the Mogollon Rim. Albert said, "It's getting late. You folks are welcome to spend the night."

Ben replied. "Thanks, but we'll ride on." He looked at Mary Catheryn. "If you want, we can come back tomorrow for you."

"No," she replied. "I'll ride back with you."

During the ride back to the Key, Ben said little. His thoughts were on J. Albert Barnett. The more he was around the big man, the more he was certain he had known him somewhere long in the past.

Chapter Nine

After leaving Mary Catheryn and her riders at the Slash Bar, Ben and his riders urged their ponies into a running two-step, anxious to reach the Key.

Within minutes after Ben and his riders rode into the ranch, a cloudburst roared through the valley, erasing all sign of the rustlers. And just before a drizzle-soaked dawn, a band of night riders came whooping down from the mountains, filling the night with gunfire and setting Ben's barn ablaze.

Staring at the blackened, but still-standing log walls of the barn the next morning, Ben rolled a cigarette and took a deep drag, sheltering the cigarette from the steady drizzle.

"We was lucky it rained," said Charlie, more to himself than Ben or the bone-weary ranch hands slogging through the mud to the chuck house for coffee and grub.

"Maybe," replied Ben. "Maybe the raiders hit because it rained."

Charlie frowned. "You lost me on that one, Ben. You mean, you think they waited until it rained, then set the barn on fire? Hell, they'd know it wouldn't burn."

Ben took a deep drag off his cigarette and dropped it into the mud at his feet. The butt hissed, and a tiny thread of smoke drifted upward. He nodded. "I wouldn't be surprised to learn that some of the other small ranchers got hit last night." He arched an eyebrow at Charlie. "Send some boys to the Slash Bar, to Colly, Ches, and Leland. See if they had trouble. If they did, and if they want to do something about it, tell 'em to meet me at Pinyon Lake up on the rim a couple hours before sundown today. The lake is about as central as we can get."

Charlie frowned. "What about Barnett?"

Ben drew a deep breath and pondered the question a moment before shaking his head. "Not this time."

"What you got in mind, boss?"

"You'll see, Charlie, you'll see."

Albert Barnett rose from the wing-back chair, tugged his woolen vest straight, and filled a fluted glass with red port wine. He sipped it and stared across the room at his foreman. "Pinyon Lake, you say?"

Borke, hat in hand, nodded. "Yeah. Sometime this afternoon."

Barnett pursed his lips and stared out the window. Below, the lush valley spread for miles, a valley so rich in nature's bounties that a man could search the world and find none better. He nodded slowly. Soon, all of which he had ever dreamed would be his. Power. And power came from the land. The more land, the more power. "He'll be at the meeting, won't he?"

Borke grunted. "Yes, sir. Soon as it's over, he'll let us know what's going on."

Barnett turned back to his burly foreman. "Make sure nothing goes wrong." His black eyes bored into those of his foreman. "It does. I hold you responsible. You understand?"

Borke gulped and nodded. "Nothing will. I promise."

"Good," muttered Albert Barnett, turning back to the window and gazing out across his holdings. Yes, everything was going as he had planned. Arizona Territory one day would be a state, but until then, immense fortunes could be taken by those wielding the most power, and power came from the land.

He had already begun to smooth the road ahead with a few dollars judiciously placed in the right hands. The Republican, Grant, would stay in the White House another four years, and talk was that Hayes, also a Republican, was a certainty for the next four. Republicans in office assured no changes in the territorial administration. That gave Barnett eight years to build his fortune.

Barnett glanced over his shoulder. Borke stood rooted to the floor. "What else?" demanded Barnett, impatient with his dull-witted but dangerous foreman.

"Do we go out again tonight, Mr. Barnett?"

Squeezing the wine glass until his knuckles whitened, Albert Barnett suppressed his temper, reminding himself he couldn't expect Borke to think more than ten minutes ahead. Releasing his pent-up breath, the cattle baron shook his head. "No. Tonight, you and the boys take some time off. Relax. Our friends have their hands full for the next few days. Then," said Barnett, holding the half-empty wine glass in a toast. "Then, I'll deliver the coup de grâce."

Borke's thick eyebrows ran together in a frown. He

shook his head slowly, clearly puzzled. "Who's she, boss? I ain't never heard of no woman around here named Grace."

Albert Barnett stared at his foreman for several disbelieving seconds. He closed his eyes and blew out a long breath. "Never mind, Mr. Borke. Just you go on back and tell the boys to stay put for the next few days."

Like a pet dog, Borke nodded eagerly as he backed out of the room.

Sipping his wine thoughtfully, Albert Barnett stared after his foreman, dreaming once again of the power coming ever closer to his grasp. Just a few more careful steps, and every inch of land, every mountain, every valley, every canyon for thirty miles in any direction would be his.

His eyes glazed over as he dreamed of his kingdom. Thirty-six hundred miles square. Thirty-six hundred sections, and at six hundred and forty acres per section, he would be the sole owner of over two million acres.

He studied the fluted glass of red port with a smug grin on his lips.

Not bad for a Union deserter.

Chapter Ten

The water of Pinyon Lake was a pale blue, blue like a robin's egg. The change in elevation dropped the temperature a few degrees, giving the air a bracing chill.

Ben and Charlie were the first to arrive. After ground-reining their ponies and loosening the double-fire leather cinches, the two men squatted by the water's edge, gazing northeast to the San Francisco Peaks on the horizon. Ben fished his Durham from his pocket and rolled a cigarette, then tossed the bag to Charlie.

Within minutes, the clatter of hooves broke the silence. From the east came a large number of riders, led by Colly Weems and Leland Pickett. When the riders were within fifty yards of Ben and Charlie, they pulled up. Colly turned in his saddle and spoke to the milling band of cowpokes; then he and Leland Pickett rode on in.

Leland touched a finger to the brim of his hat. "Ben. Charlie."

Before any further words were exchanged, a small band of riders with P. H. Hall in the lead came in from the north.

As with the other two brands, the Slash Bar riders dropped off and P.H. continued on in. "Howdy, boys."

"P.H." Ben glanced past the prune-faced foreman of the Slash Bar. "Ms. Mary Catheryn isn't coming?"

P.H. swung a bowed leg over the saddle and dropped to the ground. "Nope. Told me to listen, then let her know what's going on."

A lone rider approached from the west, Chester Lewis. The lanky Reb nodded and dismounted. "Howdy, boys. What's going on?"

Colly Weems was a short, stocky native Arizonian with a temper as quick as his mop of hair was blond. His fair complexion never browned. He lived with one sunburn after another. "That's what I was wondering. How about it, Ben? What'd you call us out here for?"

Ben leaned back against a pine. "The night riders hit each of you last night, didn't they?" Before any of the ranchers could answer, he added, "And they tried to burn at least one of your outbuildings. Is that right?"

Leland Pickett, hatchet-faced, frowned. "You too, Ben?"

"Me too. Look, boys, doesn't it strike you odd that we all get hit by riders the same night, the same way. And what they pick to hit doesn't burn because of the rain."

His cigarette bobbing with the movement of his lips, Colly Weems said, "What are you getting at, Ben?"

Ben eyed each rancher for several seconds. "Someone is trying to drive us out. All of us. I can't figure why, not yet. But I will."

"Barnett? You think Barnett's behind it, Ben?" asked Colly Weems, his words short, his tone impatient as he glanced around the small group. "He ain't here."

"I don't know, Colly. I've never seen anything to point to him behind any of the trouble. I don't think so. He's rich, and he's got more land than all of us together. I don't particularly like Albert, but in all fairness, he's never done a thing to make me think he's trying to run us out. He's not why I asked you here though."

P.H. cleared his throat. "Why did you, Ben?"

"We've got to get some help in here."

Ches Lewis grunted. "Help? You mean the law?"

Ben nodded and ground his cigarette into the grass. "One of us needs to ride down to Tucson and get the federal marshal to come up here and get to the bottom of this."

"Why not just the sheriff in Prescott? That's closer," asked P.H.

"We're not in his jurisdiction, P.H. Out here, we need a federal man."

Leland Pickett shook his head. "Hell, what good will a lawman do us, Ben?"

Ben explained. "You boys are like me. You stay so busy running your ranch you don't have time to get out and snoop around, ask questions. I'm hoping a federal man will do just that, get out and ask questions, snoop around, see what he can find."

"Hell, sounds good to me. Anything's better'n what's happening now," said Colly, removing his hat and running his fingers through his blond hair. "I'll do it. I'll ride down to Tucson tomorrow morning, full chisel."

Ben nodded. "In the meantime, the rest of us will keep our mouths shut about this and just hang tough. You let us know when the marshal comes in, Colly, you hear."

"Don't worry, Ben. I'll give you a shout."

* * *

Three days later, a grub-line drifter spotted a flock of buzzards near the base of a thousand-foot drop-off. Curious, he rode closer. From a distance, they were fluttering and stalking around a dark object. As he drew closer, the dark object took on the shape of a horse, a sorrel. He grimaced at the stench as he grew closer. Suddenly, his heart thudded against his chest. Beneath the horse lay a dead cowpoke, his skull crushed against the granite boulders on which the hapless man had landed. Blood had turned his blond hair the color of rust.

P. H. Hall stared at Ben in shock. "Colly? Dead?"

Ben watched P.H. carefully.

Upon learning of the rancher's death, Ben knew immediately that it was the result of the meeting at Pinyon Lake. One of the three remaining ranchers, Leland Pickett, Ches Lewis, or P. H. Hall was responsible. One of the three had plans of his own. Ben had already visited Leland and Ches. P.H. was the last.

"Yeah," Ben replied. "Drifter told us about it last night. He took us out this morning, and we brought Colly in. Someone ran him off the trail that leads up out of the valley."

The old foreman swallowed hard. His watery blue eyes cut to the west, then back to Ben. "It coulda been an accident. That trail is mighty narrow. Why, his horse could have shied at a snake or something." He looked back to Ben hopefully. "Don't you think so?"

"Maybe. But, I don't believe it was an accident. Someone murdered Colly, the same hombre who's trying to run us out." Ben hesitated, waiting for P.H.'s reaction.

The older man dropped his gaze to the hardpan at

his feet. "A damned shame, Ben. That's what it is. A damned shame. I just can't figure no one around here to be killing other folk. It musta been a snake or something that spooked his horse."

Ben cleared his throat. "I don't think so. I figure Colly was killed because of our meeting at Pinyon Lake. Whoever killed him doesn't want the law in here snooping around. When you told Ms. Mary Catheryn about the meeting, was anyone else around who could have overheard?"

A flash of anger darkened the old foreman's face. "You mean, you think me or someone on the Slash Bar was responsible?" His tone was sharp and demanding.

"No. Nothing like that. It's just that you came in Ms. Wills's place and you reported back to her. All I'm saying is that someone might have overheard you two talking."

P.H. shook his head emphatically, his gray eyes spitting fire. "No one overheard nothing between Ms. Wills and me. That's a damned fact."

"And you didn't mention it to the old boys who rode out with you?"

"Dammit to hell, Ben. Ain't no man going to accuse me of killing Colly."

Ben shook his head. "I didn't mean that, P.H. It's just that sometimes, a body says something sort of casual like."

"Not me. Not on something like this."

Just after riding onto the Key sometime later, Ben heard gunfire near the base of the escarpment. He drew up and listened. He arched an eyebrow. Charlie was practicing. Ben shook his head and urged the dun toward the gunfire coming from a grove of aspen lining a small creek.

Charlie spotted Ben and waved him over. A broad grin spread over his face when Ben reined up. He held up his Colt. "You wanta try again?"

Ben glanced at Charlie's six-gun. He hesitated. There was more on his mind than a shoot-off with Charlie.

Charlie prodded him. "Come on. What's the matter? Afraid I'll whip you worse than last time?"

A crooked grin split Ben's face. "Why not? Maybe this time, I'll whip you."

"Dream on, cowboy," chuckled the freckle-faced man. "You're good with that hog leg, but I taught you. Remember?"

As Ben dismounted, a flock of crows flew over. Charlie quickly counted them. He shook his head. "That's a bad sign," he said, unleathering his Colt. "Nine crows."

Before Ben could reply, Charlie quoted an old superstition. "One for sorry, two for joy, three for a letter, four for a boy. Five is for rich, six is for poor. Seven for a witch and eight for a whore. Nine for a burying. I can tell thee no more."

Shaking his head, Ben shucked his Colt and spun the cylinder. "You and those crazy superstitions. I don't know how you can remember all of them."

Charlie's face was somber. "They're true, Ben. Believe me."

Ben picked up a handful of pebbles. He extended his right hand, palm down, and placed six small pebbles on it. "Sure. I believe you. Sooner or later, there *is* going to be a burying somewhere." He laughed, and whipped his right hand into the air, launching the pebbles high overhead. His hand flashed to his Colt and the mountain air reverberated with six explosions, one on top of the other.

Three pebbles exploded.

Charlie laughed. "Only three, Ben. Only three. Hell, you did better'n that last time."

Grinning, Ben reloaded. "Just get out there and see what you can do, Mr. Big Mouth."

Deliberately faking a yawn, Charlie casually placed six pebbles on his hand and flipped them into the air. Six explosions sounded as one, and six pebbles exploded. He spun his six-gun on his finger and made a deliberate show of blowing the smoke away from the muzzle. "Well, what about that, boss?" He did a reverse spin and slipped the Colt in the holster.

Ben holstered his own six-gun. "There's always next time." He knew he could never beat Charlie. The lanky, freckle-faced man was too fast for him, but every time the two played this foolish little game, Ben remembered the big man with the eye patch. He was fast, even faster than Charlie.

Charlie's grin grew even wider. "You been saying that ever since the war, boss. I don't figure you'll ever catch up with me." He patted his stomach. "Let's git. I'm hungry."

The two men laughed and climbed back into the saddle.

Back in the chuck house, they piled their plates with grub and scooted up to the table. Ben laid his fork and knife beside the plate, the tip of the knife pointing toward him.

Quickly, Charlie reached across the table and flipped the knifepoint away from Ben, who shook his head.

"Now, what's going to happen, Charlie?" Ben said, his tone amused.

"Don't joke about it, Ben. Especially with all that's been happening lately." The skinny cowpoke dragged the back of his hand across his lips. "A knife that points at you is pointin' toward your own death."

Ben gestured to the knife. "Well, now. Look who you got yours pointing at."

Charlie's face blanched. His knife was pointing at him.

Chapter Eleven

Ben suppressed his laughter over Charlie's latest superstition. His friend had always taken such non-sensical folklore seriously, and Ben didn't want to hurt Charlie's feelings. "If it'll make you feel better, I'll be extra careful, okay?"

Charlie shook his head in disgust at Ben's lack of faith. "You better be, Ben. You just better be, or you might be sorry." The lanky cowpoke dug into his grub. Between mouthfuls, he asked Ben how the ranchers reacted when they learned of Colly's death.

"Way you would expect. All of 'em were shocked."

"You got any idea who's behind all this? I mean, the one responsible for Colly."

"Not a hint. All three seemed mighty surprised to learn Colly was dead. P.H. keeps insisting Colly's pony shied from a snake and went over the edge."

Charlie raised his eyebrows. "Could be. That trail's narrow along there. And this has been a good year for rattlesnakes."

"Yeah, but remember how Colly bragged about that sorrel of his, about how sure-footed she was?" He sipped his coffee and reached for his Durham. "I just don't figure it was an accident. Not with all that's been happening."

Absently, he rolled his cigarette, his thoughts back at the Slash Bar and P.H. "You know," he said, touching a match to the cigarette. "I think back, I wonder about P.H."

Looking up from sopping his plate with a sourdough biscuit, Charlie frowned. "Wonder what about P.H.?"

Ben considered his reply, trying to find the right words to express the vague feelings nagging at him. "Neither Leland or Ches got riled when I asked them if they'd said anything about the meeting at Pinyon Lake. P.H. did, madder'n a wet hen. I wonder why?"

For a few moments, Ben stared into the black surface of his coffee, thinking back to the first gathering of the ranchers on John Wills's front porch.

Suddenly, one or two answers slipped into place. Ben looked up at Charlie. "Remember in the chuck house after John's funeral. We were drinking coffee when Albert came in."

Charlie's youthful face beamed. "That was when you busted two of Borke's teeth out."

Ben grinned. "I wasn't thinking about that, but about what P.H. said when I told him Mary Catheryn was coming out from Baltimore."

Charlie frowned.

Ben continued, "He said that he hoped she wouldn't sell out. Remember?"

"Yeah. So what?"

"So, a couple days later on her front porch, P.H. told Mary Catheryn that Barnett's offer was a fair price."

Charlie stared at Ben, puzzled. "And that means what? So he changed his mind. Man's got a right to do that—women more so."

"Yeah, but suppose, just suppose, P.H. is working for whoever wants us out of here. He was at Pinyon Lake with us. He knew Colly was going to Prescott. He could've passed word along."

Suddenly, Ben's imagination took a giant leap, one that even surprised him. "In fact, he was the one who rode in and found John Wills in the corral."

Charlie nodded.

Ben continued, "But, what if he didn't ride in?"

"You lost me, Ben. You got to cut the deck a little deeper on that. What do you mean, what if he didn't ride in?" A frown cut deep lines into Charlie's forehead. He shook his head. "You're gettin' me confused with all this guessing."

"Just listen. What if he'd been with John at the corral the whole time. He could have knocked John in the head, trampled him with his own horse, and then turned the piebald into the corral."

Charlie's jaw dropped open. He stared at Ben, searching for words. Before the freckle-faced young man could respond, Ben banged his fist on the table. His eyes blazed with sudden insight. "That's it! It all adds up, Charlie. Don't you see? The only thing that makes any sense around here is that P.H. has to be working for someone who is willing to kill for our ranches. John Wills would never have sold out, so now he's dead. Mary Catheryn will probably sell to Barnett now, and if she does, then Ches and Leland will probably follow along. I imagine Albert is already over at Colly's place."

Charlie shook his head. "Dammit, Ben, that's the deepest pile of manure I ever heard. What do you do, stay up nights figuring all this out?"

Ben's level gaze held Charlie. "You got a better explanation?"

For several moments, the two men locked eyes. Finally Charlie shook his head. "No. I ain't, but . . . what you're saying . . . that's mighty hard to swallow."

Ben continued. "Maybe so, but listen to it again, all laid out and hog-tied. First, P.H. tells me he doesn't want Mary Catheryn to sell out. Second, he encourages her to sell. Then, he was at the ranch alone when John was killed. Finally, P.H. was at the lake, and he was one of only four who knew what Colly was up to." He paused, then added, "Maybe I'm wrong. Maybe my ideas are wild, but I'd say P.H. has given us reasons to look hard at him."

Charlie had grown solemn. "I reckon you're right, Ben. It's just that it's hard to believe all that about P.H." He paused, then added, "Sometimes Ben, I think you're too much like John. The only way anyone will take your ranch is if you're dead." He dropped his gaze to the knife on the table in front of Ben.

Ben's eyes followed Charlie's gaze to the knife. "Maybe so, Charlie. But I got an advantage old John didn't have."

"What's that?"

"I know someone's after me."

Charlie arched an eyebrow. "Someone?"

Ben read the question in his old friend's eyes. Slowly, he nodded. "Dammit, he's the only one. Nobody else has anything to gain except Albert Barnett."

"But, Ben, you ain't got no proof on Albert. Remember, you're the one who always insists on havin' all the facts."

Leaning forward, Ben said, "Remember the rustler Albert and Borke shot?"

"Yeah. What about him?"

"It slipped right past me at the time, but all this rustling has taken place at night."

Charlie frowned. "What are you driving at?"

"They caught this one in the middle of the day." Ben paused, then asked, "Whoever's doing all this rustling appears to be mighty shrewd, too smart to pull a stunt like that during the day, wouldn't you say?"

Suddenly, Charlie understood the implication in Ben's words. "You mean . . . you think they killed someone and passed him off as a rustler just to throw us off the track?"

Ben stared at Charlie. "That's exactly what I think. Some unlucky drifter came through, and Barnett killed him."

Charlie leaned back in his chair and shook his head. "That son of a bitch!"

Chapter Twelve

Albert Barnett stared at the handful of documents in his hand in satisfaction. Here they were, the key to his dream. He narrowed his eyes at the skinny, middle-aged man in the worn wool suit and steel-rimmed eyeglasses. "You made sure it's all legal, didn't you? That's what you're getting paid for."

Eustace Mooney, land attorney for the Arizona Territory, gulped and nodded emphatically. "Yessir, Mr. Barnett. Just like you wanted. The sheriff's handing out the eviction notices as we speak." He glanced around furtively. Sweat ran down the side of his thin face from his greased hair, which was parted in the middle.

The cattle baron nodded and grinned. "Relax, Eustace, relax. Like you say, it's all legal. All you have to do is play innocent. After all, these titles were filed before you were appointed to the office. You can't be responsible for your predecessor's incompetence, can you?"

The nervous attorney licked his lips. "That's . . . That's right."

Barnett gazed out the window, a smug grin on his

square face. He reckoned a heap of yelling and screaming was about to take place all up and down the valley.

A knock on the door interrupted the two men. Quickly, Albert Barnett dropped the titles into his coat pocket and peered around the edge of the curtain. He nodded to Eustace Mooney. "It's time for you to leave. Wait in the dining room until I take these folks into the parlor, then slip out. Remember what I said. Anyone starts asking any questions, just let them look at your records."

With a nervous twitch of his head, Eustace Mooney slipped into the dining room. "Yessir. Don't worry."

Straightening his coat, Albert Barnett opened the door. Mary Catheryn Wills and Zebron Rawlings stood on the porch. Albert smiled. "Ms. Wills. Mr. Rawlings, how good of you to come. Come in to the parlor. Dinner will be ready shortly."

Eustace Mooney was not a frontiersman. He was one of the large masses who followed the explorer-hunter and the hunter-farmer into the West. He detested camping under the stars, but a mere two-day inconvenience was well worth the secure future he had now provided for himself.

That night, he lay under his blankets and grinned up at the brilliant, cold stars overhead. His last thought each evening before he drifted into sleep was the second set of books he had kept for the last eight years, a set of books not even Albert Barnett knew existed.

And like Albert Barnett had said, when the fat hit the fire, all Eustace had to do was sit tight in the saddle.

The next morning, Ben and two of his ranch hands struggled to yank a bawling cow critter from a mud hole where she was bogged belly deep. The rope about her neck was dallied to the saddle on a big sorrel, whose rider was urging the pony forward. Ben was deep in the mud, twisting the critter's tail. The other cowpoke was in the mud with Ben, hauling on her horns.

A shout caught Ben's attention.

Tearing out of the tall pines and streaking across the meadow was Charlie Little, yelling and dusting his horse's rump with his hat.

The bawling cow jerked against the rope, pulling Ben back to the problem at hand. He nodded to the cowpoke on the horse. "One more time, Joe."

The men strained. The sucking mud popped as the heifer's legs broke free of its sticky grasp. Slowly, the helpless cow was dragged to firm ground where she struggled to stand upright, throwing her head from side to side and bawling wildly, scared by her ordeal and looking to fight anyone.

Charlie yanked on the reins, bringing his pony to a sliding, stiff-legged halt. His excited words ran together. "Trouble, Ben. Back at the ranch."

"Easy, Charlie, easy. What's got you all fired up?"

The other two ranch hands moved in to listen.

"The sheriff from Prescott is there, Ben. He's got a piece of paper saying you don't own the Key . . . that you never owned it."

The words slapped Ben in the face. For a moment, he stared at Charlie, looking for a hint of his old friend's sometimes bizarre humor. Charlie's freckled face was pale and drawn, his eyes wide with apprehension. Ben realized this was no joke. "I don't own the Key? Did the sheriff tell you that?"

"Not exactly. Hell, Ben, you know I don't understand all that legal jabber. The sheriff's waiting for you now."

Ben didn't waste any time. In two quick strides, he leaped into the saddle and headed for the house.

Sheriff Jess Lowry and two deputies squatted in the shade of Ben's front porch. They rose when Ben and Charlie rode up. Lowry, a balding, corpulent man, nodded. "Mr. Elliott."

Ben had met the sheriff once or twice in the past few years, but he never had the occasion to spend any time with the lawman. He knew nothing of the man. He returned the nod and climbed from his saddle. He wasted no time in formalities. "What's this about the Key, Sheriff?"

Charlie remained on his pony, his eyes on the deputies.

Sheriff Lowry handed Ben a folded document. "I'm just doing my duty, Mr. Elliott. This court order says you have ten days to get off the ranch before the real owner takes over. Seems like you never had title to this place."

Ben snapped back. "That's a lie. I filed on this ranch just after the war. My title is on record."

Lowry stiffened. He shot a glance at his deputies. He cleared his throat. "Not according to that court order, Mr. Elliott. If you read it, you'll see that you never had a title."

His eyes narrowing, Ben grabbed the document and quickly scanned it. When he finished, he looked up at the sheriff with eyes cold as ice. He glanced at Charlie, then turned back to the sheriff. "I'm not taking anybody's word on this, Sheriff." He held the document under the sheriff's nose and crumpled it. "Certainly, not something written on a piece of paper. I'm coming into town to find out what in the hell is going on."

Ben hesitated. An idea burst into full bloom. Suddenly, his theories about P. H. Hall weren't so wild after all. He eyed the sheriff. "Just for my own information, Sheriff. Who in the hell claims to have title on my ranch," asked Ben, his voice soft and controlled.

Sheriff Lowry glanced nervously at his two deputies. "Why . . . ah, I believe he is one of your neighbors, Mr. Elliott. I . . . I think his name is Albert Barnett."

Charlie Little cursed.

Ben clenched his fists. He struggled to keep his voice even. "You've done your job, Sheriff. Now, the smartest thing you and your men can do is to turn those ponies around and get off my place."

Sheriff Jess Lowry didn't argue.

Once in his saddle, the sheriff stared down at Ben. "You understand, Mr. Elliott. I'm just doing my job."

Charlie Little whirled his pony in a circle. He slapped leather, his six-gun appearing in his hand as if by magic. "Yeah, well, I'm fixing to do my job, Sheriff."

"Charlie! No!"

Charlie looked at Ben who shook his head. "Not this way, Charlie. Not this way."

For several strained seconds, the three lawmen waited, their hands poised over the butt of their own six-shooters. Sweat poured down their faces as they kept their eyes on Charlie. One of the deputies ran his tongue over his dried lips.

Ben's steady voice broke the tension. "Put it up, Charlie. You don't kill the messenger."

Jess Lowry gave Ben a weak grin that faded when Ben added, "Even though the messenger is a part of the plot."

Lowry's grin disappeared. He wheeled his horse around.

"Just a minute, Sheriff," called Ben.

Sheriff Lowry turned his pony back to face Ben.

"One question." He nodded to the sheriff's saddle-bags. "You have eviction notices for Chester Lewis and Leland Pickett?"

The dark fury on Sheriff Lowry's face answered Ben's question. He dug his spurs into his pony, cutting one-eleven's in the animal's flanks.

Ben and Charlie watched the three riders cut across the meadow toward Ches Lewis's ranch. Ben drawled, "Well, Charlie, with the sheriff in his pocket now, I reckon J. Albert Barnett figures everything's going his own way."

As Charlie looked on, Ben smoothed the crumpled document and folded it into his shirt pocket. The wiry rancher fished his Durham from his vest pocket and squatted on the porch step to roll his cigarette.

"Dammit, Ben. Ain't you going to do something?" asked Charlie impatiently. "We can't just sit around and let Barnett get away with out-and-out thievery."

Ben touched a match to his cigarette and tossed the makings to Charlie. "Fix yourself one, Charlie. And listen hard while I tell you what we're going to do."

Charlie caught the bag in midair and grinned.

Chapter Thirteen

Overhead, the Milky Way blazed a broad white path across the heavens. The crisp brace of the night magnified the sounds of the forest and the clatter of horses' hooves against the rocky trail.

"I don't care, Ben. I think we oughta go in shooting at Barnett's, not be out here heading for Prescott," said Charlie, his face taut with frustration.

Ben drew in a deep breath of crisp air. "That's playing right into Barnett's hands, Charlie. He's got the law on his side, at least for the time being." He leaned back against the cantle of his saddle and relaxed as his dun picked its way down the trail. "Like I told you, first, we got to find out about the land titles. You know as well as me that I filed title just after we staked out the Key. You were with me. If there is no trace of the filing, that means only one thing, that Barnett paid someone to make the changes."

Charlie nodded. "What do you figure Albert's doing all of this for?"

"Land." Ben removed his hat and combed his fingers through his sandy hair. "It has to be land. Give a jasper land, and with the land, comes power." He set his hat back on his head and added, "He sure had me fooled, but now, I got the feeling Albert Barnett won't be satisfied just with the Mogollon or the valley. I'm not sure just where he has his sights set, but you can bet a double eagle they're looking way past Arizona Territory."

They rode in silence. Finally Charlie cleared his throat. "So Ben, you don't really expect to find any record of your title in Prescott?"

"Not a trace."

"Then why we going?"

"You'll see."

Eustace Mooney looked up from his neat desk behind an oak railing when Ben and Charlie stomped in. His eyes quickly assessed their dress, the dusty denims, travel-stained shirts, battered hats. He pinched his lips together and sniffed. "Yes?"

Ben shoved his hat to the back of his head, laid his work-scarred hands on the rail, and leaned forward. "You the land man here?"

Mooney nodded, his small eyes peering over the top of the steel-rimmed glasses perched on the end of his nose. "Yes, I am. What can I do for you?"

Ben's voice dropped in timbre. "My name's Benjamin Franklin Elliott. I filed on a parcel of land around the Mogollons eight years ago. I've been told there's no record of it." He paused, straightened his shoulders, and laid his hand on the handle of his six-gun. "I want to see for myself."

The door scraped open behind Ben. "Hello, Mr. Elliott. It's good to see you."

Ben turned to find Sheriff Lowry and his two deputies standing in the open door. Each deputy cradled a

Winchester in the crook of his arm. "Morning, Sheriff. Funny meeting you here."

Lowry shook his head, a faint, mocking grin on his ruddy face. "Nothing funny about it at all. Just saw you ride in. Thought I'd offer you any aid or assistance you might need while you and your friend are in town."

His voice edged with light sarcasm, Ben took up his end of the charade. "Why, that's mighty decent of you, Sheriff. Does a man good to know the law is always ready to lend a hand." He narrowed his eyes and hooked his thumb over his shoulder. "But, you needn't bother. Mr. Mooney here was just going to show me the title records for 1865." Without looking at the frail man behind the desk, Ben added in a voice meant to send chills down the small man's spine, "Isn't that right, Mr. Mooney?"

Mooney coughed, then sputtered. "C . . . Certainly. I . . . I was just going to do that very thing, Sheriff."

Ben turned back to the nervous man. A broad grin cracked his hard face, but his eyes remained cold. "I certainly do appreciate your cooperation, Mr. Mooney."

Along the back wall of the land office, several large cloth-bound ledgers, six inches thick and two feet tall, were lined up on shelves like books on a library shelf. Mooney studied the gold embossed dates on the leather spine of the ledgers and pulled three from the shelf and hefted them up on the desk for Ben to examine.

Mooney stepped back against the shelf and folded his hands against his chest and waited. Charlie kept his pale blue eyes on the sheriff and his deputies; but the three lawmen remained motionless, only their eyes moving as they followed Ben's movements.

Ben had anticipated the results. He hadn't expected to find the recorded title, but he had to know for sure. He went back through the ledgers once again, the second time checking not only for his title, but for those of the other small ranchers, Chester Lewis, Leland Pickett, and John Wills. Although Colly was dead, and his wife had already agreed to sell out, Ben checked for their title also.

Finally, Ben closed the last ledger. He gave Charlie a warning glance before slowly turning his piercing eyes on Eustace Mooney. Mooney shivered. "I don't reckon this is any good either," he said, pulling his copy of the title from his shirt pocket and offering it to Mooney.

Mooney glanced nervously at the sheriff, ran his tongue over his lips, and took the title. He read it quickly. "Well, it looks legal, Mr. Elliott, but as you can see, it was never filed. They . . . They need to be filed to be legal," he added lamely.

Glancing at the sheriff, Ben pointed to the signature beneath his on the document. "George Gaspard. Wasn't he the land attorney for the territory before you, Mr. Mooney?"

Mooney gulped and shot a furtive glance at the sheriff. He cleared his throat. "It appears to be; however, the document was not filed." He shrugged helplessly. "I have no explanation for Mr. Gaspard's neglect of this circumstance. I'm sorry."

With two Winchesters looking at him, Ben was in no position to argue the frail explanation. He folded the title and slipped it in his vest pocket. His voice remained soft and calm. "Thank you, Mr. Mooney," he said. "I appreciate the time."

Ben suppressed a grin when he saw the surprised expression on the sheriff's face. Obviously, Lowry had expected trouble. For the moment, Ben's unexpected behavior caught the sheriff off guard. Ben pressed home his advantage. "Sheriff. I know for a fact I filed that record. If you have the time, I'd like to come over to your office and find out what my next step would be."

Lowry shot a puzzled look at his deputies, then frowned at Ben. "Next step? I don't understand."

"The law, Sheriff. Courts. I plan to take Albert Barnett to court. I can bring in witnesses to testify that I filed my title." He paused and shrugged. "Of course, I might lose, but I'm going to try. The problem is, I don't know exactly what I should do next—within the law, you know? That's why I'm wondering if you, since you know the law, can help me."

A smug grin broke the frown on Lowry's flushed face. "Sure, Mr. Elliott. Be glad to. When would be most convenient for you?"

The regulator clock on the wall struck four.

Ben replied. "Me and my pard are going to settle in at the hotel. How about five this afternoon? That'll give us time to clean up."

Charlie stopped in the middle of the dusty street and turned on Ben. "Dammit, Ben, what are you trying to do with all this court business." Charlie Little's face was flushed, his ears bright red. "We shoulda grabbed that scrawny pencil pusher and choked the truth out of him."

Ben nodded and continued toward the hotel. "I agree."

"I don't care what you say, Ben. We've got to do something. We can't just sit back and . . ." Suddenly, Ben's words registered on Charlie. He knitted his brows and hurried after Ben. "You what?"

"I said, I agree. And that's exactly what we're going to do, but not while the sheriff and his two hired hands are looking over our shoulder with loaded Winchesters."

Just inside the hotel door, Ben led the way through the swinging doors to the adjoining saloon. Over a glass of Old Taylor, Ben quickly laid out his plan. "I'll go over and keep the sheriff and his deputies busy when the land office closes down for the day. You wait outside and find out where Mooney lives. Tonight, we'll take care of him."

Charlie grinned and reached across the table and fished the makings from Ben's shirt pocket. "Now, you're talking, Ben. Now, you're talking."

Thirty minutes later, Charlie trailed Eustace Mooney home, then headed back to the hotel to wait for Ben. What the two had in mind wouldn't take more than two minutes.

Except for a few saloons, Prescott closed up tight after dark, preparing for another night's slumber in the chilly mountain air. Ben and Charlie ghosted through the darkness, slipping out the hotel window and leaving a deputy sleeping at the end of the hall.

Within minutes, they forked their ponies out of town with a wide-eyed, frightened Eustace Mooney between them, bouncing on a rangy, rail-backed nag. One hour into the mountains, Ben pulled up beside a small stream and dismounted. The cold moonlight bathed the mountain in an eerie glow.

Eustace Mooney started blubbering as soon as Ben tossed a lariat over a tree limb. Within five minutes, the diminutive man had confessed the entire plot, the altered records, the rustling, even the involvement of Sheriff Jess Lowry and his two deputies.

The impact of Mooney's words hit Ben. "This has been going on for the last six years?"

"Yes. Barnett paid me to change the records on all land around the Triple B." He paused, regaining some of his nerve. "I would just simply pull out the ledger page and insert another one with new information on it. Nothing to it, really, although one must know exactly what should be changed," he added with a touch of conceit.

"Suppose someone had come in to check on a title. One of those you changed."

A satisfied smile played over Mooney's thin lips. "That would never happen, Mr. Elliott. Once a man files, he never returns to check, not even when the property is sold."

"But what if someone does check?"

Eustace Mooney sniffed. "I could change them back." He shook his head. "But that has never taken place."

Ben considered the reply. He shook his head. "What happened to the original page?"

Mooney shrugged. "I burned them, but I kept copies."

Ben shot a quick glance of disbelief at Charlie. "You made copies?"

"Certainly," the small man sniffed, growing more sure of himself. "I have to provide some security for myself, don't I?"

Ben jammed his big fists into his hips and stared down at the frail man. A faint grin curled one side of his lips. He shook his head at the small man's duplicity. He figured Mooney was afraid to even raise his voice.

"Where are the records, Eustace? You want to keep Albert Barnett away from you, you'd better turn 'em over to us before he gets his hands on them . . . and you."

Eustace Mooney glanced at Charlie, who nodded. The bone-thin land attorney removed his steel-rimmed glasses and nervously cleaned the lenses with his handkerchief.

"You don't have a choice, Eustace," said Ben. "Charlie and me know your secret. Barnett will learn it soon, and your life won't be worth any more than a sour beaver skin."

Mooney's shaky fortitude crumbled. He swallowed hard and dabbed at his sweaty forehead with a handkerchief. "Do . . . Do you really think he . . . I mean, Mr. Barnett would . . ."

Charlie interjected the answer. "Faster'n you can spit, Mr. Mooney."

Mooney fumbled in his vest pocket with trembling fingers. Extracting a key, he handed it to Ben. "Here. The documents are in my safety-deposit box in Tucson. Under the name, Joseph B. Smith."

Ben grinned. "Joseph B. Smith, huh?" He tossed the key to Charlie. "There you are, Mr. Smith. Head out. Meet us at Leland's place in two days. I figure on hiding Eustace out there until we can get the federal law in. And while you're in Tucson, see if you can run down the federal marshal. Tell him we need him up here."

Chapter Fourteen

Back in Prescott, no one paid any attention when the land office failed to open the next morning at nine o'clock. By noon, however, Sheriff Lowry discovered Eustace Mooney had vanished. He quickly surmised the land attorney had not left on his own volition, for none of the small man's clothes or luggage was missing from his rented room.

To Jess Lowry, that could only mean one thing.

Ten minutes later, he was spurring his horse toward Albert Barnett's Triple B. They had come too far for the plan to fall apart now.

Two days later, Leland Pickett pulled back the curtains, allowing the morning sun to spill into the kitchen. His wife fussed about the stove, frying up slabs of venison and stacks of sourdough saddle blankets. A pot of coffee bubbled merrily.

At the table, Ben looked up from studying the ledger pages Charlie had taken from Mooney's safety-deposit box in Tucson. "You changed the titles on all of our spreads except John Wills, the Slash Bar. Why?"

Eustace Mooney glanced nervously at Charlie and

Leland, both of whom glared down at the small man. "Mr. Barnett told me not worry. That was taken care of."

Taken care of? Ben frowned at Charlie. "What do you suppose Albert has in mind?"

"No telling," replied Charlie. He patted the worn grip of his Colt. "I still say this is the only way to handle that big son of . . ." He caught himself and threw an embarrassed glance at Mrs. Pickett who kept at her work without a bobble. "Excuse me, ma'am." He looked back at Ben. "Hot lead is all his kind understand."

"No," said Ben. "Not yet." He handed Leland Pickett the ledger pages. "Put 'em somewhere safe, Leland." He nodded to Mooney. "And keep him out of sight. I'm heading down to Tucson. According to Charlie, the federal marshal is due back any day or else he'd be here with us now. With luck, I should be back in two days, three at the latest. Once we turn Mooney and those documents over to the federal government, we can get a fair shake." He gestured to Prescott to the west. "We won't get it over there, not with Jess Lowry sheriffing."

Leland Pickett, his hatchet face grim, nodded at Mooney. "Don't you worry none, Ben. This jasper'll be right here."

"Here's breakfast," Mrs. Pickett said with a smile as she slid the heaping platters on the table. "Everyone dig in."

During the ride back to the ranch, Ben laid out his plans to Charlie. "I'll pack coffee and grub in my saddlebags tonight and leave before sunup. You look after things while I'm away."

"What about Colly's widow and Ches Lewis? Should I tell them what we're up to?"

"Might as well. Don't give 'em any details. Just say we're looking for a way to get the titles cleared up."

Charlie nodded. "What about Ms. Mary Cateryn? Don't we need to tell her something?"

Ben studied the question a moment, still puzzled over Barnett's cryptic remark. What could Albert have meant by the statement, *That's already taken care of*? The title? No, the title was still in John Wills's name. Of course, now that John was dead, and once the law ruled that Mary Cateryn was his only living heir, the title would be put in her name.

"I don't figure we need to mention it to her. Her title is good. What we're doing has nothing to do with her. Besides, she might slip and give us away."

"Whatever you say, Ben," replied Charlie, his youthful face hard and cold. "Let's just be damned sure we settle up with Albert Barnett. He's got it coming."

"Don't worry, Charlie. Albert is going to get what's coming to him."

Federal Marshal Ike Hazlett stomped across the worn plank floor and sat two cups on his scarred desk. He filled them halfway with coffee thick enough to walk on and not even leave a boot print. "Reckon you like it strong. Personally, I can't stand no watery-tasting coffee." He pulled a pint bottle of whiskey from a desk drawer and filled the cups to the rim. "There. That takes the place of sugar."

Holding his cup gingerly with his fingers, Ike blew his drooping mustache out of the way, slurped the coffee, and grinned. "Ah. Now, that's good coffee."

Ben sipped his own coffee. He had run into the

marshal just outside of Tucson. During the short ride on into town and the sheriff's office, Ben outlined the problems facing the ranchers beneath the Mogollon Plateau.

Ike Hazlett set the cup down on the desk and stared squarely into Ben's eyes. "Like I said, Mr. Elliott. I got to go out to Sulphur Springs. I been puttin' off a little problem down there too long. Shouldn't take more than a few days, then I'll hightail up to your place. You'll just hafta keep your evidence hid out 'til then. If what you say is true, you ain't got no problem."

Chapter Fifteen

Charlie Little licked his lips and grinned appreciatively at Old Foss. "Them saddle blankets sure look mighty tasty," he said, bending over the breakfast table and poking down a stack of Old Foss's sourdough pancakes dotted with raisins and soaked with sorghum.

"Oughta be tasty. I cooked 'em," growled Old Foss.

The freckle-faced cowpoke didn't reply. He just shrugged and kept shoveling the grub down his gullet. Just as he washed the last bite down with a swallow of six-shooter coffee, the clatter of hooves pulled up in front of the chuck house.

The Key line rider who lived on the fence line between the Key and Leland Pickett's ranch burst into the chuck house. "Mr. Charlie! Mr. Charlie! You best come." He paused to catch his breath. "There's trouble over the Picketts'. Bad trouble."

Charlie jerked erect, his first thoughts of Mooney and the documents.

"I mean it, Mr. Charlie. Bad trouble."

"Slow down, boy," said Charlie, jumping to his feet and grabbing his hat. "I'm coming. Just what is this problem you're talking about?" He felt empty inside, hoping the trouble had nothing to do with Eustace Mooney and the ledger pages.

Half a dozen ranch hands gathered around while the young man gasped out his story. "Just after midnight, I spotted a red glow over the Picketts'. I figured a fire, so I rode over to see if I could help. While I was still out in the dark, I saw riders and heard gunshots, so—" He hesitated and ducked his head. "Well, I kinda hid out until I could see what was going on. There was a bunch of them. Ten or twenty." He paused and gulped. "Honest, Mr. Charlie. They'd of kilt me sure if I'd rode in."

Charlie nodded. "Go on."

Glancing around at those looking on, he continued. "Around sunup, they rode off. I waited until they was gone and then went in to see . . ."

He hesitated and put his hands out to his side in a gesture of helplessness. "Well, I didn't know what I could do or wanted to see. I just went in."

Charlie grimaced. He already knew the answer to his next question. "What about Leland?"

The youth shook his head, his eyes filling with tears. "D . . . Dead. His wife and child too. I . . . I couldn't tell if they was pistol shot or just . . ." He gulped and drew a deep breath. "Or just burnt up."

"Anyone else?"

"Yeah. I don't know who they all was, so I come back here, Mr. Charlie. Did I do right?"

Charlie laid his hand on the boy's shoulder. "You did just fine, Monk, just fine. Now, stay here. We'll be back later. Just you rest up and eat a bite."

The young line rider shook his head. "I . . . I ain't much hungry, Mr. Charlie. Not much at all."

* * *

One of the two ranch hands with Charlie retched when they saw the burned bodies. The other cowpokes' faces paled. They pressed their lips together in an effort to hold the gorge down.

All of the outbuildings had been burned to the ground. The rock walls of the ranch house remained standing, but the roof had caved in. Tendrils of smoke still rose from the charred timbers. Leland Pickett lay in the ruins of the porch. His wife and child were on the bed, two blackened lumps. Three ranch hands lay on the hardpan surrounding the house. And Eustace Mooney had been lashed to a snubbing post in a corral, drenched with coal oil, and set afire.

The smell of smoke and burned meat and death clogged Charlie's nostrils, reminding him of that day in the canyon of the Mohawk Mountains. He could still see the bodies strewn about as if carelessly tossed by a giant hand.

A cold fury seized him. He turned his eyes toward Albert Barnett's Triple B and laid his hand on the worn grip of his Frontier Colt. His face taut with rage, Charlie fought back the urge to ride over to Barnett's and call him out. He regretted his promise to Ben, but a promise was a promise. He would do nothing until Ben returned, but once he did, that son of a bitch Barnett was going to pay.

While the Key ranch hands dug graves, Charlie prowled through the burned remains of the house and outbuildings. With a grim shake of his head, he saw he had been right. Nothing had been spared. Barnett had made sure that neither the man nor the evidence could speak against him.

Later, after the last spadeful of dirt had been packed on the last grave, Charlie and the two ranch hands climbed wearily into their saddles and turned back to the Key.

Beneath a rose bush, Charlie spotted a small cloth doll, one with buttons for eyes and yellow yarn for hair. Instead of placing it on the child's grave, he carried it with him back to the Key, silently studying it throughout the solemn ride.

Back at the ranch, Charlie remained silent, his pale blue eyes fastened on the doll. Old Foss brought him a cup of coffee, but Charlie ignored it. Dammit, it just wasn't right, killing women and kids. Men—that's different. A man could stand up for himself, but women and kids—

The more Charlie dwelled on the death of the child, the weaker grew his promise to Ben. He unleathered his Colt and laid it on the chuck house table between the doll and the cup of cold coffee. The handgun, both cylinder and frame, was worn shiny in places, but the smooth functioning of the six-gun gave ample evidence that it had been well maintained.

Charlie had never considered seeking fame as a gunnie, but now was one of the times he was glad he was fast. He picked up the Colt and spun the cylinder. As it clicked smoothly, Charlie knew that he held the solution to their problem in his hands. He could ride in to the Triple B and call Barnett out. It was that simple.

He hesitated, and a faint grin played over his face. Well, maybe not quite so simple. Barnett had his gun hands around, so Charlie would have to take some of his own along, just to make sure no one interfered.

By the time Ben got back from Tucson, everything would be over, all problems settled. Charlie might have to leave the territory for a spell, but he could manage that. Holstering his six-gun, Charlie tucked the cloth doll under his belt and stepped outside into the blazing afternoon sun.

Overhead, a strident cry broke the still air. A flock of crows flew past. Charlie counted them. One, two, three, four, five, six, seven, eight, nine—He searched the sky for another, but there was none. He counted again. Still nine. He remembered the old superstition about nine crows.

He shook his head. "Like Ben said, superstitions is nonsense." But the last line of the superstition stuck in his head, *Nine for a burying, I can tell thee no more.*

Chapter Sixteen

Albert Barnett straightened his vest over his rock-hard abdomen. "Ben Elliott's dropped out of sight. Two days now, and no one has laid eyes on him."

Borke shoved his black hat to the back of his head and dragged his broken fingernails along the line of his jaw. "I figured he'd show up at the Pickett place, but it was that damned skinny sidekick of his what did."

Rolling his broad shoulders, Barnett peered out the window at the setting sun. "He's up to something. So far, we've stayed a step ahead." He turned back to his foreman. "Whatever he's up to, it has to be something to do with the land titles."

"So? All them pages that scrawny bookkeeper stuck back got burned up. I seen to that myself. Elliott's got nothing." The rawboned foreman paused, touching his tongue to the gap left by the two teeth Ben had knocked out. "There ain't nothing left that jasper could use to prove anything."

Barnett studied his foreman through narrowed eyes. Borke was wrong. Barnett had copies of the changes in land titles in his office. "Maybe so, but I want him out of the way, once and for all."

A knock at the door interrupted the conversation. A ranch hand stuck his head inside. "Riders coming, Mr. Barnett. Looks like them over to the Key."

A sneer twisted Borke's bearded face. "Maybe this is what you been waitin' for."

Without bothering to reply, Albert Barnett retrieved an immaculately kept gun belt from the closet and strapped it about his hips. He unleathered his six-gun, checking the action, the trigger tension, spinning the cylinder.

He handled the Colt like a baby, gently, almost tenderly. With deft fingers, he inserted six cartridges in the cylinder and slid the six-gun back in its well-oiled holster. He made one or two practice draws, then nodded to Borke. "Let's see what our neighbors want."

From the porch, Barnett and Borke watched the four riders approach. Borke frowned and spoke out of the side of his mouth. "Elliott ain't with them."

Albert Barnett didn't reply. He flexed his fingers. His eyes grew cold.

Charlie Little rode at the head of the party. His slender face was hard, his pale blue eyes dark with hate. When he pulled up at the porch, the three riders behind him angled aside.

Charlie dismounted. "I come for you, Barnett. Just you and me."

Without taking his eyes off the lean cowpoke, Albert Barnett spoke in a flat, unemotional voice. "Doesn't look that way to me, Charlie. I'd say you'd come to start a war."

"No war. My boys are here to make sure nobody makes a play except you and me." Charlie positioned himself square in front of Albert Barnett. Fifteen feet separated them. "Tell your foreman to move aside unless he wants part of it."

Borke hesitated, then stepped aside, making a deliberate show of holding his hands out to his side, palms forward.

Charlie's eyes narrowed, his body tensed. He leaned forward. "All right, Barnett. Make your play."

A crooked grin twisted one side of Barnett's square face. "Do you mind telling me what this is all about, Charlie? After all, I'd like to know why you're forcing me to kill you."

Barnett's taunt didn't faze Charlie. "Draw, child killer, or I'll shoot you down like a dog."

Barnett's face darkened. The muscles in his jaw twitched. Tension filled the air.

Both men slapped leather at the same time. Charlie's hand was a blur, but before he cleared leather, a sledgehammer blow in the chest knocked him back, spun him around. He managed to pull his six-gun, but a second blow slammed him off his feet and to the ground.

For several seconds, Charlie lay staring in disbelief at the big man on the porch. He tried to speak. "I . . . I . . ." Then he died.

Barnett coolly spun his six-gun on a finger and dropped the still-smoking revolver in his holster. Without taking his eyes off the dead cowboy, Barnett spoke to the Key riders. "Take him back. Tell Elliott it was a fair fight."

Borke shook his head and gave a soft whistle as the Key riders headed back to the ranch with their dead foreman. "I never seen a draw that fast."

Ignoring the compliment, Barnett said, "Elliott's coming after me now."

"So? Fast as you are, you don't need to worry."

With a look of disdain, Barnett stared at his fore-man. "Killing solves nothing, not in the long run. And the unexpected can always happen." He turned his eyes back on the disappearing riders, his mind working. "Didn't you hire some new hands a few days back?"

"Yep. Three."

"Just drifters?"

"Two of 'em. The other's from Tubac, outside of Tucson."

"Get one of the drifters. The three of us are going to pay a visit to Elliott's line shack tonight. I'll make sure Ben Elliott never bothers me again."

Borke asked no questions. He nodded and left to carry out Barnett's orders.

Chapter Seventeen

"He what?" Ben stared at Old Foss in disbelief.

The old cook nodded. "Shot dead. Yesterday afternoon. Albert Barnett gunned him down." He dipped his head toward a couple ranch hands seated at a table drinking coffee, their eyes on Ben and Old Foss. "They was there. Claim it was a fair fight."

"It was that, Ben," volunteered Two Bits.

"I never seen nothing like it, Ben," sputtered Monk. "Charlie never had a chance. Barnett nailed him twice afore Charlie cleared leather. And Charlie was faster than a bat out of hell."

Ben stared at the ranch hands, his face blank in stunned surprise. Finally, he found his voice. "Why in the hell did he go over to Barnett's in the first place?"

Old Foss, the cook, brought Ben up to date, telling him about the massacre at the Pickett ranch, the death of Mooney, and the destruction of the documents that would have saved the Key. "I reckon that's when the bark just up and popped off the log," the old man drawled.

Ben drew a deep breath and slowly released it. Five

minutes earlier, he had ridden in filled with hope. But now—"Where's Charlie now?"

"He's over to the bunkhouse," replied Old Foss.

The ranch hands followed Ben to the bunkhouse where they remained a respectful distance as Ben crossed the room to where Charlie lay on his bunk. He had been dressed in his Sunday suit and his new boots. His red hair was slicked down, and his gun belt lay folded on his chest.

"Them was his best clothes, Ben," whispered Two Bits. "Them's the ones he wore to church box suppers."

Ben nodded. "He . . . He looks real good. I . . ." Ben blinked at the tears filling his eyes and fought back the anger boiling through his veins. "He looks real good, boys."

Old Foss spoke up. "One of the boys is abuilding a box for Charlie right now, Ben. We dug a grave out back where Charlie always liked to sneak a nap after Sunday dinner. We can plant him soon as the box is done."

Ben forced a smile. "Thanks, boys. Charlie would appreciate all this." He looked at Old Foss. "I'll be at the house when you're ready."

Old Foss nodded.

Without another word, Ben left the bunkhouse.

With the sound of hammering echoing across the hardpan, Ben plopped down on his own bed in the main house. Lacing his fingers behind his head, he stared at the ceiling. His whole world had come down around his shoulders, but violence was not the solution, not now. Use the law. That was the only way to have a lasting peace. The law.

Ben's eyes narrowed. The best plan was to sit tight

until the federal marshal arrived. Barnett would stay close to the Triple B for the time being. The big rancher had stirred the pot. Now, he would sit back and watch it simmer, hoping someone would cause it to boil over. That was where he was wrong. Ben could watch the pot boil as patiently as anyone.

During the long, interminable wait for the coffin to be finished, Ben relived the last twelve years. 1861. That's when he and Charlie met. Since then, they'd been inseparable. He remembered the good and the bad, the funny and the sad.

Charlie was no gunfighter, but he was fast, fast enough that he could have buried a heap of gunnies had he been the sort to flaunt his speed. And somehow, it didn't seem out of place that a faster gun had taken him.

But, what didn't fit was the shooter—dignified, soft-spoken, unflappable Albert Barnett. Never, in half a dozen lifetimes, would Ben have figured the big rancher was fast enough to put two slugs in Charlie before he could even clear leather.

The fight was fair. Three Key hands swore to that fact. Damn, Albert had everyone fooled. Not only wealthy, but fast with a gun. Some combination.

A gamut of emotions coursed through Ben's veins, leaving him drained by the time the hammering finally stopped. He had to force himself from his stupor when Old Foss came to tell him they were ready to bury Charlie.

Just after the coffin was lowered into the grave, a small knot of riders came out of the pines bordering the lower meadow, heading directly for the ranch house. When they saw the hands around the grave, they pulled up. Two rode on, reining up at a respectful distance until the burying was over.

Ben paid them no attention until the last spade of dirt was packed on the grave. When he turned to the riders, he recognized Ike Hazlett, the federal marshal he had met in Tucson. He shook his head, wondering if the marshal would be able to help now that all of the evidence had been destroyed.

The marshal rode closer. He glanced past Ben to the grave, then smoothed his drooping mustache. "Made it sooner than I thought, Mr. Elliott. The trouble at Sulphur Springs took care of itself. Learned of it a few hours after you rode out."

Ben looked past the marshal at the other rider, a stranger who wore a pair of Colts low on his hips. "Coffee's on up to the cookshack," Ben said.

"Sorry, Mr. Elliott. This is business. I'm here to arrest you for the murder of William George Burgess."

Chapter Eighteen

Everyone froze, staring in disbelief at the marshal.

Ben found his voice. "What did you say?"

Hazlett rested his hands on his saddle horn and leaned forward, giving Ben ample evidence that the lanky marshal didn't plan on drawing down on him. Hazlett repeated his charge in a soft voice. "There are witnesses who swear you gunned down William George Burgess last night at your line shack by the Triple B."

An angry muttering came from the Key hands behind Ben. He held up his hand, keeping his eyes on the marshal. "I don't know a William George Burgess, Marshal, and I sure as hell wasn't out at my line shack last night. I didn't get back here until the middle of this morning from Tucson." He dipped his head toward the grave and added in a bitter voice, "Just in time to bury my best friend. I ain't even had time to take down my soogan."

"Sorry about that, Mr. Elliott. I just rode in myself." He hooked his thumb at the cowpoke with the two Colts strung low on his hips. "Me and my deputy, Billy, there. We come to see you about your trouble when

I ran into Sheriff Jess Lowry and a posse of angry cow-pokes headin' thisaway." He nodded to the forest. "Him and the others is waitin' back in the pines on the other side of the meadow."

Beyond the meadow, a band of riders milled about on the edge of the pines. They were too distant to make out individual faces, but Ben knew their identity. He looked back to the marshal. "Someone's hatched up a mighty sneaky scheme here, Marshal. Barnett figured I'd gone for you. With me out of the way good and proper, Albert Barnett has nothing to worry about. But, as long as I'm out and free, he can never rest easy."

The marshal nodded. He replied in his same calm monotone. "That might be, Mr. Elliott, but you see, I ain't got no choice. You're going to have to go with me and Billy."

Old Foss sidled up to Ben. He whispered out of the corner of his mouth, soft enough so the marshal could not hear him. "Make your play, boss. We're with you."

Ben shook his head, keeping his eyes on the marshal. "No. No gunplay, not here. Lead starts flying, people are going to get hurt. This isn't the time."

"Maybe not for you, boss, but it is for us," said one of the Key riders as eight six-guns cleared leather and centered on the marshal and his deputy.

Ben glanced around.

Old Foss had a grin wider than a river. "Git," he said. "We'll keep the marshal here while you get lost up in the mountains."

For a moment, Ben hesitated, his gaze sweeping across the meadow to Sheriff Lowry and his posse. He then realized he'd never reach jail alive. His ranch hands were giving him his only choice. He disappeared into the barn.

The deputy looked around in alarm, but the marshal didn't move a muscle. He remained leaning on his hands. He clicked his tongue and drawled to Old Foss. "This could get you boys in trouble. Best you put them hog legs down."

Old Foss spoke up. "What more trouble you gonna get us in, mister? The ranch has been took from us. We got no job no more. Winter's coming on. We're broke. Hell, I ain't all that smart, but I reckon I'd hazard a guess that we got us trouble enough here that a little more ain't goin' to hurt nothing."

Hazlett lifted an eyebrow and grinned. "Reckon you're right, cowboy."

Ben quickly saddled his dun. He had no supplies, but he'd take care of that later. Swinging into the saddle, he drove his heels into the dun's flanks, and the big stallion burst from the barn and cut northeast toward the sheer walls of the Mogollon.

Faint shouts and the distant pop of gunfire echoed up the valley as Sheriff Lowry and his men spurred their ponies across the meadow. Ben glanced over his shoulder and grinned as the Key riders stepped back and holstered their six-guns. Old Foss and his boys had given Ben the few precious minutes he needed to lose himself up on the Mogollon Plateau.

Weaving through the aspen and pine, Ben twisted through the foothills several miles before taking a winding trail to the rim. From behind a copse of pinyon on the rim, he peered down into the sixty-mile-long valley.

Far to the south, a cluster of dots moved across a meadow, disappeared into a stand of pine, and reappeared in the next meadow. For several minutes, Ben studied the approaching posse, coldly calculating his next move.

To the west, the sun dropped behind the mountains. The posse would camp soon. Until then, all Ben could do was wait and watch.

Within minutes, the posse pulled up in the bend of a narrow stream. Four small campfires soon flickered in the encroaching darkness. With a grunt, Ben turned back to the forest of pinyon on the plateau and quickly lost himself within the thick growth.

Beneath a ledge of granite from which seeped a thin rivulet of sweet, cold water, Ben picketed the dun and built a small fire over which he roasted a rabbit.

As he sat beside the small fire, peering into the darkness beyond its glow, he felt the thin veneer of the white man's civilization peeling away, replaced by the stoic fatalism of the Apache.

He had lived with the Coyoteros for almost ten years after Tin Man died. If the old peddler had not told Ben different, he would have believed he was Apache. In fact, Ben had sometimes wondered if maybe his mother or father was Apache since Tin Man had never found their bodies, only their burned-out wagon. The wagon was enough to convince Ben that his pa was white. But, he still wondered about his ma.

Moving silently, Ben extinguished the fire and lay back on the rocky ground, his fingers laced together behind his head. He stared into the starry heavens and wondered about Mary Catheryn and her sallow-faced fiancé, Zebron Rawlings. He'd heard no talk of the impending marriage, nor of the sale of the Slash Bar. Maybe she had some of her daddy's common sense after all.

Ben forced his thoughts back on his own problems.

He would give the posse another hour to settle in for the night, and then he would make his move. If he couldn't get the law to do what was right, then he would correct the problem himself.

Ben tried not to think, to put Charlie out of his mind, to forget about John Wills, about the ranches. Closing painful doors, he discovered, was much more difficult than it sounded.

Instead, he laid his plans for the next two days, plans that would force Albert Barnett to act, and perhaps make a mistake.

Ben stared at the North Star. He still couldn't believe Albert Barnett had outgunned Charlie. In all his experience, Ben had seen only one man who could have matched Charlie, the blue-belly bushwhacker who ambushed the gold wagon back in the Mohawk Mountains in 1863, ten years earlier.

Wounded and almost blinded by pain, Ben had not been able to get a good look at the man, but he was big, almost as big as Albert Barnett, he told himself, but blind in one eye. However, Ben could never forget the speed of the man's draw. One moment, the big man's hand was by his side, and the next, a Colt six-gun filled the hand. A blur. As fast—No, faster than Charlie ever was.

The recollections suddenly stirred other memories, raised puzzling questions. The two men couldn't be the same, but where did Albert Barnett get the money to buy such vast holdings? How many sections did Albert have? Twelve hundred, twelve fifty? Right at eight hundred thousand acres.

And even at distressed prices, such holdings could cost upward of four hundred thousand dollars. Where did Albert get that kind of money? Gold? Could it have been the gold from the wagon train?

Another idea struck him. The names. Jake Barnes. That was the name of the bushwhacker in the canyon. Mighty close to J. Albert Barnett.

Ben shook his head, realizing just how foolish his theories had become. "Don't be such a damned idiot, Ben," he muttered to himself. "A body can stretch anything to mean what he wants. The only problem is that if he stretches something too far, it'll pop back on him. Besides, Barnes had only one eye."

Pushing his far-fetched speculations aside, Ben fumbled in his saddlebags and pulled out the pair of deerskin moccasins he always carried. After slipping into them, he removed his hat, checked his Colt, and buttoned his vest. He wanted nothing to jangle, flap, or clatter at the wrong time. Before leaving, he moved his pony's picket. Where Ben was going, he couldn't take the dun.

Chapter Nineteen

On the rim high above the camp, Ben knelt beneath the branches of a twisted pinyon tree. The sharp fragrance of the short needles filled the air.

Below, the campfires winked in the darkness. Occasional shadows moved in front of the fires.

A cruel grin curled his lips as he remembered the lessons his Apache father, Taa-Yah, had taught him, lessons the Apaches practiced against the Mexicans and the whites.

Rising slowly, Ben glided down the mountain, pausing along the trail to rig a surprise or two for the posse. He didn't want the traps to kill anyone. He just wanted to make sure Albert Barnett got his message. The wealthy cattle baron would understand what it meant.

Despite the season, the blazing heat of the Arizona sun kept most wildlife forted up during the day. At night, the mountains and valleys abounded with the creatures of nature searching for food. Ben took advantage of their habits, imitating the cry of a wounded rabbit.

Within moments, the beating of wings swooped just above Ben's head. He gave the cry again. Finally, he spotted what he had been waiting for, a dark, sinuous shape slithering across the rocky ground, a rattlesnake looking for an easy meal.

When the serpent spotted Ben, it immediately coiled into its defensive posture, rattles buzzing like a hive of bees. Ben quickly pinned its head; then, using a stiff branch the size of his little finger, he pressed against the venom sacs behind the fangs, voiding them of their poison, a dark, viscous liquid in the moonlight.

He slipped the rattler in a bag and knotted the top. Then he gave the wounded rabbit cry again and waited. Soon a second rattler glided from the darkness. Quickly, Ben voided the venom sacs on the second serpent.

He glanced through the pines toward the camp. A wicked grin played over his face. Jess Lowry was about to get the hell scared out of him.

Holding the rattler firmly behind the head with one hand and the rattles with the other, Ben slipped in close to camp. He spotted the two guards, both of whom had fallen asleep. Three of the fires were almost out, but the fourth burned brightly. Three cowpokes squatted beside it, their voices soft murmurs.

Lowry was not one of the three. From the darkness, Ben studied the sleeping figures, but he could not pick out the sheriff. There was only one thing to do. He called the sheriff by name. "Lowry! Jess Lowry!"

Ben's voice broke the silence of the night like an alarm bell.

The sheriff jumped to his feet, his six-gun in his hand. "Who the hell . . ."

A sudden buzz broke the silence, and Sheriff Jess Lowry's voice froze as a ropelike object came twisting from the darkness, wrapping about his throat. "Yaaaa," he screamed, frantically grabbing at the writhing, twisting rattlesnake. "Snake, snake, snake," he screamed again, dancing a war dance around the fire.

The other cowpokes, guns drawn, stayed well away from the high-stepping sheriff. Finally, Lowry dislodged the snake, which slammed to the ground, then managed to slither into the darkness unharmed despite the barrage of .44's directed at it.

Jess dropped his six-gun, grabbing his neck and shoulders to see if the rattler had struck him. "Oh, no," he groaned. "Please, please, dear Lord. Don't let me be bit." After a few terrified moments, he realized his hurried prayer had been answered. With a long sigh, he sat heavily on the ground by the fire.

At the same time, Ben heard the crashing sounds of the two guards behind him rushing to camp. He knelt in the shadows at the base of a pine as they hurried past.

Before the men in camp could gather their thoughts, Ben called out again. "Jess Lowry!"

As one, the cowpokes about the fire froze. Sheriff Lowry shot a frightened look at the federal marshal, then, mustering his courage, turned back to the encroaching darkness. "What do you want, Elliott?" Shaken bravado trembled in his voice.

Ben watched in amusement as Lowry frantically signaled his men to disperse into the night in an effort to surround Ben. "Tell Barnett he bit off too much this time. Things are going to get a hell of a lot worse before they get better."

Without another word, Ben slipped back into the night and headed for the trail, deliberately creating enough noise to be heard in camp.

"The trail. He's headin' up the trail," came a cry.

"Shut up. You want him to hear you?" cried out another voice.

Ben grinned to himself as he skirted his traps. He paused and tossed a rock back down the trail.

"Up there. I heard him up there."

The scraping, clattering sound of boots against rocks echoed through the darkness. Suddenly a swishing noise and a sharp cry split the night. A deep silence followed.

"Jesus," came a muffled groan. "My nose . . . my nose is busted."

After a few moments, the sound of pursuit continued up the trail, this time not quite as rapid. One cowpoke whispered, "Careful. Look out for any more of them tra—Yahhhh."

"What the hell . . ."

"Cut me down. Dammit, you hear me. Cut me down."

Ben grinned as he imagined the cowpoke swinging by one leg ten feet off the ground. Now was the time to get their attention. "That's far enough, boys," Ben called out.

Immediately, the night grew still.

"Next time, I get serious. Whoever comes on up here won't be going back." Ben reached behind a small boulder and pulled out the bag with the second rattler.

"What do you want, Elliott?" It was Ike Hazlett, the federal marshal.

"Justice, Marshal. That's all, justice."

"This ain't no way of getting it."

Ben had pinpointed the location of the men below him, about a hundred feet or so down the steep trail. He pulled the rattler from the bag. "I'm tired of talking, Marshal." He hurled the snake out over the treetops, aiming for the patch of men below.

When the snake hit the treetops, Ben called out, "Another rattler coming down, boys. Better cover your heads."

A frozen silence filled the night; then as the heavy body of the rattlesnake dropped from the treetop, crashed from limb to limb, and plopped to the ground, the night exploded into a frenzied dash for anywhere except where they were.

Ben had one or two more matters to take care of before he disappeared back onto the rugged Mogollon. He slipped off the trail and circled the camp, arriving before the posse. Within seconds, he stampeded their horses and disappeared into a grove of nearby pines with the marshal's pony, a roan. He waited, watching for the federal marshal.

The posse broke up in pursuit of their ponies. When Marshal Ike Hazlett approached the grove of pines, Ben spooked the roan. It whinnied, catching the marshal's attention.

Crouching behind a tangle of briars, Ben watched the marshal approach his horse through the shafts of white moonlight penetrating the pine grove. "Easy, fella," the marshal whispered. "Easy." He reached for the bridle and his hand froze in midair when he saw the roan was tied to a pine.

"That's right, Marshal," said Ben, gliding forward and shucking the marshal's six-gun. "You been taken. Now, turn around."

Maintaining the same laconic manner he had always worn, the marshal grinned at Ben. "You kinda stirred up some excitement around here, Mr. Elliott. Almost makes a man feel right unwelcome. Them rattlers might have kilt someone."

"Not likely. I took the poison out of them."

"Now why would you do that?"

Ben studied the man before him. He holstered his own six-gun. "I don't want to hurt no one, Marshal, but right now, you are unwelcome. The best thing you can do is leave this part of the territory. Law or not, I can't keep watching out for you. Things are going to start moving fast. I wouldn't care to see you caught up in it."

For several long seconds, the marshal studied Ben. He cleared his throat. "It appears this is between you and Barnett."

"That's about the size of it."

The marshal took a deep breath and released it slowly. He stroked his drooping mustache. "Wish I could do what you say, Mr. Elliott, but there's the murder of William George Burgess, and I don't reckon I can ride away from my duty when a killing is involved."

Ben stared hard at the lanky, mustachioed marshal. His first impression of Marshal Hazlett back in Tucson was that the man was honest, that he hid out in no one's pocket. And nothing had happened to make Ben change his mind.

He grinned, drawn to the lanky marshal's sense of duty. "I didn't figure you would, Marshal. I just don't want to see you or your deputy hurt. You can't stop what's going to happen here. As sure as the sun rises, there's bound to be bad trouble in the valley. But for your information, I didn't kill that hombre you're talking about."

"I believe you. But the court's got to make that decision. Come on back. Let the judge decide."

"I can't. Don't you understand? Barnett is behind all this. He wants you on my tail so he can pull off this scheme of his, whatever it is. He figures I'll be so busy dodging you that I can't be any trouble to him until he's got his plan all packaged nice and neat." Ben hesitated. "No one is going to stop me from taking care of Albert Barnett. No one," he added, his voice cold and threatening.

Ike Hazlett sighed. "That's what they pay me for, Ben. I couldn't take their money no other way."

"I understand." Ben shook his head. "I'm going to have to tie you up, Ike. I can't have you tagging after me."

Ike Hazlett glanced at Ben's holstered six-gun. He stroked his mustache. "No need to. I'll give you fifteen minutes. That's about how long I figure it would take me to untie myself."

Ben chuckled. "Not if I tied you."

Ike grunted. "Maybe so. Fifteen minutes."

With a grin, Ben nodded, and like a ghost disappeared into the night.

"But, I'll be coming after you," the marshal called into the darkness. Lowering his voice to a whisper, he added, "After I get back from Tucson." He squatted by the pine and rolled a cigarette, after which he casually untied his roan and patted the animal on the neck. "Let's go, fella. And take it slow and easy. That hombre needs some time to take care of problems around here. We'll be back in a few weeks."

Chapter Twenty

"He did what?" Albert Barnett exploded, smashing his wine glass against the wall. "Dammit, man," he yelled at Sheriff Jess Lowry. "There were a dozen of you, and you let one solitary man run you off."

Jess Lowry tried to explain about the rattlesnakes again, but the broad-shouldered cattle baron waved his words aside.

"What about that damned federal marshal? What did he do?"

Lowry shrugged. "He couldn't do nothing more than we did. It was dark, and we couldn't see nothing."

"The hell you say," snapped the irate cattle baron. "Where in the hell is he now?"

"Gone back to Tucson with his deputy. Said he had some business to take care of, but he'd be back."

Barnett closed his eyes and clenched his teeth. "He can't do that. What about the murder of Burgess? What'd he have to say about that?"

Lowry shook his head. "Nothing. He didn't have nothing to say about it."

Rafe Borke leaned against the wall, his black eyes

mere slits, his thin lips sneering. "Want me to take care of Elliott, boss?"

His square face dark with anger, Albert Barnett spun on his foreman. For a moment, he considered Borke's offer, but he had more use for the burly foreman here. He could hire the gunnies to take care of Ben Elliott. "No. Not you. Cherokee Jack. Where's Cherokee Jack?"

Borke pursed his lips and pushed away from the wall. "Last I heard, out east in New Mexico Territory."

Barnett's eyes narrowed. "He as good as I hear?"

The bearded foreman grinned evilly. "Better."

"Get him. Tell him to bring five or six of his best men." The large man crossed the room to the window and stared up at the Mogollon Rim. "I want Ben Elliott dead."

With a curt nod, Rafe Borke left. Barnett turned to the sheriff who remained standing in the middle of the room, hat in hand like a recalcitrant schoolchild. "You're sheriff because I put you there. I put you there, and I can take you out, and that's exactly what will damned well happen if you don't do your job."

Jess Lowry nodded hastily. "Yes, sir, Mr. Barnett. Yes, sir." He reached for the door, then paused.

Barnett snapped at him. "Now what?"

Lowry turned back, his cheeks coloring. "What . . . What should I do first . . . I mean, about Elliott?"

Albert Barnett drew a deep breath and held his temper. What could he expect from men like Lowry, dull, unimaginative, incapable of seeing beyond the first move in a game of checkers?

Shaming the man would solve nothing, only undermine the intensity of Lowry's support, not that Albert Barnett had even sought Jess Lowry's aid, but the man was sheriff, and the position did carry a certain amount of power and influence that Barnett could use. No sense in turning down any help.

In a level, patient tone, Barnett told Lowry to place guards around the ranches, the Key, Leland Pickett's spread, Ches Lewis's spread, and Colly Weems's place. "I don't think Elliott will show up, but there is an outside chance." His smooth voice slid into a patronizing tone that Jess Lowry failed to recognize. "So, that's where I need your help, Jess. I want *you* to cover them for me, you hear? And when Elliott shows up, and he will, kill him."

After Lowry left, Albert Barnett rigged up his buggy and rode over to the Slash Bar. The time had come for Zebron Rawlings to start pulling his weight.

Remembering his years with the Coyoteros, Ben moved his camp into a jumble of house-size boulders a mile back from the Mogollon Rim, a thousand-foot escarpment that marked the southern boundary of the plateaus and mesas of the Colorado Plateau.

The years had dimmed his memory, but quickly, Ben discovered the hidden trail winding between boulders back into a ten-acre meadow lush with rich grass and bisected by a clear stream with a small, deep pond bristling with trout.

Astride the dun, Ben rode slowly around the meadow, his dark eyes searching for any evidence of recent camps. What few horse biscuits he spotted disintegrated upon touch. He discovered the remains of a campfire that was nothing more than a black stain on the ground.

Ben nodded with satisfaction. This was from where he would mount his campaign against J. Albert Barnett.

Back among the boulders was a natural cave, deep enough to shelter him from rain. A fissure in the back of the cave allowed smoke to drift among the boulders. Yes, he decided, looking back out over the small meadow, he had found the ideal hideaway.

He removed the saddle and gave the dun a good rubdown and turned him loose. Like a young foal, the dun dashed across the meadow, whirled and pranced, then fell to the grass and rolled from one side to the other.

Ben gathered an armload of kindling and built two fires outside the cave. Once the flames were hot, he added damp wood. A thick column of smoke from each rolled high into the sky, sending a special message.

After a few minutes, he extinguished the fires.

Though some of the skills he had learned from the Coyoteros had lost their edge, Ben quickly speared four fat trout and spitted them over a small fire he built inside the cave. He put on a pot of coffee. As the sun began its drop behind the mountains, he checked his gear, noting that he only had ten or twelve cartridges for his six-gun.

An unbidden grin played over his face. After tonight, ammunition would be the least of his worries.

Later, as the early evening stars began appearing in the sky, Ben had visitors, two Apaches, White Eye and Tree That Shakes, Coyotero warriors with whom he had grown up.

Ben explained why he was in the mountains.

"We will help Little Tin Man," replied White Eye.

"No. This is for me to do, not my brothers, though I am very honored that you so offered. The white man hates the Apache. I do not wish to cause my brothers any more pain. I must do this myself."

White Eye nodded. "We know of what you speak, and it is true; but never forget us, Little Tin Man. We will watch and come whenever you call."

"Good. There is a man, a lawman with a mustache." He dragged his finger across his upper lip. "He follows me. I wish him no harm, but I must know where he is."

Tree That Shakes grunted. "The one of which you speak rides the trail to Tucson with the rising of the sun."

Ben frowned, surprised at the news. Why would Hazlett suddenly ride out?

White Eye spoke up. "You wish for us to bring him to you?"

"No." Ben shook his head. "Let him go. I didn't figure he'd leave so soon, but I don't want to stop him. He is a good white man." He gestured to the fire. "Come. Eat." White Eye and Tree That Shakes squatted and drank coffee and ate broiled trout.

After the Apaches left, Ben departed his camp, riding along the rim well into the night until he spotted Barnett's ranch in the valley. Dismounting, he slipped the bit from the dun's mouth and picketed the animal in some browse.

Barnett's headquarters was a little over four miles distant, no more than an hour's travel on foot.

A sense of strength, of sheer indestructible power flooded through him as he wound his way down the red sandstone and basalt rim. He remembered the first time he had ever experienced such a feeling.

He was fourteen, only a short distance from completing his first twenty-mile run holding a mouthful of water. When he finished the run and spit out the water before his Apache father, Taa-Yah, he experienced a pride that would remain with him the rest of his life, always reminding him that he was Apache, that he was one of the Human Beings, that he was a special man among a special race of special people.

Ben soaked up the teachings of his Apache father like sand absorbing water. He came to know, without having been told, that a single Apache, fighting by himself against any odds, was invincible, indomitable, unconquerable.

And the driving force of those beliefs now coursed through Ben's veins as he loped across valleys and through pine groves to Albert Barnett's headquarters.

Chapter Twenty-one

Falling to his stomach in the lush blue grama meadow abutting the hardpan around Barnett's ranch house, Ben studied the dark shadows surrounding the main house and outbuildings. He grinned to himself at the irony of his strike.

From the very man he had sworn to ruin, Ben planned to steal the tools and weapons necessary to carry out such a task.

First, he would set the barn afire and then, while the ranch hands were attempting to extinguish it, slip into the main house and take an armload of Winchesters and ammunition.

With the patience of a mountain lion, Ben waited and watched. Soon, he pinpointed sentries deep in the shadows and marked their locations, especially around the main house.

At midnight, the shift changed, and in the confusion, Ben glided like a wraith through the darkness to lie in the shadows beneath the lower rail of the corral near the barn. That was his destination; the barn and the side door less than ten feet from him.

Crickets chirruped, and a light breeze sprang up,

moaning through the nearby pines and rustling the slender stems of grama. The nearest sentry was in the shadows at the end of the barn, some thirty feet distant.

From time to time, the guard walked from one corner of the barn to the other. Ben waited until the sentry turned, then dashed into the barn by the side door and pressed against the wall and listened, waiting for his eyes to adjust to the blackness around him. He felt along the wall with his hand, not wanting to stumble into anything that would create a disturbance and draw the sentry.

Suddenly, he stiffened. His hand rested on a wooden box. Running his fingers over the box, he guessed it to be about a foot by two feet. Below it were more boxes of the same size.

Could it be? Barnett used dynamite. All the ranchers had used it for the last three years. The new explosive had proven to be much safer than black powder.

Ben itched to strike a match, but he couldn't take the chance on being discovered. Fumbling with the top of the box, he discovered it to be loose. He reached inside. His fingers touched a cool, cylindrical object. "I'll be damned," he muttered, unable to believe his luck.

Outside, the jangling of the sentry's spurs kept Ben alert to the guard's location. Altering his plans, Ben waited until the sentry crossed to the far corner of the barn and silently carried two cases of dynamite out to the meadow, stashing them just inside the grove of pine a mile from the main house. He glanced at the Big Dipper. Almost two. A waning moon shone from directly overhead. He was running late.

Back at the ranch, Ben slid into the shadows of the

corral. The sentry had left his post. Ben strained to pick up any sounds. All he heard was the soughing of the early morning breeze and the whispering murmur of the pines.

Ben took a deep breath and dashed across the clearing to the side door. Just as he stepped inside, a match flared, and Ben stopped in his tracks. The sentry stood frozen, so shocked to see a man the cigarette went unlit, the match inches from its tip. He gasped. "What the . . ."

Ben wasted no time. He took advantage of the sentry's surprise. He slammed the muzzle of his Colt across the man's temple. The cigarette and match flew through the air and landed in the straw strewn across the floor of the barn. If the straw had been doused with kerosene, it couldn't have ignited any faster.

The guard on the floor groaned.

Grabbing him under his arms, Ben hauled the unconscious man out to the corral and dropped him away from harm. In a crouch, he ran into the meadow and then sprinted to the far side of the ranch house and waited.

Within minutes, yellow flames leaped into the dark sky, illuminating the surrounding buildings with an eerie glow. Shouts filled the air, and the sentries rushed to the barn.

Ben waited. So far, so good.

Moments later, his nightshirt tucked into his pants, Albert Barnett hurried onto the porch. Without hesitation, the big man leaped to the ground and shouted, "The horses. Get the horses out. There's dynamite in there."

With the cunning of an Apache, Ben slipped into the main house, grabbed five Winchesters and a mixed case of .44's, rimfires and centerfires. Just as silently, he disappeared back into the night.

No sooner had he reached the meadow than the dynamite in the barn exploded, sending shards of flaming timber high into the sky like Fourth of July rockets.

"The house," someone shouted. "There's fire on the roof."

"On the cookshack too," another voice shouted.

Ben laughed to himself and fell into a mile-eating trot across the meadow to the dynamite. He enjoyed the moment. "The fun's just starting, Albert," he muttered; but he didn't fool himself. Albert Barnett knew damned well who was responsible, and he would come looking for Ben Elliott, one way or another.

Mary Catheryn Wills looked at herself in the mirror, patted one side of her hair in place. She smiled when she thought of the upcoming cotillion. The bawling of cows caused her to look at the reflection of the window in the mirror.

For a moment, she pondered the last weeks back home. She had not been as miserable as she had expected. In fact, she rather enjoyed the physical demands such a life put on a person, whether riding a horse or branding stock, not that she had actually branded any stock, but the bawling of the cattle, the shouting of the cowboys, the smell of blazing wood and burning hair, all enveloped in clouds of choking white dust brought back forgotten memories of her childhood.

She vaguely remembered her mother. Her father, big, robust, always laughing, had been her life until he sent her to Baltimore so she could become a lady.

A wry grin curled her red lips, and she arched an eyebrow at her reflection. A lady. She studied her image in the mirror. Yes, she was a lady, and Zebron Rawlings always treated her in that manner. She studied the sudden knit in her eyebrows, wondering why she should be unhappy with Zebron's constant attention. She should be pleased he was always around to help her make decisions, but—

A knock on the door interrupted her thoughts. "Yes," she called.

Zebron Rawlings's silky voice came from the hallway. "Albert is here, Mary."

"I'll be right out." She studied her face, noting the healthy tan on her cheeks, a tan most women would hate. She remembered the first time she and Zebron had dined with J. Albert Barnett as well as the subsequent occasions. She had been thrilled to dine with one of the most influential men in the territory, but now— why didn't she feel the same way? He was courteous and gentlemanly as always. Nothing had happened to make her feel different, but she did, and now she almost wished she had not agreed when Zebron told her Barnett was coming to dinner. "Business," he had explained simply. "Cattle business."

Dinner that night was strained. Albert Barnett was not his usual ebullient self. Instead of the after-dinner retirement to the parlor for brandy and chitchat over news from the east, Albert excused himself, claiming pressing business back at the Triple B.

After Albert Barnett paid his respects and departed, Zebron Rawlings asked Mary Catheryn to set a date for their marriage. For some reason not even she understood, she begged off, promising instead to set the time at the cotillion in three weeks.

* * *

While Mary Catheryn and Zebron Rawlings entertained Albert Barnett, Ben glided through the darkness to the Key. He dropped to one knee behind a twisted pinyon less than fifty feet from the burned-out barn.

Throughout the day, he had kept watch on the ranch from the aspen grove above the south meadow. Two of his hands had ridden out, their war bags tied behind the cantle. They were replaced by two or three strange faces, one of which seemed to have taken over the main house. Lowry's compadres, Ben guessed.

With the stealth of a wolf, Ben slipped into the dark shadows of the cookshack and pressed up against the wall outside the window under which Old Foss slept.

Softly, Ben tapped on the window.

Immediately, Old Foss returned Ben's signal.

Ben slipped inside. "I hoped you was by yourself," he said into the darkness.

The disembodied voice of the old cook cackled. "You best know that, boss. Ain't nobody but me sleeps in here. Them punchers got their own bunks."

Ben's voice dropped into a whisper. "What's been happening around here?"

"Not much. Barnett's foreman, Borke, he told us to be off here by Saturday. Frank and Sawtooth rode out today."

"Damn," muttered Ben, peering into the darkness, looking for the silhouette of Old Foss, but the darkness was so complete that Ben could not even see the proverbial hand in front of his eyes. At least Barnett hadn't come in shooting. Of course, Ben reminded himself, the rancher was too smart for that. "I'm sorry about gettin' you boys mixed up in all this."

"Hell, boss. It ain't your fault. It's that damned Albert Barnett. I'd like to cut his balls off."

Ben chuckled. "That's why I'm here."

Hope flooded Old Foss's voice. "You got something cooked up?"

"More or less. Here's what I want you to do. Go over to Prescott. Tell our boys to do the same."

"Why Prescott?"

"I'll know where you are when I need you. Besides, in the next few days, I figure lead plums are going to be flying pretty thick around here. I don't want you fellers catching any of it."

Old Foss was silent for a moment. Then, "You figure on being right in the middle of it, huh, boss?"

"Smack-dab in the middle. That's why I want you boys out of here. I don't want any of my people hurt, and I damned sure don't want Barnett to come after you because of me."

"Yeah, and he's just the worthless, egg-sucking kinda mongrel to do something like that," Old Foss replied. "But, you figure. You start something, someone's gonna get bad hurt."

"It won't be me. Anyway, stop by the other ranches. Pass word on to the others. If I need you, I'll get word to you in Prescott, you hear?"

"Okay, boss. We'll be up there waiting. But, I'd sure like to join you. Do me good to put a hot chunk of lead in Barnett's butt."

Ben remained silent a moment, filled with gratitude at the old man's offer. "Thanks, but you're best off not involved right now."

Old Foss hesitated. "How you fixed for grub?"

Ben chuckled. "I can use some."

"Wait here."

For the next few minutes, Ben sat motionless, listening to the whisper-faint rustlings in the darkness as Old Foss packed grub into a denim bag.

Suddenly, the bag was thrust in Ben's hands. "Here. There's cigarette makin's in case you run out."

"Thanks."

"And a man's gotta sin. I even stuck the last of my medicinal whiskey in for you."

Ben chuckled, then grew serious. "Remember, Foss. You and the boys get out of here, pronto."

"We will. Don't worry."

After Ben rode away, Old Foss gathered his plunder. He'd do what Ben wanted, except him and the boys would camp alongside the Prescott road at the base of the mountains. That way, Ben wouldn't have to ride all the way to Prescott to fetch them.

Chapter Twenty-two

Early next morning, Ben, perched high on the Mogollon Rim smoking a Durham, watched the movement below as Old Foss and the last of the old Key riders departed the ranch. He remembered the work, the sweat, the money put into his spread, and he damn well regretted what was going to happen to the entire valley, but he had no choice.

When the old cook rode out and headed for Ches Lewis's spread, Ben grinned and turned the dun back to the hidden valley.

Back in the cave, Ben spent the remainder of the day in preparation for the fighting to come. After fully loading each of the Winchesters, he opened the boxes of dynamite and began lashing the sticks together, two in a bundle. Without blasting caps, he would have to place the charges where he could reach them with a .44. Then he fashioned shoulder straps for the denim bag Old Foss had given him.

By the time Benjamin Franklin Elliott finished with Albert Barnett, the cattle baron would wish he had never heard of Arizona Territory.

* * *

Ben's plan was simple. Harass Barnett until the man made a mistake. And when he made that mistake, Ben would be damned certain he was there to take advantage of it.

It was midafternoon when he finished the last pack of dynamite. A distant gunshot broke the silence of the mountain air. Moving quickly, but without alarm, Ben stacked the bundle of dynamite with the others, and then climbed into the boulders surrounding the small valley.

From behind a pinyon on the rim, Ben saw a small party of men on the edge of a meadow far below. Two were stringing up a deer while a couple more built a fire, opting for an early camp and fresh meat.

Idly, he rolled a cigarette and lit it. "Barnett's started the ball," he muttered, blowing out the match. A strange excitement possessed him, and he recognized it as the Apache's desire to fight, the primary purpose in an Apache warrior's life.

Back in the cave, Ben packed several bundles of dynamite into the knapsack he had fashioned from Foss's denim bag. He strapped on his gun belt and grabbed a Winchester.

Now he would see if the kind of men Albert Barnett was hiring had cojones or not.

For once, Ben was surprised. From his vantage point behind a snarl of briars, he studied the man squatting by the fire. Cherokee Jack! He studied the squatting hombre's long black hair under a flat-brimmed hat with a brightly beaded hatband. "Thought he was over in Texas or New Mexico," he mumbled, recognizing that

Albert Barnett was not losing any time with second-rate gunnies.

Ben was not anxious to kill anyone. If driven to it, he would, but he'd prefer scaring them out of the valley instead of planting them six feet under. Of course, if a jasper got right down to the nut-cutting, one way was as effective as the other.

He scrutinized the other five, but none of them were familiar. A frown wrinkled his forehead. At one time, Jack had run with a psychotic killer with the misleading handle of Happy Schmidtkye, a German immigrant who fancied slicing his enemies into separate pieces. Ben had seen him once.

He studied the camp for another few minutes. No sign of Schmidtkye. The men finished their chow, wiped their plates clean, and squatted around the fire, laughing and drinking coffee fortified with rotgut whiskey.

With a grin, Ben faded back into the forest and bounded back up the mountain to a large boulder overlooking the camp. He pulled one of the dynamite bundles from the knapsack and jacked a live round in the chamber of the Winchester. "Okay, boys," he whispered. "Time to get the dance started."

He measured the distance to the fire and hurled the dynamite far out over the forest below. He jerked the Winchester into his shoulder and set the sights on the falling bundle.

The dynamite missed the fire by inches, but the sudden appearance of an unknown object striking the ground between the squatting cowpokes startled them, for the moment, freezing them in their squat.

"What the . . ."

Ben did not give them a chance to react. No sooner had the dynamite sticks slid to a halt than he squeezed the trigger. The crack of the Winchester was lost in the resounding explosion that rocked the camp, blew apart the fire, and knocked the gunnies on their backsides, filling the air with a cloud of red and yellow embers. Frightened horses snorted and reared, jerking their pickets loose and disappearing into the forest.

Before any of them could react, Ben raked the campsite with gunfire, sending the squalling toughs scrambling for nearby trees. When the hammer fell on an empty chamber, Ben dropped down off the boulder and raced silently through the forest to an ancient windfall north of the camp. Excited voices and painful moans drifted to him. Quickly, he reloaded.

"Who in the hell did that?" said Cherokee Jack, his husky voice rough as gravel. From where he was crouched behind a pine, he scrutinized the forest around him, looking for any movement at all in the fading daylight.

"Jack. Jack. I'm hurt."

"Shut up." Jack snapped back with a curse. "Whoever's out there don't need to know where we are."

A taunting voice off to Jack's left cut through the silence. "Forget it, Jack. I got each one of you set up."

Jack grimaced. His thin fingers gripped his .44, and his lips were stretched tightly over his clenched teeth. Who in the hell is that sumbitch? And what does he want?

On either side of him, Jack heard moans. His own ears still rang. He felt a warm liquid on the side of his face. He touched his fingers to the stiff beard. Blood!

A blinding fury filled his muscles, but he forced

himself to remain calm. He didn't know who he was facing. He didn't know how many.

"Who in the hell are you? What do you want?"

"You!" The voice came from Jack's right this time. He jerked his head around. Whoever was out there had covered a hundred yards without a sound. Only a damned Injun could move like that, but the voice sounded white.

Jack motioned one of his men to circle behind the disembodied voice in the forest. "Why me? What'd I ever do to you? Hell, I don't even know who you are."

In answer to his question, another bundle of dynamite flew through the air in the direction of the sidekick Jack had sent after Ben. Jack saw it and shouted, "Duck!"

The report of a Winchester punctuated Jack's shout, and the dynamite exploded in a yellow ball above their heads.

"Stay put, Jack," came the voice. "All of you. I don't want nobody hurt, but you push it, I'll plant every one of you under a pile of rocks."

Jack doubled his left fist and slammed it into the pine behind which he was hiding. Frustration seared his bearded face, scorched his ears. With a supreme effort, he held his temper. "What do you want? Tell me."

The voice remained silent for several seconds. Then, "Out of the valley. Let someone else do Barnett's dirty work."

Cherokee Jack cursed when he realized the identity of his antagonist. Elliott! Ben Elliott! So that's who had them pinned down. Just a damned rancher. His eyes narrowed. There was not a rancher in the territory who could stand up to Cherokee Jack Crater, and this one wasn't going to be the first.

He sneered. He stuck his head around the pine. No common rancher would tell him what to do. "Go to hell, you . . . owww!" He grabbed his burning cheek and jerked back as the crack of a Winchester echoed through the forest.

"Next one is between the eyes, Jack. You best listen to what I say. Come morning, I start burying you old boys."

Chapter Twenty-three

Ben moved back up on the rim where he could watch the camp throughout the night. The campfire was never rekindled, an effort on Jack's part to hide his activities from Ben. Such an effort didn't bother Ben. Either the men would leave the next morning, or they wouldn't. If they didn't, then he would carry out the promise he made Jack.

Just after false dawn, the camp awakened. Four men, their eyes constantly searching the heights around them for their assailant, climbed from their blankets and stomped their feet to put circulation back in their bones. One kindled a small fire, and soon the rich aroma of boiling coffee reached Ben. Two cowpokes were missing.

Ben rolled a cigarette and lit it, blowing the smoke into the crisp morning air, unperturbed by the missing men.

Clustered around the fire, the men sipped their coffee and talked, throwing occasional glances over their shoulders, hoping to spot anyone, anything.

Ben looked on without emotion, waiting for Cherokee Jack to make his move. The outlaw was well-known for his bluster and bravado, but he always had half a dozen hardcases behind him. The same reputation law-abiding citizens despised was the reputation men like Barnett called on when there was dirty work to be done.

If Cherokee Jack backed away, word would spread like a prairie fire throughout the territory. With a sigh, Ben crushed the cigarette against the rocky ground and watched the small party break camp.

Down below, Cherokee Jack looked up the mountain and cupped his hand to his mouth. "Elliott!" The gravelly voice carried up the rim and echoed down the valley.

Ben remained silent, watching Jack without emotion.

"I know you're up there, Elliott." Jack made a quarter turn to his right and yelled, "We're leaving now. That's what you want."

Jack paused, staring into the heights around him. Finally, he shrugged and swung into his saddle. In single file, the riders disappeared into the pine grove and headed out of the valley.

From a distance, Ben followed on foot, always keeping the four outlaws in sight and keeping his eyes peeled for the two missing owlhoots. Despite the years in the saddle, Ben had forgotten none of the skills he had learned from his Apache father, Taa-Yah of the Coyoteros. He clambered over boulders effortlessly; glided through stands of pines like a puff of smoke; crossed open meadows like a vagrant breeze.

At noon, Jack reined up.

Ben slipped behind a vine-tangled windfall within hearing. He had expected Jack to pull up around midmorning and make his plans. Maybe the burly outlaw figured Ben was following them. But then, perhaps this was just what it appeared, a noon stop for coffee. Perhaps Jack had taken Ben seriously. Perhaps the gunsel was riding out of the valley.

An hour later, Jack and his band swung back into their saddles and continued on their original course. Ben remained crouched behind the windfall. He pondered the whereabouts of the two missing killers. With a shrug of finality, he grunted. If any of them came back, he would learn of it.

Back in his hidden valley, Ben boiled coffee and roasted a slab of venison. Then he slept. Waking just before dusk, he saddled the dun and made his way down the rim into the valley. He had a piece of ground to cover tonight.

His first stop was at Colly Weems's old spread, which he reached an hour after sundown. Leaving the dun deep in the forest, he slipped through the aspen and pine toward the main house, a sturdy, rock-walled structure with a single window lit.

At the edge of the forest, he dropped to his knee and waited, studying the shadowy buildings. The burned timbers of the barn jutted into the night like spectral fingers, twisted and clawed. Behind the remnants of the barn, several horses milled about in the corral.

Silently, he stole down to the corral. In the starlight, Ben made out the brand on one's rump, a Triple B. Just as Ben figured. Colly's widow and her children had already moved out. The horses belonged to Barnett.

He opened the corral gate, then tossed a bundle of dynamite at either end of the bunkhouse and hurried back to his lineback dun. Swinging into the saddle, he shucked his Winchester and quickly placed lead slugs in each of the two bundles of dynamite.

The explosions lit the night and ripped off either end of the bunkhouse.

Stunned cowpokes stumbled from the burning building. A satisfied grin played over Ben's lips as he wheeled his pony about and headed for Ches Lewis's place.

At midnight, Ben reached Lewis's spread. Within minutes, he discovered Barnett's men had moved in there also. That meant Barnett had taken over all of the small ranches in the valley.

He knew old Foss had done as he had asked, that the old cook had got word to all the spreads for their hands to move out. He just hoped that the cowpokes on the other ranches listened to the old cook, because from now on, Ben couldn't afford to look after anyone except himself.

Sitting astride the lineback dun, Ben studied the shadowy buildings below. The raiders who burned his barn bypassed Lewis's barn, burning instead the hay shed. And in all probability, some of the very raiders who had hit his place were sleeping down in the bunkhouse at this moment. He considered burning the bunkhouse, then decided to just blow off a corner to get Barnett's attention.

Ben glanced at Ches Lewis's barn.

All of the ranchers used dynamite. Maybe, with a little luck, Ben could steal some blasting caps and fuses for his dynamite. Tying the dun securely, Ben slipped back to the barn. He had visited the old Rebel enough to know where Ches stored his supplies, so finding the fuses and the caps in the dark was no problem.

Within minutes, his pockets bulging with blasting

caps and fuses, Ben slipped from the barn and disappeared into the night.

When he reached his horse, he transferred the stolen items to his war bags, then swung into the saddle. He stared back down at the silent buildings.

Pausing on a rise behind the cookshack and bunkhouse, he inserted a blasting cap in a stick of dynamite and fused it. Touching a match to the fuse, he hurled the stick at the bunkhouse. The hissing fuse reminded him of Fourth of July fireworks as it tumbled through the dark night.

When it struck the side of the building and bounced to the ground, Ben jerked his Winchester to his shoulder and jacked a cartridge in the chamber and raked the bunkhouse with fourteen 250-grain .44's, deliberately aiming high. With the last two slugs, he blew the stove chimney off the roof. He paused, grinning at the thought of a cloud of black soot filling the bunkhouse.

Moments later, the dynamite exploded, ripping off one corner of the bunkhouse.

An hour later, Ben reined up in the shadows of the forest overlooking his own spread. He had one more task before he was finished for the night. He had taken care of Chester's and Colly's, now it was time for his.

He paused, remembering the hours of labor and sweat and money that went into the spread below. For a moment, he hesitated, but then, clenching his teeth, pulled out two bundles of dynamite and fused them. Taking a deep breath, he muttered, "Here we go, Charlie." He lit the fuses, then dug his heels into the dun's flanks and sped down the slope. Moments later, he lobbed a stick through the front window of his house, and the second one at the front door of the bunk-house.

Seconds later, two explosions shook the ground, one on the heels of the other.

Ben rose early next morning. After coffee and a ciga-rette, he opened a can of tomatoes, drinking the juice after eating the peeled halves. He replenished his sup-ply of cartridges and packed several bundles of dy-namite as well as caps and fuses in his saddlebags along with enough coffee and grub to last three or four days.

Just as the sun peeked over the eastern treetops, Ben rode out, heading for the Triple B. It was time to put more pressure on Albert Barnett. As far as Ben was con-cerned now, any rider he came across was one of Bar-nett's men, and he would be treated accordingly.

Less than an hour later, Ben reined up on the edge of an escarpment and surveyed the valley below. Almost directly below him, five cowpokes drove around fifty head of cattle to a small stream.

Ben pulled out two bundles of dynamite. Inserting the cap and fuse, he touched a match to the first bundle. The fuse hissed and sputtered, but remained lit. Ben watched, waiting for the right time to drop the bundle. The night before, he had burned two fuses, counting off the seconds for each inch of fuse. He concluded two seconds for each inch of fuse.

When there was three inches of fuse left, Ben tossed the bundle over the edge, aiming it in front of the cat-tle. As it tumbled end over end, he lit the second bundle and hurled it behind the cowpokes pushing the small herd.

Holding the dun on a tight rein, he grinned as the

first bundle exploded with a deafening roar, hurling rocks and detritus into the air. The startled cattle swapped ends instantly, bawling and grunting as they stampeded back on the riders.

Fighting to control their frightened horses that were pawing the air and dancing on their hind legs, the five cowpokes were too busy to give a damn about the cattle.

Suddenly, a second explosion rocked them from behind, turning their ponies into sun-fishing, cartwheeling wild broncs, snorting and squalling as they spun and twisted. One sorrel dashed into a stand of pines, dragging his rider into a pine limb knocking him from the saddle. Two other ponies collided, spilling their riders in the middle of the stampeding beeves. A fourth horse grabbed the bit in his teeth and tore across the meadow like he'd been given a dose of Tabasco and castor oil. The fifth pony, a large Appaloosa, pawed the air and squalled. His rider clung to his back, yanking too hard on the reins, which caused the horse to topple backward, crushing the rider between the granite wall of the escarpment and the fifteen-hundred-pound App.

When the dust cleared, four cowpokes lay groaning on the rocky soil and fifty head of Lewis's stock had lost itself in the pinyons beneath the Mogollon Rim.

Deliberately, Ben lit a cigarette and flipped the match over the edge, watching the thin whisper of smoke tumbling end over end until it went out. Now, it was time to pay Albert Barnett a visit.

Chapter Twenty-four

Albert Barnett resisted the urge to smash his glass of rye whiskey against the wall. His fingertips whitened as he gripped the glass, glaring at the somber face of Rafe Borke. "You said he was good," he growled, his tone accusing, sarcastic.

"He is, Mr. Barnett. I—"

Cherokee Jack interrupted. "Hold it, Barnett. You wanta talk to me, talk to me . . . not your hired man there." His face was sullen, and his black eyes measured the big rancher before him. "You want my answers, you ask me."

Albert Barnett snapped his head around to face Cherokee Jack. His eyes burned holes in the owlhoot. Very deliberately, without taking his eyes off Jack, Barnett set his half-filled glass on the highboy. A sense of anticipation coursed through his veins as he read the contempt in Jack's eyes. He knew what the dangerous outlaw was seeing, a well-dressed, rich rancher who hired other men to fight his battles, who either couldn't or feared to fight his own.

Cherokee Jack was no different than a dozen other hardcases Barnett had handled the last ten years. He took a step toward Jack, whose body tensed instinctively. Jack's eyes narrowed. His Adam's apple bobbed once or twice. "Sure, Jack, I'll talk to you," the rancher said, jabbing the outlaw in the chest with his finger. "I'll be happy to talk to you," he said, continuing to jab the finger in the smaller man's chest, driving him back to the wall.

Jack swiped at Barnett's jabbing finger with his left hand. "That's enough of that sh—"

The words choked off in his throat as Albert Barnett's plate-size hand grabbed a fistful of vest and shirt and slammed Cherokee Jack against the wall, banging his head and knocking his dirt-stained hat from his head.

Jack grabbed for his six-gun, but Barnett's free hand seized his wrist and held it in a grip of steel. Then, his face a mask of cold fury, Albert Barnett flexed his arm and slowly shoved Cherokee Jack up the wall until the outlaw's boots were six inches off the floor.

Jack's eyes opened wide in fear. His spurs drummed against the wall. His eyes sought out Borke, begging for aid, but the burly foreman remained leaning against the wall, watching the unfolding events without emotion.

Albert Barnett spoke in a soft, well-modulated voice. "Now, I'm talking to you, Jack. And you better listen and listen good. I want Ben Elliott dead. That's the only way you'll get out of this valley alive yourself. You try to run out on me, I'll hunt you down and squash you like I'd stomp on a spider."

For interminable seconds, Albert Barnett held Jack aloft, his eyes boring into the outlaw's, accentuating his own determination, warning that his words were no idle threat.

Abruptly, he released his grip and stepped back.

Jack dropped to the floor. His legs buckled, but he caught his fall and pulled himself erect. He opened his mouth to speak. His lips quivered, and he clamped them shut to still the tremors wracking his body. Beneath his heavy beard, his face had paled noticeably.

Picking up his rye, Albert stared coldly at the outlaw. In a voice that froze Cherokee Jack's blood, Barnett said, "We understand each other now, don't we, Jack?"

Jack cast a quick glance at Borke, who continued to stare at him with all the indifference of a man staring at a dead lizard. He looked back to the big rancher. "Yes, sir, Mr. Barnett. We understand each other."

A faint grin ticked up the corners of Barnett's lips. "Good. See that you handle Ben Elliott this time."

Rafe Borke followed Jack outside, but moments later, he hurried back in, followed by a breathless, middle-aged cowpoke.

Albert Barnett had seated himself at his rolltop desk and opened a ledger. The glass of rye sat on the edge of the desk. He looked up when Borke came in. "What?"

"Elliott again, Mr. Barnett."

"Damn!" Barnett jumped up, knocking his chair on the floor. "What the hell now?"

Borke nodded to the cowboy. "Jerny here said that someone stampeded the horses out of the Weemses' corral last night and blew up the bunkhouse. They blew up the bunkhouse at Ches Lewis's place too." Borke paused, his eyes narrowing. "And later, both the ranch house and bunkhouse at the Key was blown to pieces."

Barnett stared at his foreman in stunned disbelief. He shook his head slowly. "Elliott! I didn't know he could be so cold-hearted. I misjudged him." He drew a deep breath and stared at the ceiling. Slowly he released his pent-up breath. "Well, I sure as hell won't make that mistake again."

"That ain't all, Mr. Barnett, sir," said Jerny, hat in hand. "This morning, five of the boys was pushing stock to the box canyon, and someone tossed dynamite on them. Hurt two purty bad. Kilt one. Lost the stock."

Barnett exploded. "Damn him!" He clenched his fists and turned on Rafe Borke, who took a step backward. For several seconds, Albert Barnett stood like a colossus, arms bowed, fists clenched, jaw set. That bastard Elliott was not about to get away with this. Not if Barnett had to spend five thousand dollars on hired guns.

Jerny glanced nervously at Borke, who nodded for the old cowboy to leave the room. He scurried out.

After a few moments, Barnett calmed, but it was a superficial calm for his blood still boiled with anger. When he spoke, his voice was tight with controlled rage. "Borke, I don't have any faith in Cherokee Jack. He'll go out there and get himself and his men killed. We've got to be ready. Hire more men. Bring in as many as you think we need. You understand?"

"What about that federal marshal that rode out of here? You want me to get him back?"

The big rancher's eyebrows knit in an angry glower. "To hell with him. The best thing he did for us was to leave. I don't want any lawmen around who can stir up trouble later."

Rafe Borke's thick lips twisted in a sneer. "Let me take care of Elliott, Mr. Barnett. You don't have to spend no money on nobody that way."

The broad-shouldered rancher shook his head. "You're

too important to me here, Borke. No, hire someone to do the job. Today."

"I can send a rider down to Tortilla Flat. Bobby Siringo and Buckskin Johnny Starr hole up down there."

Barnett grunted. "What about the Apache Kid. He still in the territory?"

"I reckon. Ain't heard of no one stringing him up yet."

"Get him too. All three of them and all of their boys. I want Ben Elliott dead."

With a departing nod, the burly foreman left the room.

Barnett downed the remainder of the rye and refilled the glass. He crossed the room to the window and pulled back the curtain. Outside, the valley spread to the north as far as the eye could see. Toasting the vista, the rancher turned up his tumbler of rye whiskey and drained it. "Hope you enjoyed the fun last night, Elliott," he growled. "That's the last you'll see in this lifetime."

Cherokee Jack splashed cheap whiskey into the tin cup and leaned back in the chair. Rafe Borke sat across the table from him in the Triple B bunkhouse, a rectangular structure with a dozen bunks lined up against each wall. In the space between the foot of the beds sat several tables and chairs. Cowboys were seated around the tables, drinking whiskey and playing poker.

Jack spilled some whiskey down his chin as he guzzled the fiery liquid. He slammed the cup down and reached for the half-empty bottle. "I'll kill that *el hijo de una ramera*," he growled, his voice husky and slurred.

"How?" Rafe Borke leered. "You gotta catch the bastard first. There ain't no love for him on my side, but he's part Injun. You'd have better luck tracking an owl at night than runnin' him down."

Jack's beady black eyes glared at the burly foreman. His raspy voice heavy with sarcasm, he demanded, "What in the hell would you do, Borke?"

Borke refilled his own cup. "Easy. I'd make him come to me."

"Yeah, and just how would you go about that?"

"Get something that means a lot to him, something personal, something valuable." Borke eyed him shrewdly.

"Like what?" He snorted. "Hell, Barnett's got the Key. He killed Elliott's best friend. Why don't Elliott come after Barnett for that?"

Rafe Borke shook his head. "That's another one of your problems, Jack. You don't understand the man. Ben Elliott can't call Barnett out for that. Even his own men swore it was a fair fight."

Cherokee Jack snorted again and gulped down another shot of whiskey. "Who cares whether it be fair or not?"

"Ben Elliott cares," said Rafe Borke, nodding his head emphatically. "Ben Elliott cares."

The bearded outlaw studied Rafe Borke for several moments. He pursed his lips. "How? How do I bring him to me? With his ranch gone, what's important enough to bring him in?"

"Old Foss."

"Old what? What's a foss?"

The burly foreman sneered. "Old Foss is Elliott's cook. Next to Charlie Little, that cantankerous old man means more to Ben Elliott than even the ranch."

Suddenly a light penetrated the dull mists in Cherokee

Jack's alcohol-fogged brain. "Yeah. Just where is the Foss hombre?"

"Word is him and some of the Key wranglers is camped west of here in the foothills where the mining camp road cuts north to Prescott."

Jack slid back from the table, rose to his feet, and belched. "I reckon me and the boys'll just pay this feller a visit." He hesitated and nodded to the main house. "What is it about this Elliott jasper that riles Barnett? Why does he want him dead so bad?"

Borke leaned back in the cowhide-bottomed chair and eyed Cherokee Jack thoughtfully. That was the one question that Borke had tried to figure out himself. He shrugged. "*Quien sabe*. Maybe because he's standing up to Barnett. He's the last of the small ranchers. All the others are either dead, or they've left the territory. I reckon Barnett don't want none of them around as a reminder."

Jack nodded his understanding. "Sounds reasonable to me."

"Yep. Me too," responded Borke, reluctant to tell the outlaw the real reason, that Ben Elliott frightened the hell out of Albert Barnett. He had no proof that was true. It was a gut feeling, a gunfighter feeling, but every time Albert Barnett spoke of Ben Elliott, the feeling was reinforced. But the way Borke saw it, the really strange part of it all was that Barnett himself was not aware that Elliott frightened him.

Chapter Twenty-five

The next morning, Cherokee Jack and his men surprised Old Foss and a handful of Key riders in their camp, riding in unexpectedly and pulling down on the Key hands. The old cook, cantankerous and belligerent, bellied up to squint-eyed half-breed like a banty rooster. "Just who in the hell you think you are, riding in on a camp without asking." He gestured to the dust stirred up by the horses. "You done ruint breakfast for us."

Jack laughed and faster than the eye could follow, laid the barrel of his .44 across Old Foss's head, knocking the old man to the ground. "Put a plug in that talk box, you old geezer, or I'll plug it for you." He climbed down from his saddle.

A mutter of protest sounded from the Key riders, but the cocking of hammers silenced them. Jack grinned. "That's it, boys. Just you settle down and nobody will get hurt."

Old Foss moaned and struggled to sit up.

The sneer on Jack's face vanished, replaced with cruel anger. He kicked Old Foss in the side, spinning him over to his back. In the next instant, he shot the cook in the meaty part of his calf.

Foss screamed and rolled over on his side, bending double to clutch his bleeding leg.

A young cowboy stepped forward. "Why you . . ." A muzzle jammed in the cowpoke's side silenced him.

Another Key rider, sixteen-year-old Billy Joe Tolliver from Mesilla, started toward Foss.

"Hold it right there," barked Cherokee Jack.

"Hell, all I wanta do is help the old man, mister," said the youth, his voice pleading.

Jack shook his head. "No one ain't helping him. Only Ben Elliott can help that old man."

The young man looked at the blood running through Foss's fingers. "To hell with you," he said, taking another step.

Jack's .44 belched an orange flame. The slug caught the young boy in the chest and knocked him off his feet. The sneering half-breed turned his six-gun on the other three Key riders. "Any of you want the same, step forward."

As one, they shook their heads, their gaze jumping between the dead youth, Foss, and Cherokee Jack. "I didn't think so," said Jack with a smirk. He motioned to their horses. "Now you boys saddle up. Tell Ben Elliott I got this worthless piece of trash here. Tell him I'll kill the old man come sundown unless Elliott shows up first. I'll be on the north road between here and the mining camps."

The three Key riders nodded and quickly saddled up and rode out. When they were out of sight of the camp, they reined up. Monk frowned. "Where do you reckon Ben is?"

Two Bits shrugged. "I don't know, but I ain't crazy

about hangin' around and gettin' shot down like the kid back there."

"Look, let's split up. I'll go up on the rim. One of you head south down the valley, the other back north."

"Not me. I ain't going north," said Two Bits, nodding in the direction from which they had come. "That damned crazy half-breed's headin' up that way."

"Okay. You take the rim. I'll take the north end of the valley," said Monk, reining his pony around and digging his spurs into the pony's flanks.

"And hurry," he yelled. "It's Old Foss we're talking about."

Jack trailed north along the mining camp road until he found a small box canyon. He grinned with satisfaction. Exactly what he had been looking for.

When they pulled up, Old Foss was weak from loss of blood. He slid from the saddle and slumped to the ground. One of Jack's men looked at his boss, his eyes questioning. "You want me to bandage the old man up, Jack? He's lost a heap of blood."

A cruel sneer distorted Jack's bearded face. Astride his horse, he stared down at the old man, whose face was contorted in pain. "Naw," he growled. "Don't bother." In one slick motion, he shucked his six-gun and blew the back of Old Foss's head off. Holstering his .44, he leered at his men. "See? Now, he ain't no bother at all."

"But . . . what about when Elliott gets here, boss? What then?"

"Build a fire over near the canyon wall. Lean that body against the wall like he was sleeping. We'll kill Elliott before he ever gets close enough to see the old man's dead."

Two of Jack's men raised their eyebrows and shrugged at each other, but they did exactly as their leader instructed.

Ben received the message in midafternoon. After sending the Key rider out of the valley, he headed north, cutting through the forest and over the foothills, always keeping the road in sight, regretting now that he had spared Cherokee Jack and his men two nights earlier.

Chapter Twenty-six

Ben knew he was riding into an ambush.

In the decade he had lived with the Coyoteros, he learned the secret for their survival in a world with rapidly increasing numbers of hostile white men, knowledge—knowledge of the country in which they lived. The Apache knew every stream, every ridge, every valley, every cave, almost every shrub within a hundred-mile radius.

Ben had put his early training to practice as soon as he settled beneath the Mogollon in 1865. He disappeared for days at a time, often pushing a few head of unbranded cattle ahead of him when he returned, an unexpected windfall for the Key. Charlie Little ran the spread when Ben was gone.

So, Ben knew the valley and the plateau, and though there were hundreds of sites for ambushes, he knew exactly where this one would take place, a box canyon east of the mining camp road. Though not the most ideal, it was the most obvious site for ambush that any jasper new to the country would pick.

He circled wide to the east, ascending the mountain and coming up on the canyon from the rear. Leaving his dun picketed in some forage, he eased through the pinyons and slithered up to the rim of the canyon on his belly, peering between clusters of small boulders to break his outline.

The three walls of the canyon were sheer, about three hundred feet. The mouth of the canyon faced west, the opening partially blocked by boulders that had split from the north wall, leaving a narrow pass beneath the south wall. The horses were picketed at the rear of the canyon. A small fire emitted a thin stream of smoke near the north wall. A blackened coffeepot sat in the edge of the coals. At the base of the wall, Ben saw Old Foss lying on a blanket, his battered Stetson pulled down over his eyes. Sleeping?

Ben's blood ran cold. The old man was either dead or unconscious. He seldom slept, even at night, and in the eight years Ben had known Foss, he had never known the old cook to nap during the day.

Carefully studying the lay of the land below, Ben pinpointed six outlaws, all situated in the boulders around the mouth of the canyon. Six. Same as two nights ago. His eyes narrowed. Obviously, neither Jack nor his men had taken Ben seriously.

Overhead, a buzzard circled.

Frowning, Ben looked back down at the still form of Old Foss, then at the sun.

Jack had given him until sundown. An hour left. He could afford to wait. From his vantage point, he could stop Jack's efforts to harm Old Foss simply by calling out.

As he waited, Ben studied the canyon walls, searching for a way down. On the north face of the box canyon, a slender fissure stretched from the canyon floor to the rim. Shadows filled the interior of the fissure.

Suddenly, from the base of the fissure, a tiny ground squirrel scurried along the base of the wall to the camp, drawn by crumbs from the outlaw's meal. The squirrel paused and, perched on its hind legs, looked around, then darted toward Old Foss. The tiny creature paused again, then scrambled on the cook's chest.

The old man didn't move. For several seconds, the animal remained on Old Foss, sniffing and digging in his vest pockets.

Ben closed his eyes and dropped his head between his shoulders, a vast emptiness enveloping him. Still, he told himself, raising his head and focusing on the men below, he had to be certain. Perhaps the old man was unconscious, or hurt bad.

Leaving his Winchester, Ben eased around the canyon rim to the fissure. Only a few feet wide, it reminded him of a chimney with one side missing. Bracing his feet on the irregular surfaces of the fissure, Ben slowly clambered down to the canyon floor.

At the base of the fissure, Ben slipped behind a scrub of manzanitas. He peered through the dull green leaves at the still form of Old Foss thirty feet distant. The old man had not moved a muscle. A bag of Durham lay on the ground by his side, fished from his vest by the curious ground squirrel. Ben reached for a pebble, but before he lobbed it at Foss, he noticed a shadowy stain beneath the old man's head, the color of the dark red-purple bark of the manzanita behind which he was hiding. Blood.

He looked back to the bushwhackers. They were still watching to the west. From the layout, only one of Jack's men could see Foss, a narrow-shouldered yahoo wearing a black-and-white cowhide vest. Ben had to know about the old cook before taking any action. He couldn't afford to open up the game with his old friend lying in the open.

There was little cover between Ben and the owlhoot in the cowhide vest, but it was enough. Taking his time, Ben eased along the base of the canyon wall behind the boulders and undergrowth of mesquite and brittlebush. The evening shadows lengthened. From time to time, one of the bushwhackers called to the other. Each time, Ben froze, his heart thudding against his chest.

Once the nearest outlaw turned and looked at the camp, his eyes completely overlooking the wiry man who had blended in with a jumble of boulders.

Then, as silence filled the canyon once again, he continued stalking the jasper in the cowhide vest. Ben gripped his six-gun tighter as he drew within a foot of the outlaw. Suddenly, the cowpoke stiffened and started to turn around, but Ben whacked him across the temple with the muzzle of his Colt. The outlaw fell like a poleaxed steer.

Quickly, Ben bound and gagged the outlaw, then hurried back to Old Foss. Kneeling by the rail-thin cook, Ben cast a hurried glance in the direction of the bushwhackers. They were all out of sight behind boulders and underbrush.

He laid his hand on Foss's shoulder, then recoiled as soon as his fingers sensed the stiffening flesh. "Damn," he muttered, his eyes turning to ice, any clemency he might have felt completely forgotten. Cold, calculating fury swept over him as he laid his hand over Old Foss's heart.

He cut his eyes back to the bushwhackers just as a voice cut through the growing dusk. "Whatta you think, Jack?"

"Shut up."

"I don't see nothing."

"Me neither," said another voice.

Several moments of silence passed. Finally, Jack called out, "What about you, Curly?"

"I ain't seen nothing, Jack. Maybe he ain't coming."

"Dave? What about you? See anything?"

No answer.

Ben nodded briefly. Soon someone would come looking for Dave, and he sure as hell wasn't going to like what he found.

"Dave? You hear me?"

"Hell, maybe he dozed off."

"Shut up, you," snapped Jack. "Dave? You hear me?"

Ben faded back into the undergrowth at the base of the canyon wall.

"Curly, go see what's doing with Dave."

"Why me?"

" 'Cause I said so."

"Okay," Curly mumbled as he clambered down from his niche in a jumble of boulders. His boots clattered and clacked on the rocky soil.

Behind the mesquite and brittlebush, Ben palmed his knife and waited as Curly's footsteps grew louder. The bearded outlaw rounded a large boulder, and Ben released the knife. In the growing dusk, the shiny blade was almost invisible.

Curly called out in a loud whisper. "Dave? Dave? Where in the hell are y—" He rocked back on his heels. He stared in disbelief at the knife handle protruding from his chest. His eyes opened wide. "I . . . I . . ." Then the pain struck. He grabbed the handle and tried to pull the blade from his chest, but his fingers refused to function. His legs buckled. Curly was dead before his alcohol-ravaged face slammed into the ground.

Several moments passed. Jack called out, his harsh voice rough as sandpaper. "Curly! What's going on over there?" Silence. Then, "Answer me, Curly. What's going on? Where's Dave?"

Might as well start the ball, Ben decided. He shouted back. "Curly's dead, Jack. He's holding the gates of hell open for the rest of you."

A deathly silence froze the canyon.

Without wasting a second, Ben eased along the north wall, wanting to take refuge in the shadows cast among the boulders by the setting sun. There were still four killers out there.

Cherokee Jack's voice sounded from beyond the boulders. "You're a dead man, Elliott. I'm goin' to make you beg like I did the old man. Then I'll open your belly and leave you for the buzzards."

Ben knew Jack's game. He remained silent and waited.

The distorted whisper of voices carried on the evening breeze, indistinguishable, but Ben knew Jack was giving out orders. Sure enough, a few minutes later, a single cowpoke crawled around the base of a boulder on his stomach, hitching himself forward with his elbows, trying to sneak a look at the camp.

From Ben's hiding spot near the canyon wall, he had a clear shot. Despite the anger, the fury driving him, Ben could not deliberately kill the man, not from ambush. Taking aim, Ben shot the bushwhacker in the right shoulder, breaking the collarbone.

The outlaw screamed in pain and rolled several feet into the canyon, clutching his shoulder. Even before the outlaw stopped rolling, Ben had climbed fifteen feet higher among the boulders. He eased into a small opening and waited. Three remained.

Several wild shots ricocheted off the canyon wall behind Ben, followed by enraged cries as two more bushwhackers rushed around the boulder and emptied their six-guns into the undergrowth behind the camp. Ben grimaced as he saw Old Foss's body jerk from the impact of wild shots.

Jack called out from behind the two bushwhackers. "You get him?"

They kept their six-shooters leveled on the camp even though the handguns were empty. "Looks like it," one replied tentatively. "He ain't shootin' back."

Jack laughed, the rollicking bray of a donkey. "Guess that shows him." He holstered his revolver as he stopped beside his men. He peered into the dusk. "Where is he?"

Ben rose from his hidey-hole fifteen feet above the three men. "Right here, Jack."

As one they spun. Jack grabbed for his six-gun, but Ben blasted a chunk of flesh off the outlaw's ear. "Don't try it, Jack." He gestured with the muzzle of his own handgun. "Leather the hog legs, boys."

The outlaws did as ordered. Behind them, the cowpoke with the broken collarbone sat on the ground, doubled over, clutching his shoulder and crying. Slowly, Ben, his eyes never leaving the three owlhoots, walked down the tumble of boulders just like he was descending a flight of stairs. With each step, the suppressed anger grew, threatening to explode. He resisted the urge to gut-shoot all three and watch them die, moaning and crying.

Cherokee Jack clutched his ear. Blood ran through his fingers. All three glared with murderous hatred at

Ben. He stopped in front of them, his teeth clenched. He stared deep into Jack's beady eyes. "You better make your peace, Jack. It's time."

Whining like a cowards, Cherokee Jack took a step backward. "Without a chance? That ain't fair."

Ben cut his eyes to the other two. "Load them hog legs, boys. Never let it be said Ben Elliott refused to give even the sleaziest cockroach a fair chance." He cut the muzzle of his .44 toward them. "Be damned careful. Point that six-gun anywhere in my direction, and you're dead."

Jack grinned, a lopsided sneer. "Hell, Elliott. You ain't got a chance, not up against the three of us. Even me. I can take you."

Backing off several steps, Ben kept his six-gun trained on the three outlaws. After reloading, the two outlaws holstered their six-guns and stepped apart. Ben kept the muzzle lined up on the three, all of whom had broad sneers plastered across their faces.

Lowering the hammer, Ben dropped his Colt back in his holster. He flexed his fingers and bent his knees. His voice was cold as a blue norther. "Now, it's fair, and I won't have to lose any sleep over killing three mange-eaten mongrels."

His words slapped the sneers from their faces. "Why, you . . ." Jack grabbed for his six-gun.

Ben's hand blurred. Even before Jack cleared leather, Ben's .44 boomed three times, three slugs, one in the chest of each outlaw. The impact of the slugs knocked them backward, flinging their arms aside like they were in some kind of gangly dance, and sent them sprawling limply on the rocky soil.

Ben didn't move for several seconds, his eyes carefully studying the men before him. Slowly, he relaxed.

Taking a deep breath, he looked over at the still form of Old Foss while ejecting the empties and filling the chambers with fresh cartridges. "That's the best I can do right now, old man," he said.

To the west, the last of the bloodred sunset slipped beneath the mountains, pouring deathlike blackness into the valley. The stars overhead gave off a ghostly glow. Ben untied the outlaw he had knocked out and sent him and his wounded compadre back to Barnett after taking their gun belts.

"Tell Barnett I'm coming to get him," he said.

"What about horses?" whined the outlaw. "It's ten miles to Barnett's."

Ben's voice chilled the owlhoot's blood. "Walk or join your friends."

The two killers disappeared into the night.

Ben brought the horses up, removed the gun belts from the four dead bushwhackers, and hefted Foss over a saddle. He'd bury the old man on the Key.

Chapter Twenty-seven

Picking up his own pony above the canyon, Ben rode back to his valley and turned the horses out to graze, all except his dun and the pony carrying Foss. He stashed the gun belts and saddles in the cave.

Later that night, Ben buried Old Foss on the Key, next to Charlie Little.

"Well, I'll be damned." The middle-aged gunhand stared down at the fresh grave. He read the wooden marker. FOSS COLLIER, 1873. KILLED BY BUSHWHACKERS WHO WAS KILLED BY BEN ELLIOTT. He looked around at the handful of paid gunsels. "That took one hell of a lot of nerve, burying the old man with us snoozing just over there," he said, nodding to the bunkhouse a hundred yards distant.

All of the gunhands nodded, but one seemed particularly thoughtful as he studied the marker and chewed his tobacco. He shifted the wad to his cheek. "I don't know about you fellers, but I got the feeling, this is going to be a mighty rough poker game." He switched the tobacco to his other cheek. "I don't mind admittin' that any hombre who's got this kinda nerve scares the hell outta me. Like he don't care, and that's dangerous. I been up the river and back again, so none of you know me as a coward. I seen many a rogue wolf." He nodded to the grave. "This one appears to be mighty bad, so I reckon I'll just fold up my hand and ride out."

Rafe Borke rode up to the Key just as John Turner climbed into the saddle. The burly foreman frowned. "Where in the hell you think you going?"

Turner, lanky, lean, and soft-spoken, aimed a stream of tobacco in the dust. "Don't like the looks of this game, Rafe. I ain't collected no pay from you boys yet, so it don't bother me to ride out."

Borke's bearded face darkened. "What's the matter? You turnin' yellow?" The moment Borke finished, he regretted his words.

The lanky outlaw didn't move a muscle, but his pale blue eyes burned a hole in Rafe Borke. Turner grinned, but there was nothing friendly about it. "You know me better'n that, Rafe. I'm just gonna forget you even said anything."

Borke and Turner had worked together before, and one of the few men Rafe Borke could never call yellow was John Turner, yet he couldn't understand why the lean gunfighter wouldn't hang around. "You're right. But, hell, John, there's a lot of money to be made. Barnett, he's figuring on gettin' rich, and we can tag right along after him. He needs gunhands like us."

John Turner shrugged. "Maybe so, Rafe, but I got the feeling that neither Mr. Barnett or anyone hooked up with him against that Elliott feller is gonna get anywhere. You included, I'm sorry to say." He touched his fingers to the brim of his hat. "You and me, we had some good times." A crooked grin played over his grizzled face. "You might be a worthless old bastard, but you take care, you hear? I reckon I'll head over Texas way." He clucked his tongue and rode around Rafe Borke.

Borke watched his old acquaintance head up the road to Prescott. Sure, it was a gamble, but hell, what wasn't? Life was a gamble. And with Barnett, there was the chance to shuck these dirt-encrusted clothes and go East. Maybe New York, or Baltimore where that Wills girl went to that finishing school.

When he was younger, the excitement and thrills in his chosen profession meant more to Rafe Borke than the money he stole; but now—well, he was growing long in the tooth. This was the last time. And nothing would stop him. He'd kick, stomp, or kill any hombre to get what he wanted this time, and if that meant Ben Elliott, that was fine with him.

The frown on his face deepened. He squinted after John Turner. The outlaw had pulled up and was talking to two jaspers on foot who had just stumbled out of the pines beyond the meadow. After a moment, Turner rode on, and the strangers headed in Borke's direction.

Borke watched impassively as Albert Barnett reacted to the news about Cherokee Jack. The cattle baron was furious, hurling a cut glass decanter of brandy through the front window. The narrow-shouldered cowpoke who had brought the bad news cowered, his hat in his hands.

Barnett glared at his foreman. "You do what I told you?"

"About the others, Siringo and Starr? Yeah."

"And the Apache Kid?"

Borke nodded. "Almost two days back. As soon as you told me, Mr. Barnett. They should be here tomorrow or the next day at the latest."

Barnett grinned with satisfaction. "Now, get that damned sheriff out here."

"The sheriff?" Borke frowned.

Barnett grinned. "Yeah. Jess Lowry. He doesn't know it yet, but he's going to deputize them. We're sending a legitimate posse after Ben Elliott."

Upon returning to his hidden valley, Ben shed his gun belt and moccasins and went down to the trout pond. Shucking his clothes, he waded into the icy pond and washed his dust-caked body. Easing onto his back, he floated about the pond, staring at the puffy white clouds in the deep blue sky. While drifting on the surface of the still pond, Ben wondered about Mary Catheryn Wills. Had she already sold out to Barnett? As far as he knew, she could already be on the stage back to Baltimore.

When he first met her, he couldn't believe she was the daughter of John Wills, but the day she apologized when they were all out following the trail of the rustled cattle, Ben recognized his old friend's common sense and levelheaded thinking. While Ben felt no personal obligation to the young woman, he felt obligated to John Wills to offer his daughter a shoulder if she needed one.

"But, she won't believe a word I say," he muttered, kicking his feet and paddling with his hands. Overhead, wings extended, a hawk rode the air currents.

Whether she believed him or not, Ben decided to

pay her a nocturnal visit and reveal all that had happened—if she hadn't moved out. Once he did, he could rest easier for he would have done all he could for his old friend's daughter. She could then make her own choice.

Back on the grassy shoreline, he shaved with his knife, and then washed his clothes, wishing for a second set while these dried, but, he told himself, looking around the valley, he was all alone, so wandering about in his birthday suit would offend no one.

He draped his clothes over some boulders just outside the mouth of the cave. Taking his six-gun and knife, he crawled between the blankets in his soogan, planning on catching up on his sleep in the cool depths of the cave.

Near dusk, he arose, dressed, and fed kindling to the banked fire. Soon, small, hot flames illumined the darkness of the cave. Ben slid a coffeepot into the coals and laid a venison steak on a facing slab of granite to broil.

While his meal was cooking, Ben cleaned his six-gun and filled the empty cartridge loops in his gun belt. After his meal, he completed outfitting himself for the coming night. Barnett was bringing in more gunmen, of that Ben was certain. The cattle baron had no choice now. He had to kill Ben, for the younger man had refused to run. He had chosen to remain and fight, fight with a cold-hearted ferocity and steel determination that surprised even J. Albert Barnett.

Ben rode out as the waning moon rose over the plateau. Tonight, he would give Albert Barnett a lesson in cold-blooded destruction. By tomorrow night, the big cattle baron would be searching for a cave of his own. But first, he had a quick stop to make.

Riding down off the rim, Ben circled the Triple B, heading for the Slash Bar. With luck, he would find Mary Catheryn alone.

Lights shone from the parlor window when Ben slipped up to the Slash Bar and hid in the shadows of the well house. Above the small shed, the Eclipse windmill was silent, its maroon-tipped blades locked.

Behind the curtains in the parlor window, he spied two silhouettes, a woman and a man, Mary Catheryn and Zebron Rawlings in all probability. As he watched, a third shadow stopped in front of the window, this one short and rotund, wearing a dress. Teresa. The Willses' housekeeper and cook.

Moments later, Zebron Rawlings stepped onto the porch, spoke back into the open doorway, and closed the door. He pulled his hat down on his head and fished a cigar from his pocket. Lighting it, he strolled across the hardpan to the bunkhouse.

Back in the main house, the parlor light dimmed, then went out. At the back of the house, the light in Mary Catheryn's room came on. Ben waited.

Soon after the bedroom light was extinguished, the bedroom light behind the kitchen where Teresa slept went out. Ben continued to wait.

Thirty minutes later, he knocked softly on Mary Catheryn's window. He glanced over his shoulder toward the bunkhouse, then tapped again. The curtain moved, revealing a dark strip between the two panels. Mary Catheryn was peering out, trying to discern the man at her window.

Ben struck a match and cupped it against his chest, dipping his head so she could make him out. Seconds later, the window slid up. "What are you doing here?"

Her voice was an urgent whisper. She must have heard the stories about him, but her reaction indicated she didn't believe them, or at least, she had some reservations about the stories.

"To see you. To tell you what is going on."

The pale light of the moon gave an eerie glow to her face. She sniffed. "I know what is going on."

"All you know is what Albert Barnett wants you to know."

"And you plan on telling me something different?" Her voice was heavy with skepticism.

Ben knew then he was wasting his time. The one thing that puzzled him was why she was even bothering to speak with him. If she believed Barnett's lies, why hadn't she screamed when she recognized him? Why didn't she give an alarm? He asked her.

"Because," she replied, her tone cool and distant. "You were a friend of my father's. I owe it to him to give you a chance to escape. Next time, I'll give the alarm as soon as I see you."

At least she was honest. Ben figured he might as well be the same. "You're right about why I'm here. Your pa was a good friend. I'll sleep better knowing I've told you what I've found out. What you do with it is your business. If you ignore it, that's your problem." He paused. "Fair enough?"

"Fair enough."

Ben told her about the rustling, the raids, and the killings.

She interrupted. "I suppose you'll try to tell me he had my father killed also. Mr. Barnett said you would."

Frustration washed over Ben. He bit his tongue to keep from retorting angrily. Finally, he said, "He was right about that. That's exactly what I think. I can't prove it, but yes, I think John was killed, and Barnett was behind it. And one of these days, I will prove it."

He paused. Several seconds passed.

Finally, from the darkness of the bedroom, she said, "Was that all you wanted to tell me?" Without giving him time to reply, she added, "Then you have fulfilled your obligation just as I." She closed the window and pulled the curtains.

Chapter Twenty-eight

As he made his way back to the dun, Ben considered their none-too-congenial conversation. Albert Barnett had her attention, her confidence. No way she would even consider contrary information or details. At least, he told himself as he swung into the saddle, I tried. John can't blame me now.

Ben cut back north. He planned to hit the Triple B before midnight. The Triple B. Straight to the heart of Albert Barnett. The cattle baron had already had a taste of payback when Ben dynamited the barn. This time, Ben would see what he could do about the ranch house.

A mile from the southern boundary of the Triple B, Ben reined into a grove of aspen, their moon-splashed leaves rattling in the soft breeze. Wary of guards, Ben moved out slowly, remaining among the pines and aspen while he skirted a thousand-acre meadow. The moonlight filtered through the treetops, laying pale ribbons of light on the forest floor.

Soon, Ben moved onto Triple B land. After he left the guards behind, he urged the dun from the pines and into a running walk, staying near the edge of the meadow just in case he should need cover quickly.

An hour passed.

Other than sleeping cattle, grazing deer, or prowling coyotes, Ben saw no trace of life. Finally, he topped out on a shallow hill overlooking the ranch two miles below. The ranch was dark, but Ben knew Barnett had guards stationed around the spread. With luck, most of them might be dozing.

Fishing about in his saddlebags, he pulled out two bundles of dynamite, each with a three-minute fuse, and nudged his pony in the flanks.

A quarter of a mile from the ranch, Ben reined into a grove of pine and pulled out a match. He studied the ranch, its dark buildings set on a broad expanse of hardpan in the middle of a large meadow. Beyond the corrals and remains of the barn ran a narrow, twisting stream. He planned to sprint past the ranch house, toss one bundle on the porch and the second against the outside wall of the cookshack.

With luck, Ben would have ten seconds or so after he threw the dynamite, time enough to escape the blast. And, if his luck held, by the time anyone could pull down on him, he'd be out of handgun range. Taking a deep breath, he struck a match and touched it to the fuses.

"Hope you're a sound sleeper, Albert," he said, digging his heels into the dun's flanks.

With a leap, the big dun burst from the pines and raced toward the darkened buildings. The animal's hooves thudded in the meadow, then moments later, chattered like drumbeats when they struck the hardpan. Just before Ben reached the ranch house, a light flickered in a back window. Ben cut the dun toward the porch and lobbed the sputtering dynamite at the front door, but it struck a post and bounced to the ground.

Lying low over the neck of the dun, he squeezed his left knee, turning the animal to the right toward the cookshack. He placed the second bundle exactly where he intended and buried his face in the whipping mane of the lineback dun. Mentally, he counted the seconds as the racing animal thundered down the road.

He reached the count of fifteen before the first explosion. The second echoed the first, and behind him, yellow flames leaped into the black night.

Suddenly, from the meadow, bursts of orange erupted from either side of the road. Barnett's men had been stationed in the meadow, not in the forest. Slugs whistled past. Something stung his arm. Abruptly, he reined the dun off the road, directly toward one of the gunmen.

In the next instant, Ben felt a thump and heard a yell. The dun stumbled, caught its balance and continued into the forest less than a half mile distant. Behind, the firing continued, but the shots flew wild.

Reining up behind a motte of pinyon on the rim of the Mogollon next morning, Ben peered down on the Triple B. That there was little effort to clean and rebuild the destruction he had wreaked only hours earlier did not surprise Ben.

Had he been in Barnett's boots, he too would have been more concerned to first halt the destruction. There was no sense in rebuilding or repairing anything as long as Ben Elliott was alive.

A crooked grin twisted Ben's lips. He shoved his hat to the back of his head. He figured if he kept up the pressure on Barnett, the rancher would soon be panting like a lizard on a hot rock. If he wasn't mistaken, after last night, probably more gunsels should be showing up in a day or so.

That didn't worry Ben.

If he couldn't take care of them with the ways of the white man, he could always do it the Apache way. Sooner or later, Albert Barnett would run out of hired guns and would be forced to come out himself.

With a click of his tongue, he reined his pony around and headed for his hidden valley. Time for grub and sleep. Tonight, he would hit his own spread, the Key. He planned to level any building still standing. By the next morning, J. Albert Barnett would fully understand just how serious Ben Elliott was.

Mary Catheryn set her jaw and stared up at Zebron Rawlings. "I told you exactly what happened last night, and I will not stand here and be questioned about my actions." She jammed her fists into her narrow waist, her eyes hurling knives at her sallow-faced fiancé.

Rawlings attempted to pacify her. "All I mean, Mary, was that you should have called someone. You could have been hurt. A man like Elliott isn't to be trusted."

"Nonsense," she retorted, turning on her heel and reaching for the pot of tea. "One sugar or two?"

"One, thank you. But you understand how dangerous Ben Elliott is. Why, after he left here last night, he . . ."

She tossed her head, slinging her red hair in a sweeping arc. "I know what he did. You've told me twice." She poured two cups of tea and sniffed. "Besides, I won't be seeing him again. I warned him that next time I would send up an alarm."

Zebron Rawlings nodded in satisfaction. "Good. And don't worry. I'll have men out."

"Poof!" She sniffed with disdain. "Don't waste your time. I just told you he won't come back."

For a fleeting moment, Zebron Rawlings's eyes turned hard as granite, but quickly softened.

Mary Catheryn Wills sat on the edge of the wing chair and sipped her tea. Although she would not admit it, she was curiously intrigued by this man who so disturbed not only her fiancé, but also the richest, the most powerful man in the country, perhaps even the territory, J. Albert Barnett.

Chapter Twenty-nine

Late that afternoon as Ben squatted at the mouth of his cave oiling his Colt, he spotted his dun's ears perking forward. The other ponies in the meadow followed the dun's gaze. Moments later, the clatter of iron shoes on rocks and the murmur of voices reached his ears.

Moving quickly and silently, the wiry rancher holstered his Colt and ghosted through the boulders and pines in the direction of the newcomers.

He sprawled on his belly and peered over a granite ledge at the five hardcases below. While they were too distant for him to make out their words, Ben knew who they were though not by name—more hired guns Albert Barnett was bringing in.

On feet silent as a spider on a web, Ben followed until the small party camped on the rim of the Mogollon just before sunset. He crept forward until he could make out their words. When he heard the name *Buckskin*, a crooked grin played over his rawhide-tough face. Silently, with the cold-blooded intent of a rattlesnake, he headed back to his valley, deciding to hold off torching the Key. He had a surprise for Buckskin Johnny Starr, a surprise that would perhaps send Albert

Barnett the same message as burning the Key to the ground.

Early next morning, Red Davis stretched the sleep from his bony frame and scratched the week-old beard on his pointed jaw. "You ever hear of this hombre we're after, Buckskin? I ain't." Three other members of the outlaw band climbed from their bedrolls, yawning.

Buckskin Johnny Starr shook his head. "Name's Ben Elliott. Never heard of him neither, but he's causing quite a ruckus up around here. He kilt Cherokee Jack Crater and some of his boys. Three in a stand-up draw down so the story goes."

Red squatted by the small fire and filled his cup with coffee. He rose and stared at the sprawling valley a thousand feet below. "Why'n the hell we gotta get up so early, Buckskin?" He stretched. "It probably ain't no more than five o'clock." When Buckskin failed to reply, he shivered. "Damn, it's nippy up here," he mumbled, pouring a cup of coffee and squatting on his bedroll. "I just want to get on with it, get this job over with fast. I got me a new little dove back in Tortilla Flat just awaiting for me."

One of the other gunnies spoke up. "Might not be as easy as you think, Red. Word I hear is that Bobby Siringo and his boys is coming to give a hand."

"Yeah," chimed in another. "And the Apache Kid."

Red snorted. "So what?"

Buckskin Johnny Starr spoke up, his deep voice rumbling like thunder. "So, it could be this Elliott yahoo ain't no one to sniff at."

"Well, they can sit back and cry," growled Red. "It ain't goin' to take no more than us right here to settle that old boy's bacon."

Suddenly, the early morning darkness erupted with gunfire. Slugs smashed into the campfire, sending fire and branches flying. A burning brand slammed into Red's chest. He dropped his coffee in his lap and slapped at the embers burning small holes in his shirt.

A slug caught the coffeepot, sending it spinning across the fire, sloshing out the coffee in brown spirals.

Within seconds, the camp was in bedlam. Picketed horses squealed. Men shouted. Pots clanged against rocks.

"What the hell . . ." Buckskin Johnny Starr leaped from the firelight and forced himself into the rocky soil behind a pinyon.

Panicked by the sudden onslaught, Red Davis jumped to his feet and took off running into the night, away from the gunfire. Thirty feet from camp, he ran off the rim of the Mogollon Plateau. At the same time, the gunfire stopped.

Starr jerked around when he heard Red's scream, which seemed to go on for hours before it abruptly ceased. The realization of just what had taken place slowly sunk in on the outlaw. In his own twisted way, he regretted Red Davis's fate, but whether it was a 250-grain slug or running off a cliff, death was going to get them all. Red just got his sooner.

He turned back on his belly and peered around the base of the tree, trying to pick out any movement in the darkness behind the scattered campfire, which was now no more than a few embers winking in the early morning darkness.

He thought he heard the clatter of horseshoes on rocks in the distance, but he couldn't be sure. Shifting around to ease the pressure of the rocks digging into his belly and chest, Johnny Starr strained his eyes to penetrate the darkness.

A frightened voice broke the silence. "Buckskin? You there?"

Buckskin Johnny Starr didn't answer. Suddenly, a strange light came looping through the night toward them. Instinctively, the outlaw pressed up against the pinyon. When the light struck ground near the scattered campfire, Starr realized what it was, the burning fuse on a stick of dynamite.

The voice called out again, this time more insistent. "Buckskin? You hear . . ."

The night exploded.

Starr buried his head under his arms as rocks and debris flew through the night air and clattered to the ground. The echoes of the explosion faded away, and the night fell silent once again.

For several minutes, the outlaws lay unmoving. Only when an owl hooted, and a cricket chirped did they climb to their feet and gather back at their smoldering bedrolls.

Buckskin Johnny Starr stared into the darkness surrounding the camp. Now he understood why Rafe Borke had called him and Siringo and the Apache Kid. This Elliott hombre had slipped in like the wind and destroyed the camp without an eye being laid on him.

"Saddle up, boys," said Starr. "Dark or not, we're getting down to the valley right now. Run down your ponies. We ain't staying on this rim with that waddy out there."

"What about Red's horse and saddle?"

Starr grunted and tightened the cinch on his pony. "Split it up between you. It ain't doing Red no good now."

The outlaw leader could hear the whispering among his men, too soft to distinguish their words, but he knew what they were saying, and the uneasy feeling on the back of his neck made him wish he too had never agreed to come into the valley. But he had given his word. And he couldn't back down now. None of them could.

The trail down the rim was narrow and tortuous, a sheer granite wall on one side and a thousand-foot fall on the other. Given the choice, however, the outlaws much preferred the hazards of the trail than remaining on the plateau with Ben Elliott.

Once, during the journey down the trail, Buckskin Johnny Starr thought he glimpsed a shadow near a boulder on the trail, but when he looked closer, he saw nothing.

Finally, they reached the valley.

Starr reined up and stared back at the rim, now a dark line against the graying dawn. He chided himself for being spooked earlier. Elliott was a man, no more, no less.

He nodded, his eyes fixed on the rim. He muttered, "I'm coming back up there, Elliott. I'm coming back up there, and I'll cut out your liver and feed it to the buzzards."

"Hey, Johnny. Look there. Is that him?"

The outlaw leader reined around and stared into a grove of aspen a quarter of a mile distant. The vague outline of a man stood with his back against a tree. Elliott! Starr grabbed for his six-gun, then hesitated. There *was* something familiar about the man, but the early morning light played tricks with his eyes.

"Let's go see, boys," he said, cocking his handgun

just to be on the safe side. There was no way Ben Elliott could have beat them to the valley, but Starr wasn't
about to take any chances.

An ominous premonition came over the outlaw
leader as they rode closer to the man. The hombre's chin
was resting on his chest, like he was sleeping standing
up. His hat was pulled over his face. Starr glanced
around, suddenly looking for an ambush.

The other outlaws sensed Starr's apprehension. They
bunched together, guns drawn, hammers cocked.
They looked around nervously. "What do you think,
Johnny?"

Starr shook his head, remaining silent, his eyes focused on the man in the aspens. They drew closer. Now,
Starr noticed that the clothes looked familiar. "Son of a
bitch!" The words exploded from his lips, and he yanked
on the reins, spinning his pony onto its hind legs. "Son
of a bitch!"

The sudden spin of Starr's horse spooked the other
horses.

"What the hell," yelled one of the outlaws.

The outlaws pulled their horses under control.
"Dammit, Johnny. What's wrong with you?"

Starr pointed at the man. "There. That's Red. Don't
you recognize him. That's Red Davis!"

"What?"

"Yeah. Hell, it sure is," said a second outlaw, looking
over his shoulder, his frantic eyes now searching the
forest around them.

One grew silent. "How'd he do that?"

Starr looked at the speaker. "What do you mean?"

The outlaw nodded at the body of Red Davis, a rope
looped under his arms and tied around a limb. His
thumbs had even been hooked in his pockets, giving

the impression of an afternoon drifter on the streets of Prescott. "How'd he do it so damned fast . . . get down here, pick up Red, and tie him here where we could find him?"

The implications of the question silenced the outlaws. Shaken, they looked around, their handguns cocked and ready.

"He coulda got down here ahead of us," said Starr. "But he'd been mighty hard-pressed to git all this done with any time to spare."

The sun rose above the rim behind them, a brilliant glare in their eyes.

Suddenly, a chunk of ground exploded at their feet, spooking the horses. The roll of a gunshot echoed down the valley as the outlaws fought to steady their animals.

"There. Up there," yelled one of the outlaws, pointing to the rim a thousand feet up.

Silhouetted against the rising sun, a dark figure of a man with a Winchester stood watching them for a few seconds, then vanished.

The outlaws looked at each other. "It was him," said one. "Ben Elliott."

"Ain't likely," retorted another. "No way he coulda got Red strung up like this and then got back up there without us seeing him."

"Don't kid yourself. He probably knows a dozen ways up that rim."

Buckskin Johnny Starr didn't join in the discussion. He was remembering the shadow he'd glimpsed during the ride down from the rim.

Chapter Thirty

His hand on the neck of the bottle of Yellowstone whiskey, Bobby Siringo stiffened when Rafe Borke ushered Buckskin Johnny Starr into the parlor in the main house.

Johnny Starr froze.

The two gunmen glared at one another. They had met once, years earlier.

While they had never drawn down on each other, they each knew the other's reputation. Borke took the bottle from Siringo's hand. "You know Starr here?"

Ignoring the foreman, Bobby Siringo leaned his chair back against the wall and stroked his thin mustache, his eyes still fixed on Starr's. His voice was guarded. "Long time, Johnny."

An amused gleam in his own eyes, Borke splashed whiskey into two glasses as Starr stared down at the grinning Bobby Siringo.

Starr said, "Heard you were up here." He hesitated, then added in a chilly tone. "Missed you down in Tucson."

Siringo turned up his glass and downed it. He looked up at Starr, a wry expression on his face. "No sense in it, Johnny. Charley Benson skipped with the loot. You and me, we'da killed each other for nothing."

"Two thousand ain't nothing, Bobby."

"Maybe not, but my hide's worth more than that. And to tell the truth, I ain't never been certain just which one of us is faster. I figure I am, but I ain't gambling on it for only two thousand."

Starr grinned and picked up a glass of whiskey. "You're probably right." He swung a leg over the back of a chair and plopped down.

Siringo looked up at Rafe Borke. "This hombre we're after must be mighty tough for your boss to bring both of us in." He turned back to Buckskin Johnny Starr. "How many boys did you bring with you? Five, six? Me, I got five. Six counting me."

The grin faded from Starr's face. "Don't kid yourself about this jasper, Bobby. We run into him up on the Mogollon. There was five of us and now there's four."

Borke stiffened. "Elliott? You run into Elliott?"

Starr shook his head. "He didn't bother to leave a name, but whoever that hombre was, he seemed mighty unhappy to see us. Shot our camp up early this morning. Red Davis run over the rim trying to get away."

Bobby Siringo hadn't moved a muscle. He remained leaning back in his chair, his smile frozen on his face. "Old Red, huh? Never cared for him, but that's a helluva way to cash in."

Borke spoke up. "You get a shot at 'em?"

Starr sipped his whiskey. "Never seen him. Like a damned ghost. He come in, shot up the place, then heaved a stick of dynamite at us."

Siringo cut his eyes toward Borke who was leaning forward, his beady eyes narrowed on Johnny Starr. The burly foreman grunted. "What else happened?"

Before answering, Starr chugged the whiskey, dragged the back of his hand across his mouth, and refilled the glass. "We hightailed it off the rim fast as we could, but when we got to the valley, we found Red strung up by his arms to one of them aspens. Next thing we knew, Elliott was standing up on the rim looking down at us."

Siringo drawled. "Sounds like this feller moves purty fast."

"Crap," snapped Borke. "He ain't no faster than any other two-legged yahoo."

The slender man arched an eyebrow and smoothed his mustache. "I don't know, Rafe. Any hombre who can scoot down a thousand-foot drop, string up a dead body to a tree, and then hustle back to the top as quick as Starr here says he did is faster'n any man you or me has ever knowed."

Borke wanted to argue, but Starr added, "And faster'n I even seen."

A thick silence hung over the room as the three men sipped their whiskey. Bobby Siringo maintained his ever-present grin. Buckskin Johnny Starr stared into his glass solemnly. Rafe Borke sneered.

Finally, Siringo broke the silence. "What do you got in mind, Johnny?"

Starr hooked his thumb over his shoulder. "Countin' me, there's four of us. You got six. That's ten." He paused and looked straight into Rafe Borke's eyes, daring the burly foreman to dispute him. "That ain't enough."

Borke's eyes narrowed, spitting fire. His voice charged with sarcasm, he replied, "The Apache Kid is coming in. That gonna be enough for you, Mr. Starr?"

Johnny Starr's grim expression faded into a smirk. "Why don't you come with us, Rafe?" He indicated the interior of the parlor with a nod of his head. "Must be mighty boring for a top gun like you to always stay behind when the rest of us is out doin' the fighting."

The big foreman jumped to his feet, grabbing leather. "Why you tinhorn son—"

"Gentlemen." Albert Barnett strode into the parlor. He jerked to a halt when he saw Borke and Starr standing nose to nose. His face grew hard, and the muscles in his jaws twisted like a clutch of snakes. "You're not getting paid to fight each other." He spat out the words.

His cold gaze settled on Rafe Borke, who met his eyes for a moment, then dropped his gaze to the floor. Johnny Starr stared defiantly at the broad-shouldered cattle baron. "I don't know about Bobby Siringo, Barnett, but me and my boys ain't tackling this rogue wolf for no measly five hundred dollars."

Albert Barnett faced Starr, legs spread, his massive fists planted on his hips. "Welching?"

"Nope. Call it renegotiating if you want. I don't give a damn. But what I'm saying is that the boys and me, we done run into this feller up on the Mogollon. He's a thousand-dollar kill. Maybe more."

"A thousand for one hombre is mighty steep."

A faint smirk spread across Starr's face. "You don't understand, Mr. Barnett. A thousand for me and a thousand for Siringo. Two thousand, all totaled."

His jaw set, his eyes blazing, Barnett studied the faint, almost daring smirk on the face of Buckskin Johnny Starr. He flexed his fingers, opening and closing his fists. "If anyone else told me that, Starr, I'd figure him for yellow. But you're not. I know that for a fact." The anger fled his face. "I don't particularly cotton to being backed up against the wall like this, but because I know what you can do, I'll go along with what you want . . . this time. Two thousand for Ben Elliott. Dead."

Starr patted the grip of his worn .44. "For that kinda money, Mr. Barnett, you ain't got nothing to worry about." He glanced past the big rancher. "What about you, Bobby? You go for this deal?"

Siringo grunted. "Why not? Sounds good to me."

"That's what I like to hear," said Albert Barnett, becoming convivial. He handed the bottle of Yellowstone whiskey to Starr. "Now you boys take this bottle, and Rafe'll find you a spot in the bunkhouse. You'll push out first thing in the morning . . . after you're deputized."

Starr's eyes widened in surprise. "Deputized? What the hell's going on here, Barnett?"

Barnett shrugged. "Making it legitimate. You boys will be a posse going after a wanted man. Simple."

Starr glanced at Siringo, who arched an eyebrow. "I ain't never been no deputy. Might be fun. Come on, Bobby." Taking the bottle, Johnny Starr led the way from the parlor.

Barnett held Borke back. He lowered his voice. "As soon as those bastards get Elliott, kill them."

Rafe Borke nodded and followed the two outlaws to the bunkhouse.

Albert Barnett crossed the parlor to the highboy and poured a brandy. He swirled the golden liquid in the snifter, staring absently out the window. Ben Elliott had caused him enough trouble. With a satisfied nod, he sipped the brandy.

Later that night, the Apache Kid rode in. After listening to the plan, he refused to ride with Starr and Siringo. "Ain't nothing 'gainst you boys. I don't trust nobody. I'll ride by myself. I tree him, I get the two thousand. You or your boys get him, I get nothing."

Chapter Thirty-one

Back in his cave, Ben Elliott stirred the banked fire and considered the last few hours. From all he had heard, Buckskin Johnny Starr figured he was a big-time gunnie stomping around in the footsteps of Clay Allison or Bill Longley, but the truth was, the yahoo was nothing more than a two-bit back-shooter who rolled drunks in dark alleys. Word was that he and his gang had hit a bank or two over near Mesilla and then up to Stinking Springs, all in New Mexico Territory, but no evidence or proof ever came to light.

He dropped two handfuls of coffee in the pot and scooted it to the edge of the small fire. He poured out some flour on a flat rock and sprinkled water over it. He stirred the mixture, adding more water until he could roll it into a ball. Deftly, he patted the dough into pancake bread and flopped it on a flat rock he had tilted to face the fire.

Next he sliced venison and laid the strips on the rock beside the bread dough and leaned back against the cave wall, his eyes fixed hypnotically on the fire. There could only be one reason Starr and his band of ridge runners were in the territory. Albert Barnett had sent for them, and if he'd sent for this bunch, he'd probably sent for more.

Using the tip of his knife, Ben turned the sizzling venison and flipped the bread. The rich aroma of brewing coffee filled the cave. His stomach growled. He couldn't remember the last substantial meal he'd put himself around, but this morning he planned on making up for it. This might be his last chance to stoke up on grub for a spell. Unless he was badly mistaken, action was going to start picking up around here come morning.

Ben regretted the deaths that had already occurred. Tin Man had taught him to respect the sanctity of man, but Ben also realized that in a land without law, every man had to take care of what was his. He wanted to run the hired guns out of the country without any killing; but if they forced his hand like Cherokee Jack, then he had no choice.

That afternoon, Ben saddled his dun, tied three lassos to the cantle, and snapped a lead to the bridles of two of Cherokee Jack's horses and led them down the trail to the valley below. He planned on setting up a few surprises for those jaspers coming after him.

A single road wound through the valley, bisected by several small trails leading into the forest or up to the rim of the plateau. Off the main road in a small clearing in the pines, Ben staked out the two horses, easily visible from the road. He sliced through the picket ropes, leaving the two pieces bound by only a few strands. At the base of each of three pines on the clearing's edge nearest him, he buried a stick of dynamite, leaving one end exposed. If he calculated right, the trees would fall into the clearing. At the sound of the explosion, the frightened animals would break the few strands holding the picket rope and scamper to safety.

Another quarter mile down the narrow trail, he reined up at a boulder. He flipped a loop over a head-high limb on one side of the trail and tossed the other end over a limb on the opposite side of the trail. The slack rope lay across the trail. Ben kicked dirt over it. Then, he tied the loose end to a thirty-pound stone balanced on the larger boulder. Bending a small pine, he fastened a trip rope to the straining arch of the small tree. Then he tied the stone to the tip of the pine.

He stood back and measured his handiwork. When he cut the trip rope, the pine would spring up, yank the stone off the boulder, and the hidden rope across the road would be snapped taut, neck high for a man on horseback. Might not hurt them, but it would get their attention.

The road curved and paralleled the base of the sheer escarpment of the rim. Ben pulled up under an over-hanging ledge of granite, and in a head-high crevice, placed a dynamite charge, using a fuse several inches long.

Another mile down the road, he urged his dun up a slope of talus to a ledge that opened to a trail to the top. Dismounting, he rolled several boulders to the edge, against which he leaned three Winchesters. At the rear of the ledge grew a cluster of twisted pinyon. There he would picket the dun.

To the west, the sun rolled behind the mountains, spreading a blanket of shadows across the valley. Pausing, Ben rolled a cigarette and gazed back across the valley in the direction of the Triple B. He inhaled deeply and blew a stream of smoke into the crisp autumn air. He shivered. Winter was fast approaching.

For a moment, he permitted himself the luxury of reminiscing, of harking back to those years when he was building the Key—the Key, so named because Tin Man always insisted that the key to success was honesty, fair play, hard work, and perseverance.

He and Charlie Little had come out of the Civil War battered and worn, but with a determination to build something of their own. Both men had spoken of marriage, of a family. They even had plans for another main house for Charlie and his family, but with all the work on the ranch, neither ever got around to going out to look for a wife.

Despite Charlie's protestations, Ben had made him an equal partner.

"I don't feel proper about that, Ben. You're the one who came up with the gold, the money to buy this spread."

"Not buy, Charlie. Just the down payment, and it wasn't me, it was the Coyoteros."

Charlie clicked his tongue. "Sure surprised me. Where do you reckon they got the gold?"

Ben arched an eyebrow, and with a crooked grin, replied, "You wouldn't believe me, Charlie."

"Yeah, I would. Come on, Ben. Tell me. Where'd they come up with all that gold?"

The wiry rancher gestured to the mountains around them. "Out there. If they had to, they could bring in a wagon full of gold. But, they don't have to," he added. "They got all they want . . . go where they want, live how they want, do whatever they care to." He shook his head. "They got a good life."

Charlie grunted. "Well, it was mighty white of them, but they was your friends, not mine. It still bothers me about you making me a partner."

"Don't let it, Charlie. You and me, we been partners long before we started this ranch. Have been since Mesilla. Look at the times you pulled my bacon out of the fire. Hell, I'd be dead and gone six times over if it hadn't been for you."

"Well, you saved my skin enough times."

"That's what I'm getting at, Charlie. We're a matched pair, like two high-stepping thoroughbreds in fancy harnesses."

Charlie laughed. "More like two jackasses in trace chains."

They worked from *can't see* to *can't see*. Slowly the ranch grew. And six months ago, Charlie told Ben he was ready to find a wife and start a family.

Suddenly, Ben realized the cigarette was burning his finger. He dropped it and crushed it out with his boot heel. "Damn," he muttered, blowing on his fingers. A gust of cool air brushed his cheek. Dark purple scars of clouds marred the fiery western sky as the sun set behind the mountains.

He rode back to the picketed horses and eased into a vantage point overlooking them. When Starr and his men showed up, they would find a hell of a lot more than they expected.

Glancing in the direction of the Triple B, Ben decided to make one last effort to run the gunslingers out of the valley before the ground began soaking up blood. Making his way through the dark forest, Ben eased up in the rear of Barnett's ranch. A stack of new clapboard sat on the ground beside the burned barn, which was now in the first stages of repair. Moving silently, Ben leaned over in the saddle and opened the corral gate, then eased up beside the barn. He pulled out two sticks of dynamite and struck a match.

Abruptly, a voice from the bunkhouse broke the silence. "Hey. What'n the hell's that light out at the barn?"

Ben touched the match to the fuses and hurled the sticks at the bunkhouse, one at either end, deliberately missing the house by several feet. Before they struck the ground, he wheeled the dun and disappeared back into the darkness.

A cacophony of yells erupted behind, but then two ear-shattering blasts, one right after the other, smothered the shouting. Beneath the echoes of the explosions came the frightened squeals of stampeding horses.

Ben rode back to his vantage point above the picketed horses where he napped throughout the remainder of the night. Because of the stampeded horses, he didn't expect Barnett's hired hands to move after him that night, but he was not about to get careless. The unexpected had sent more yahoos down that stairway to hell than he cared to think about. Well before false dawn, Ben tugged his blanket over his shoulders and pulled out a couple strips of venison. It was dry and tough, but its bulk filled his belly. He took a long drink of water and settled back to wait.

As the morning sky grayed, he readied the dun, snugging down his gear behind the cantle and jacking a cartridge in the chamber. His face expressionless, he took his place behind a boulder and waited.

Later, far to the north, hoofbeats echoed through the fading darkness. Ben flexed his fingers and squirmed into a comfortable position against the boulder, sighting the Winchester at the picketed animals below. There were no butterflies, no nerves, no shortness of breath, only a matter-of-fact anticipation of the coming fight.

Ben had no idea how many he would be facing, five at least; but from the sound of the hooves, there were more. A faint grin played over his face. Five, ten, fifteen. He would handle what he had to handle.

Not wanting to take a chance on the hired guns passing the picketed horses unnoticed because of the darkness, Ben waited until the riders drew closer, then slapped the rump of his dun. The animal whinnied and the picketed horses replied.

Ben hurried back to the boulder and slid the Winchester across the top.

The riders had stopped. They were too distant to discern their words, but their attention was drawn to the picketed animals. Ben squinted into the gray light. He counted ten riders, three of whom were pointing to the horses.

Two other gunnies looked up and down the road nervously.

For several seconds, the riders milled about, discussing the horses. Finally, they rode into the clearing, guns drawn, their eyes constantly searching the forest about them.

"Come on, boys. Just a little closer," whispered Ben, waiting for the last rider to enter the clearing.

As soon as the last rider reined up by the picketed horses, Ben snapped off three quick shots. The second and third were lost in the roaring explosion of the first stick of dynamite.

Horses whinnied, reared, and pawed at each other.

With lightninglike cracks, the ponderosa pines shuddered, then toppled.

Men yelled and shouted.

A thick cloud of dust billowed up, enveloping the clearing.

When the dust cleared, one man was down, an arm crushed beneath one of the large pines. Ben snapped off two more shots, then leaped into his saddle and raced down the road.

Behind him came shouts.

"There he is!"

"Get after him!"

The sunlight rolled down the mountain slope, brightening the shadows in the road. Ben glanced over his shoulder. Nine riders were in pursuit. Slugs whined past him. A sharp burning sensation stung his arm. He glanced down and saw the stain of blood on his shirtsleeve. Just a scratch, but it burned like hell.

Ahead lay his second trap, but he had to draw his pursuers closer; otherwise, they could pull up before the trap caught them. But, the closer they came, the more accurate their gunfire.

He tightened the reins. The owlhoots drew closer, still firing. A slug gouged out a chunk along the top of his thigh. He clenched his teeth and palmed his knife. As he swept past the boulder, he reached out and slashed the trip rope. The top of the pine sprang upward, dropping the boulder, and yanking the rope taut across the road, neck high.

Two gunnies were knocked out of their saddles. One landed on the back of his head, snapping his neck. The second turned a complete somersault and landed on his belly. Just at the last moment, he rolled from beneath the trampling hooves of the galloping horses.

Ben urged the dun faster. At the third trap, he paused, lit the dynamite, then headed for the ledge just above the slope of talus. Behind, he heard hoofbeats, then a racketing explosion.

With a grim smile, Ben urged the dun to the ledge where he picketed the laboring animal in the pinyons near the trail.

He grabbed the first of the three Winchesters and knelt behind the boulder, waiting for the appearance of the riders. Moments later, six rode from the forest.

Ben drew down on the first. When they were fifty yards from him, he placed three 250-grain slugs in the man's chest, and then sprayed the other riders with the remaining slugs. He dropped that Winchester and grabbed the second.

Riders yanked on reins, trying to untangle the horses. Buckskin Johnny Starr tossed off two wild shots, but two slugs caught him in the neck, sending him sprawling.

Bobby Siringo saw Johnny Starr slammed from the saddle. He wheeled his pony and screamed at the top of his lungs. "Why you dirty son—" Those were the last words the mustachioed gunslinger uttered. Two blazing chunks of lead blew his head apart.

As suddenly as it began, the fight was over. The remaining three gunfighters threw up their hands, screaming for mercy.

Ben had already swung the muzzle onto one of the men, and his finger had begun squeezing the trigger. He hesitated, fighting back the anger and fury coursing through his blood, anger and fury heated by the battle. He fought against the bloodlust of killing coursing through his veins.

He rose from behind the boulder and stared down at the three men. He drew a deep breath and released it. "Turn those ponies around and get. If I see you around here again, you're dead men."

Nodding obediently, the men turned their ponies about and dug their spurs into their flanks.

A hundred yards down the road, they reined up, arguing with each other. One yanked his horse around and rode across the valley as fast as he could. The other two shucked their six-guns and charged Ben.

He knocked them both from the saddle, one with a slug that blew apart one hombre's heart and a gut shot to the second.

Ben remained motionless, unable to believe the foolishness of the owlhoots. Such stupidity was one of the reasons the Apaches considered the white man subhuman, the fact that they recklessly threw away their lives instead of waiting until another time.

Moving cautiously, Ben rode down the talus, removed all nine jaspers' gun belts and looped them over his saddle horn after which he threw the dead gunhands over their saddles and sat the gut-shot cowpoke on his pony. He snaked out a lasso and tied the horses in tandem and led them back down the road.

By the time Ben had picked up all the bodies, he had three living and six dead, and chances were the seventh would expire before reaching the Triple B.

With nine ponies tied in tandem, Ben led them back toward the Triple B. Just before he rode out of the forest into sight of the ranch, he pulled up and gave the reins to the cowpoke with the broken arm. "Tell Barnett he's wasting his money."

With a sharp *gee-up* and a slap on the croup, Ben sent the horses back to the ranch with their loads.

Chapter Thirty-two

Rafe Borke saw the plodding horses first, heads down, shuffling along the dusty road that cut across the meadow. He froze in the chuck house door, stunned by the sight, unfeeling of his burning fingers that clutched a tin cup filled with steaming coffee.

Suddenly, his brain picked up the frantic signals sent by the nerve ends in his fingers, and he dropped the cup, cursing.

Other cowpokes gathered about the chuck table looked up, curious. When the burly foreman cursed and stepped outside, they followed, as he, jolted by the chilling sight of two crippled hardcases leading seven dead men being hauled in like sacks of grain.

Borke threw a fearful glance at the main house. He grimaced. Albert Barnett stood on the porch, his face stony, his lips twisted in fury.

Behind Borke, a voice muttered, "I'm hauling my ass outta here."

The burly foreman spun and glowered at the speaker, a young gunhand not yet twenty. "The hell you say. You hired on, cowboy. You're gonna stay or be hauled out like them jaspers yonder."

The young cowpoke gulped and nodded.

The foreman glared at the other ranch hands. "Understood?"

As one, they nodded.

"Borke!" Barnett's voice thundered across the hardpan.

Giving the young cowboy one last glare, Borke hurried to the main house. Without waiting for the foreman, Barnett stormed inside. Borke followed.

Watching the burly foreman's back, the young cowpoke glanced at his compadres. "I don't know about you old boys, but first chance I get, I'm lighting a shuck out of here."

Barnett was in the parlor, killing a glass of Pennsylvania Club rye whiskey. He slammed the empty glass down on the table and grabbed the white pottery jug of rye and filled the glass once again. He turned his blazing eyes on the foreman. "What in the hell happened? What in the damned hell happened?"

For the first time since Rafe Borke had known Albert Barnett, the big man seemed to be tottering on the verge of losing control; he could not give Barnett the answer the rancher wanted. Borke couldn't give Barnett any answer because he himself didn't know what in the hell had happened.

"How could ten paid-for-hire killers come back in less than three hours with six strung across their horses like drawn–and-quartered beef? Well?"

Borke eyed Barnett. "They were good men. They . . ."

Barnett snorted. "Good? Good? And one man takes them?" He shook his forefinger in the air. "One. You hear what I'm saying, Borke?" His face darkened, and his voice rose. "Do you hear what in the hell I'm saying? One damned, single, solitary man killed six." He hesitated, drew a deep breath, then gulped the entire contents of the second glass of rye.

The two stiff drinks fueled the rage blazing within Albert Barnett.

Rafe Borke stared at the big man before him, suppressing the sneer that tried to twist his lips. Barnett was scared. The rich, blustering cattle baron was frightened like a two-year-old child who had wet his pants.

And with that flash of comprehension, in that brief moment when the sharp blade of understanding slashed old perceptions apart, separated old concepts, when he realized Barnett was no different from any other man, Borke's ambitions trebled.

Hell, he'd been with Barnett for years. He knew the wealthy cattle baron's interests. He could handle the affairs of the Triple B just as good, probably better than Barnett. And, if he studied on it, he could probably figure out some way to use this Ben Elliott business for his own gain. But he had to move carefully. No sense in giving Barnett any ideas.

He said, "The Apache Kid is still out there."

Those words tempered the irate cattle baron's anger slightly.

Borke continued, "Ben Elliott growed up with Injuns. Maybe that's where *we* was wrong." When he saw the questioning arch of Albert Barnett's eyebrows, he added hastily, "I mean, that maybe it takes an Injun to catch an Injun."

Barnett opened his mouth to speak, then thought better of it. Instead, he filled his glass to the brim once again. Then he muttered, "Maybe."

* * *

After turning the horses loose with their grisly loads, Ben headed back to his hidden valley, avoiding the meadows, taking care instead to remain within the forest of aspen and pine.

He was drained, physically and emotionally. He longed for the sanctuary and security of his cave high on the Mogollon Plateau. Tend the wounds, feed the belly, rest the body.

An hour later, Ben paused just outside the hidden entrance to his valley and scanned the pinyon-and-pine forest around him. Nothing seemed out of place. Clucking his tongue, he urged the weary dun into the twisting corridor of boulders that led to the valley.

Once in the corridor, Ben relaxed, closing his eyes and enjoying the slow rocking motion of the dun. He was looking forward to a refreshing swim in the trout pond, a cup of steaming coffee and a slab of fried venison or even some baked trout if he got lucky.

Then sleep. But, not too long. Albert Barnett was still out there.

Once in the valley, Ben turned the dun loose, stashed his own gear and the ten gun belts in the cave, stirred up the fire and put on the coffee and venison. Down at the trout pond, he peeled out of his clothes and washed them, laying them out on the ground. Back at the cave, he would spread them on boulders to dry in the sun. Then, he swam, enjoying the frigid tingling of the water as it stimulated his skin, stirred his blood, sharpened his senses. The water burned his wounds, but they were superficial, although his thigh would be sore for a few days.

Afterward, he slipped into his still-wet long johns, figuring on letting them dry on him. His gun belt slung over one shoulder and his clothes over the other, he headed back to the cave, whistling, picking his way over the rocks and around the red-capped bull thistles in his bare feet.

Despite the trouble facing Ben, he was cheerful. He remembered his Apache father, Taa-Yah, who always cautioned him to enjoy each day, each hour, each minute. Face your enemies when they come, but do not let them steal seconds from your life by worrying of them.

At first, Ben had not understood his Apache father's cryptic words, but as he grew older, he came to perceive their meaning, the belief that for everything, there was a time and a place, a time to fight, a time to love, a time to cry, a time to laugh. "Don't cheat yourself by carrying one time into another," Taa-Yah had counseled.

Ben's grin grew broader as he pictured the pan-shaped face of his Apache father.

Above, the blue sky was without clouds. In the distance, a hawk screeched. Behind him, Ben heard the splashing of trout breaking the water after insects.

Yes, Taa-Yah had been right. Enjoy while you may. He filled his lungs with the clean, crisp air, and smelled the fragrance of the pinyons and pines.

He stepped into the cave and stared down the muzzle of a .44.

Instantly, Ben threw himself aside and hurled the armload of wet clothes at the man behind the .44 just as the handgun boomed and an orange flame leaped from the muzzle. The report was deafening in the closed quarters. The exploding powder burned his skin.

Ben bounced off the wall of the cave and swung his gun belt at the .44, knocking it from the man's hand;

but Ben's own six-gun flew out of the holster, clattering against the rock wall. He started for it, but the man jumped him, arm upraised. In the dim light of the cave, Ben glimpsed sunlight reflect off a knife in the assailant's hand, and then a searing pain struck his chest.

Ben swung the belt again, striking the man in the head, staggering him momentarily. He fumbled with his gun belt. His fingers closed about the reassuring bone handle of his own knife, and he slid it from its sheath and dropped into a crouch, arms extended. In his left hand, he held on to the gun belt.

Blood stained the chest of his long johns, but the wound was merely a scratch, deep enough to bleed profusely, but not to incapacitate. "Looks like you missed your chance, hombre," Ben growled, studying the man before him. Indian—Apache or Ute. Not Navaho. Round face, hair black as midnight, high cheekbones, cruel lips curled in a half smile.

The Apache's lips twisted, and he shuffled to one side, knife extended. His black eyes exuded a cockiness, a conceit. "Do not mistake yourself, gringo. I never miss," he said in the white man's vernacular. He waved the double-edged blade slowly, continuing to shuffle to his right. "A matter of time. That is all."

Ben flicked the gun belt at the Indian, hoping to distract him long enough to make a move, but the Indian was quicker than Ben expected. His hand shot out and grabbed the gun belt and tried to yank it from Ben, but the wiry rancher held tight, and suddenly, the two men were tied together by the belt, neither relinquishing his grasp.

They continued to circle, feinting, waiting for an opening, tugging at the belt, each hoping to yank the other off balance.

Abruptly, the Apache Kid jerked on the belt and made an upward thrust for the belly. Ben leaned back and parried, forcing the knife above his head. In the next instant, he shifted to his right, away from the downward cut of his assailant, and slashed down and across with his knife.

The Kid screamed and jerked against the belt. Blood stained his greasy cotton shirt from his right shoulder to his left hip. The sureness fled his eyes, leaving behind fear and concern. He dragged his tongue over his lips.

Slowly, deliberately the two men circled, each searching for an advantage. The Kid thrust, and Ben parried a horizontal slash. The bolster on his knife locked against the Kid's, the wicked blade scant inches from his own throat. The Kid tried to force his knife, and suddenly, the match became one of sheer strength.

Sweat beaded on Ben's forehead as he forced the blade away from his neck. The Kid groaned through clenched teeth, his muscles bunched, struggling futilely to resist the strength in the wiry man's body.

Without warning, Ben aimed a kick at the Kid's knee, slamming his leg from under him and knocking him off balance. In the same motion, Ben yanked on the belt, spinning the Apache killer to the ground and knocking his knife from his hand.

In an instant, Ben was on him, his knees pinning the Kid's arms, his knife at the Kid's throat. Breathing hard, Ben gasped. "It's over. Give it up."

The Apache Kid struggled, but he was held too firmly. Slowly, his struggles ceased. He looked up at Ben in fear.

Ben relaxed. There had been too much killing. His eyes less than eighteen inches from the Kid's, Ben glared at him. "I oughta rip your throat from ear to ear, but I'm not. I'm giving you a break."

The fear vanished from the Kid's eyes, replaced with cool wariness.

Ben read the change. He pressed his knife tighter against the man's throat. The Kid's eyes bulged. Ben warned him, "Cross me, and you're dead. You understand?"

The Kid tried to nod.

"All right," Ben replied, removing the knife from the Kid's throat. He pushed himself to his feet. "Get up."

As the Apache Kid sat up, Ben turned his back, reaching for his six-gun. A satiny noise from behind caused him to look over his left shoulder in time to see the Kid raising a derringer, cocking it in the same motion.

Ben whipped his knife under his left arm. It turned over once and buried itself hilt deep in the Apache Kid's heart.

The Kid stiffened; his eyes protruded; then he shuddered; he tried to level the derringer, but his eyes rolled up into his head, and he slumped to the floor.

Ben stumbled backward and sat heavily on the ground beside the banked coals. Without taking his eyes off the dead man, he pulled out a bag of Bull Durham and with shaking hands, rolled a cigarette. He smoked it, trying to understand the last futile action of the dead man.

Finally, he flipped the butt into the coals and stood up. He removed the Kid's gun belt and tossed it with the others. He grabbed the Kid's ankles. "Come on, partner. Let's get you on your pony."

Chapter Thirty-three

Zebron Rawlings pulled up at the hitching rail in front of the main house and dismounted. He wrapped his reins around the rail and took the steps two at a time. Without bothering to knock, he opened the door.

"Albert!" The front hall was empty. "Albert!" His strident voice echoed through the house.

The broad-shouldered rancher appeared from the parlor. "You don't need to shout, Zebron. Jesus! You'd think you were born in a barn."

Rawlings allowed a faint smile to flicker over his thin lips. "Hell, maybe I was."

Barnett laughed. "Sure. And my mother was a mountain lion." He poured them a drink and handed one to Rawlings. "Thanks for coming over. How's everything at the Slash Bar?"

The lanky man nodded and sprawled in a chair, arms draped over the arms and legs stretched out in front, very unlike the proper gentleman he portrayed at the Slash Bar. "Behind schedule if you still want the ranch by the end of the year. On schedule if you're willing to wait some."

Barnett cursed. "What's the problem?"

"We've talked some about getting hitched, but for some reason, she's gotten spooky about it."

The big man's eyes flashed. "What in the hell did you do?"

"Nothing. Not a damned thing. She's a woman. That's what happened."

Barnett pursed his lips. "I don't like rushing things, but with Elliott out there, we could be running out of time. You need to push her."

Rawlings snorted and gulped down half the glass of whiskey. "How can Elliott hurt us? The sheriff's bound to be after him now that he killed those deputies."

It was Barnett's time to snort. "Deputies, hell. They were two-bit gunfighters."

"Maybe so, but Jess did swear them in. Your idea, and officially, they was lawmen, lawmen murdered in the line of duty." He chugged the remainder of his drink and reached for the bottle.

The broad-shouldered rancher grunted. "Jess'll do what I tell him. Right now, like you say, Ben Elliott can't hurt us, but the longer he stays out there, the better his chances are that someone important will come along and listen to him. That federal marshal, for example. The one who rode back to Tucson that night Elliott was tossing around all those rattlesnakes. What was his name?"

"Hazlett. Ike Hazlett."

"Yeah. Hazlett."

Rawlings arched an eyebrow. "Why would he come back?"

Albert Barnett shook his head wearily. "There's still the killing of Burgess. Remember him? The one Borke killed, and we blamed on Elliott."

"Yeah. I'd almost forgotten about that."

"Well, don't. Don't forget a thing. We can't afford to, not until everything is in place. Once it is, once I have clear title to thirty-six hundred square miles of the territory's finest land, no one can stop me. I've got the other ranches, all four of them. All I'm missing is the Slash Bar, and that's up to you. I don't care how, but get that girl to marry you."

Rawlings eyed the larger man for several seconds, then slowly drained his glass and unfolded his lanky frame from the chair. "We're planning a cotillion in a couple weeks. It'll be taken care of by then."

Albert Barnett fixed his gaze on the sallow-faced man before him. "And in the meantime, we'll run Ben Elliott to ground."

The next morning just before sunup, Albert Barnett was awakened from a sound sleep by someone jerking on his arm. He rolled over and blinked the sleep from his eyes. Slowly, the bearded face of his foreman came into focus. "Yeah?"

"You better see for yourself, boss. The front porch."

Swinging his feet over the edge of the mattress, Barnett slipped on his trousers and tugged his suspenders over his shoulders. "What is it?"

Borke shook his head. "Like I said, you gotta see it."

Puzzled, Albert Barnett picked his way through the dark house. He swung open the front door and halted in his tracks. His mouth dropped open.

In the middle of the porch was a pile of gun belts. Beyond the belts, the body of the Apache Kid sat propped against one of the posts supporting the porch roof.

Albert Barnett stared unbelieving at the corpse and

the gun belts. Finally, he managed to croak out the question, "When did he do this?"

Borke grunted. "Nobody heard nothing, Mr. Barnett. Like you ordered, we had two men patrolling the ranch last night. Good men. They didn't see or hear nothing."

A month earlier, Albert Barnett would have scoffed and called the guards liars and slackers, but in the last few weeks, he had witnessed enough of Ben Elliott's moves to realize the tough rancher was perfectly capable of slipping into a roomful of people, undressing every one of them, and slipping back out unseen, unheard, even unfelt.

Albert Barnett had never worried about the success of his plan, not once in the eight years he had owned the Triple B. But now, a tiny, nagging doubt flickered to life in his brain, ignited by Ben Elliott, who had thoroughly defeated every move Barnett had made to kill him.

He lifted his gaze to the pines beyond the meadow. It would be just like that damned Ben Elliott to be sitting out there watching, and laughing. Well, let him laugh. "I'll have the last laugh," the big rancher muttered.

"What's that, Mr. Barnett?" Borke leaned toward him to hear better.

"I said, get that body out of here and then come in the house. I've got a chore for you."

Ben sat in the pines beyond the valley watching the two men on the porch. A tiny grin tugged at his lips as he imagined the chagrin of Albert Barnett.

So far, Ben's harassing had been successful, but he knew well enough that sooner or later, his luck would run out. Continual harassment meant nothing unless the wealthy rancher became careless. He had to force Albert Barnett into a mistake, a mistake serious enough to pull him from the throne he had built on murder and theft.

One of the figures on the porch went inside. Barnett. The other strode to the chuck house and stuck his head inside. Moments later, two cowboys emerged and headed for the porch.

Ben didn't wait to see them dispose of the corpse. He turned the dun back into the forest, his mind working hard to come up with an idea that would force Albert Barnett to destroy himself.

By the time Ben reached the valley, he had discarded a dozen impractical and far-fetched ideas. Barnett was playing every move close to the vest. He would not be stampeded into a hasty decision that could cost him all he had built. Ben could continue burning outbuildings, but Barnett would simply rebuild them. Every window Ben shot out, the cattle baron could replace five times over.

He wondered about Zebron Rawlings. In Ben's scrutiny of the Triple B in the last few weeks, he had witnessed the lean man visit the ranch at least twice a week. Why would a man reputedly from Baltimore visit Albert Barnett so frequently? What could the two men have in common?

After turning the dun loose in the small valley, Ben put coffee on to boil and plopped the last of his venison on the stone to broil.

The more Ben thought about his last question, the more intrigued he became. What in the hell could the two men have in common? On the surface, nothing. But—suppose there was some kind of connection, some link.

He shook his head. "Don't be an idiot," he muttered.

The aroma of the boiling coffee filled the cave. Ben poured a cup and sipped at it while the venison sizzled. His unbidden thoughts kept going back to Rawlings and Barnett until he finally decided to snoop around to see just what he could find.

Back at the Triple B, Rafe Borke climbed into his saddle and headed for Tucson with a letter to Columbus Delano, secretary of the interior in Washington D.C., and a second letter to Marshal Ike Hazlett.

Hazlett read the letter with a growing irritation, not so much because of the contents or even the smug sneer on the face of Rafe Borke when he delivered it, but because J. Albert Barnett had him pinned to the wall. The rich cattleman suspected Hazlett was deliberately dragging his feet in his pursuit of Ben Elliott, and he had so claimed in the letter to Delano, the influential politician who had pressured the president into appointing Ike Hazlett federal marshal.

Ike started to reread the letter, but the hulking figure of Rafe Borke standing on the other side of the desk caught his attention. He looked over the top of the letter at the sneering foreman. "You got any more business here?"

Borke shrugged. "Nope."

The marshal nodded to the door. "Then get out."

The sneer broadened, carving a ragged gash across the foreman's face, revealing the gap where the missing teeth belonged. "Whatever you say, Marshal."

After Borke left, Hazlett reread the letter once again,

crushed it into a ball, and threw it in the trash. "Damn," was all he said.

The next morning, Ike Hazlett gave instructions to his deputy. "I'll be up at the Mogollon Rim. You handle things here. Keep the drunks outta the middle of the street. And keep a close eye on any jasper new to town."

The deputy grunted. "Don't worry, Ike. You sure you don't want me to ride along with you. Earl can take care of the town as good as me."

"Nope," replied the marshal, stuffing a shirt, canned tomatoes, and crackers in one side of his saddlebags. In the other side, he dropped a couple boxes of .44's. "This is strictly a one-man job."

Chapter Thirty-four

Ben tied the dun in a small clearing with thick browse. Overhead, the moon bathed the forest in a pale glow, its beams vertical shafts of light penetrating the forest of pines. Staying in the shadows of the tall, slender trees, Ben ghosted through the forest to the meadow.

He planned on slipping up to the house in an effort to see just what was taking place. And if the opportunity presented itself, he might even sneak inside and prowl through the cattle baron's desk.

Like a phantom, he drifted across the meadow and blended into the shadows of the main house, the front of which showed the effect of the dynamite. The Triple B hands were in the bunkhouse. The murmur of their voices floated across the hardpan to Ben as he eased along the house to the lighted window.

Inside, Barnett sat at a desk, busily scribbling in a ledger. Backing away, Ben then slipped to the bunkhouse, noting that the foreman, Rafe Borke, was at neither place. Usually hooked on to Albert Barnett's coattails, the burly foreman's absence puzzled Ben.

Staying in the shadows, Ben made his way back to his pony. Tightening the cinch, he mounted and headed for the Slash Bar, not at all anxious to speak with Mary Catheryn Wills, but curious as to what was taking place at the ranch.

Mary Catheryn had been home almost a month now. Zebron Rawlings still lived on the ranch, but the arrangement was completely innocent, especially with the presence of Teresa Martinez, the rotund Mexican housekeeper who raised Mary Catheryn from childhood.

Ben wasn't sure just what he might find at the Slash Bar. Anything, a stray word, a suspicious act, but the ranch was dark when Ben reined up just inside the forest at the edge of the meadow.

Astride the dun, Ben studied the ranch for several minutes before turning back to his valley.

Two days later at sunset, Rafe Borke returned to the Triple B and rode straight to the main house. Ben watched from the shelter of the forest as Barnett stepped onto the porch and gestured the foreman inside.

The ranch hands had already chowed down in the newly repaired chuck house and retired to the bunkhouse where they engaged in their nightly poker games. A couple cowpokes squatted near the front door, smoking and seeing who could come up with the biggest windy.

Ben frowned when the light went on in the parlor. He'd cut off his arm to be beside the window, listening to the conversation between Barnett and Borke. The cowpokes outside the bunkhouse rose and sauntered inside.

Dusk had settled over the valley, casting shadows and distorting vision. Though uneasy over moving out before complete darkness, Ben knew he had no time to waste if he wanted to eavesdrop.

On foot, he slipped across the meadow, staying in a crouch in the taller grass. If he were spotted, with luck, his silhouette might pass for a small deer. But, he reached the main house unseen and crouched in the deep shadows beneath the parlor window.

The harsh voice of Rafe Borke tumbled out the open window. "That's right. He's coming up here." Borke laughed, a cruel snarl. "You shoulda seen him. His ears got red and his neck swoll up. I figured he was goin' to pop he was so mad."

"You sure he's coming?"

"Well, he rode out next morning. I drifted back over to the marshal's office and asked for the marshal. The deputy told me he'd be back in a couple weeks."

Barnett brushed his hands together as if he were wiping dirt from them. "Finally. Well, maybe with the federal marshal on Elliott's tail now, he'll be too busy to fool with us."

"I still think you oughta let me handle him," said Borke.

"Haven't you learned anything about Ben Elliott, Rafe? He's put a heap of gunslicks in the ground. No way we can run him down. He's like the damned wind, but this way, we're letting the law do our job for us. I know Ben Elliott. He won't kill a lawman."

Ben backed away into the darkness, disturbed, but not surprised that Ike Hazlett was coming back after him. Despite the unspoken understanding between Ben and Hazlett, the marshal had no choice. He had a job to do, and Albert Barnett was somehow forcing Ike to do it. Ben glanced over his shoulder, half expecting to see the marshal who was probably already in the area.

He wished he had more time before having to worry about Hazlett. Ben had accomplished nothing significant in the weeks the marshal had been away. He'd burned some outbuildings, dynamited a few bunkhouses, rattled some cookshacks, tore up a few houses, but as far as prying Barnett's fingers from the ranches, he had been unsuccessful.

He had no hard proof of any of the rancher's misdeeds. The documents had been destroyed; Eustace Mooney, the title clerk, murdered; all he had was the truth, but with no one to back him up, he might as well be spitting into the wind.

Back in the forest, Ben mounted the dun and sat staring at the pale yellow rectangles of light dotting the darkness surrounding the Triple B. Damn. If he could only find someone with the knowledge to back him up, but the only one who knew was Barnett's foreman, Rafe Borke, and he'd die before he opened his mouth.

Like a stroke of lightning, Ben remembered P. H. Hall, John Wills's foreman. "Why didn't I think of him before," he muttered, suddenly excited. His theory of John Wills's death came rushing back.

P. H. Hall, the foreman of the Slash Bar, rose well before sunup. He groaned, stretched the sleep from his bony frame, and scratched his ribs through his long johns. The rich, full aroma of boiling coffee had awakened him as it did every morning. He pulled on his duds, stomped into his boots, and grabbed his gun belt, buckling it around his waist as he stepped out of the bunkhouse.

Before he took a step, a gun muzzle jammed him in the back. Ben whispered, "Don't say a word, P.H. It's me, Ben Elliott. Just do what I say, and there won't be no trouble."

Abruptly, the old foreman spun and grabbed for his six-gun. In the next instant, his head exploded with a brilliant display of stars, and he felt himself falling into a deep black hole.

Ben grabbed the limp body of the foreman and tossed him over his shoulder and disappeared back into the early morning shadows. A few horses nickered as he hurried past, heading up the road to where the dun was tied.

He wished there had been some other way to get to the old foreman, but this was the surest, and for Ben Elliott, the safest. If he were wrong about P.H., then he'd apologize like hell and offer his chin as a target to the old man.

But, deep inside, and though it made him sick to his stomach, he knew he wasn't wrong.

The dun lifted its head and jitter-stepped a few times when Ben lashed P.H. over the saddle. He swung up behind the cantle and headed for his hidden valley, planning exactly what he would ask the old man when he awakened.

Chapter Thirty-five

When the old foreman came to, he was propped against a ponderosa pine. Squatting in front of a nearby pine was Ben Elliott, hat shoved back, smoking a cigarette.

Ben nodded. "Sorry about the bump on the head, P.H. You brought it on yourself. I only wanted to ask you a couple questions without any commotion."

P.H.'s wrinkled face twisted in anger. "You ain't got no right coldcocking me like that, then hauling me off to the middle of nowhere."

"You should've listened to me then. I only wanted to ask you a few questions."

"Well, I ain't answering nothing," he retorted, growing angry. "Especially not for no killer."

Ben shook his head and flipped his cigarette to the ground. "I reckon you'll answer for me, P.H. The Apache taught me ways to help folks talk." He hoped to bluff the old man.

The old man gulped, and some of the defiance fled his face, but his eyes were still flinty, and his thin lips pressed tightly together.

Ben had considered his questions. He decided to

proceed as if his theories were true, that P.H. was working for Albert Barnett, and that P.H. knew a hell of a lot more about the death of John Wills than he let on.

The first question smacked P.H. between the eyes. "How long you been on Barnett's payroll?"

The old foreman's mouth dropped open, and his eyes grew wide. He stammered. "I . . . I mean . . . what are you talkin' about? I ain't on Barnett's payroll."

Ben shook his head. He lied in a calm, self-assured voice. "Don't lie to me, P.H. You might not be on the monthly payroll, but you get paid. I heard Barnett tell Borke about you. Now, tell me how long you been taking money from Barnett."

P.H. looked around in desperation, seeking someplace to run, to hide. Ben read the body language and suppressed a grin. His guess was right on target. The old man was trying to hide something, his tie-in with J. Albert Barnett.

Encouraged by P.H.'s nervousness, Ben pushed his bluff. "Answer me, P.H. Now!"

He shook his head. "I told you, Ben. I . . . I don't work for Barnett." He climbed to his feet, but Ben remained in his squat.

He looked up at P.H. His voice remained soft and low. "Well, now, P.H. I'm not so dumb that I can't spot a goat in a flock of sheep." He rose to his feet. "So, I reckon, I'll just brush off a couple tricks I know about helping folks talk."

"Not with me, you ain't," he croaked, grabbing for his handgun, but all his fingers found was empty leather.

Ben patted the six-gun stuck in his belt. "Figured something like that, P.H. So I just made sure neither one of us would accidentally get hurt." He hesitated, eyed the older man a moment, then growled, "Turn around and put your hands behind your back."

P.H. glared at him defiantly.

Shaking his head at the stubborn old man, Ben shucked his six-gun and leveled the muzzle on the old man's belly. "I mean it, P.H. Get those hands behind your back and turn around unless you want another knot on that thick head of yours."

Reluctantly, P.H. did as he was ordered. Holstering his six-gun, Ben bound the old man's hands quickly. "You might as well watch, P.H.," Ben said in a soft drawl as he picked up a lasso and threw it over the limb of the ponderosa pine. "Give you an idea of what's in store for you."

The old man turned to run, but Ben's warning voice stopped him within the first half dozen steps. "Waste of time, P.H. There's only one way out of this valley, and you don't know it." Fearfully, the old foreman turned and watched helplessly as Ben gathered kindling.

In a casual voice, as if he were patiently describing the steps in baiting a hook to a young boy during his first fishing lesson, Ben explained what was going to happen. "You see, P.H., the Apache puts a lot of stock in a man's courage." He picked up dry branches and kindling and stacked it near the base of the pine. "Fire tests the hell out of a man's courage."

P.H. sucked in his breath noisily. Ben glanced over his shoulder. "What I'm going to do, P.H., is loop this rope around your ankles and dangle you headfirst over a fire."

The old foreman took a step backward, then turned to run, but in his hurry, he stumbled over his own feet and sprawled to the ground. Before he could roll over, Ben had lashed his ankles together and then jerked his feet above his head. "Now, P.H., you can stop this right here if you want to. Just answer some questions about Albert Barnett such as how long you been on his payroll and this goes no further."

His voice quivered. "I told you, I ain't on his payroll. I got nothing to do with Albert Barnett."

Ben shrugged. "Wrong answer, P.H." Ben dragged the old man to the pine and looped the rope around his ankles. He grabbed the other end of the rope. "Last chance." Ben prayed the old man would talk. He knew he could never go through with the torture.

P. H: Hall pleaded. "I told you the truth. I . . ."

Ben yanked him into the air, tying off the end of the rope when P.H. was eight feet above the ground. Taking his time, he placed the tinder directly under P.H.'s head. Next, he stacked the kindling over the tinder. "We start with a small fire first, P.H. Then, if you don't tell me what I want to hear, I make it larger." He fished a match from his vest pocket and held it for P.H. to see. "Well?"

The old man's face was flushed a deep red. He shook his head.

Ben struck the match.

P.H. caught his breath. "You ain't really goin' through with this?"

"Barnett's ruined me. I got nothing left, P.H. I got nothing to lose." His eyes cold, Ben touched the match to the tinder and a small flame leaped up, igniting the kindling. He added a few small, dry logs. Within moments, the flames grew larger, leaping and dancing two or three feet into the air.

"The law will get you for this, Ben," the old man choked out.

Ben untied the rope. "Makes no difference to me, P.H. You know Barnett has got me framed for murder.

The federal marshal is on my tail. So if I bake your skull and explode what brains you got all over the place, what more can they do to me?" He paused, muttered a hasty prayer, then lowered the old man.

He stopped after a foot, tied the rope off again, and squatted by the fire and rolled a cigarette. P.H. twisted and moaned. Blood rushed to his head, turning his face the color of canned tomatoes. His thinning hair hung straight down.

Ben pulled a stick from the fire and touched the flame to his cigarette. He inhaled and blew the smoke into the fire. "First thing that's going to happen, P.H., is that your hair will burn. Then your skin will blister and swell up with water. When the blister breaks, the fire will bake your brain and start boiling the blood. It'll push against your skull, but bones won't swell, not like skin. Your skull will finally explode and dump your brains on the fire, but you won't smell the stink of frying brains because you'll be dead."

P.H. twisted and jerked in a futile effort to swing himself beyond the heat of the fire. Ben laughed. "Won't work, P.H." He flipped his cigarette into the fire and rose. "Well, I'm tired of listening to your lies, old man. Don't worry though. I won't let the buzzards and coyotes get you. I'll at least give you a decent burial."

He reached for the rope.

P.H. gagged and vomited into the fire below. He blubbered and cried. Tears ran over his forehead and dripped in the fire. "Please, please, don't. I'll tell you whatever you want. Just please get me down. I don't want to die."

Ben breathed a sigh of relief. He kept his voice hard and cold. "You better not be lying to me. You do, I'll drop you in that fire and fry you like a johnnycake."

"I won't. I promise, I won't."

Kicking the fire aside, Ben lowered the old man and propped him against the trunk of a tree. "All right. First question. How long you been on Barnett's payroll?"

He blinked the tears from his eyes and coughed. "Thr . . . Three years this winter."

"What were you supposed to do for him?"

"Nothing . . . not really. He just said he wanted me to keep watch . . . see what was going on and let him know."

"Going on? About what?"

"He . . . He said whatever was different or unusual."

"How'd it come about? Barnett come to you?"

P.H. nodded emphatically. "Yeah. Yeah. That was it."

"John Wills. How'd he die?"

Shaken by his close call with death, P.H. blurted out the truth. "Borke. Rafe Borke knocked him in the head and threw him in the corral with the horses. He run them over Mr. Wills until he was dead. Then he run them out and put the piebald in."

A red film of anger blinded Ben. His hand reached for his knife, and he took a threatening step toward the bound man.

P.H. squealed like a pig. "Honest. I didn't know nothing about it 'til it was done. I tried to back out, but they wouldn't let me. Said I was as guilty as they was."

Ben halted, his knife half drawn. He glared down at the frightened man, fighting back the urge to kick the hell out of P. H. Hall, to cause him the pain he and Albert Barnett had caused Mary Catheryn Wills and Ben.

The thought of her raised another question, which he posed to the old foreman. "Barnett's been visiting the Slash Bar considerable. And on the days he doesn't, Rawlings shows up at the Triple B. What's going on?"

P.H. shook his head. "Honest to God, Ben. I don't know. Rawlings, he comes over, and him and Barnett disappear into the parlor of the main house. Barnett don't let no one around them except Borke."

Ben believed the old man. Tears had carried dirt and grime into the deep wrinkles on his ancient face and dripped onto his vest, staining it an even darker brown. "You never heard any kind of talk between the two?"

"No. I never did. I . . . Yeah, once. Once." He looked at Ben eagerly, like a mongrel hound seeking a gentle pat on the head. "I didn't hear much, but it was Borke and Barnett talking about the war and Rawlings."

"What did you hear?"

P.H. gulped. "Not much. All three was in the war together, best I could make out."

A different perspective of the Barnett-Rawlings relationship began to open for Ben. "What else?"

"Something about land titles in Barnett's office."

A frown knit Ben's forehead. "What titles?"

The mossy-backed foreman hesitated, then mumbled, "The ones he had changed so he could steal the ranches in the valley."

Ben's pulse raced, but he retained his outward calm. "Keep going."

"No more. That's all. I swear to God, that's all."

Ben studied the old man for several seconds. P. H. Hall was telling the truth. He had spilled all he knew, and it was enough to provide Ben with a more detailed picture of all that had been taking place in the valley.

But, what in the hell was Barnett doing with copies of the original titles? The sensible move would have been to burn them. Puzzled, he knelt and removed the rope from P.H.'s ankles, leaving the grizzled old fore-man's hands bound. The next step was to see Mary Catheryn Wills. Explain to her just what was going on and get her to safety, not that he believed Barnett and Rawlings would deliberately hurt her, for even back-shooting murderers respected the women in the West, but in the heat of battle, accidents could happen.

"Get up," he told P.H. Before he went to the Slash Bar, he had to take care of the old foreman so he couldn't warn Barnett and Borke.

Turning his back on the old man, Ben kicked the smoldering branches back together, rebuilding the fire, adding damp wood to create a thick smoke, which streamed into the clear sky in a solid column. After five minutes, Ben extinguished the fire. He turned back to P.H. and nodded to the cave. "Over there."

P.H. frowned at the remains of the fire, but quickly he did as Ben ordered. In the cave, P.H. gathered his shattered nerves. "What . . . What are you goin' to do with me?" His voice cracked.

Ben shoved the coffeepot in the coals and looked up at P.H. His face was hard, his eyes cold. "You're my hole card, P.H. When the time comes, you're going to tell the marshal just what you told me."

P.H. nodded, but his eyes took on a wary, scheming look. "What makes you think I'll talk to him?"

The grim expression on Ben's face turned into a grin. A shadow appeared in the mouth of the cave. P.H. looked around, and his heart leaped into his throat.

Four sneering Apaches glared hungrily at him.

Chapter Thirty-six

A puzzled frown on her heart-shaped face, Mary Catheryn stood on the front porch staring out over the ranch. She wore riding breeches, a becoming blouse with a lace collar buttoned snug around her neck and a black flat-crowned hat with a straight brim. "You sure he isn't out on the range somewhere?"

Zebron Rawlings stood beside her, his lean body slouched, his thumbs hooked in his gun belt. "One of the boys saw him leave the bunkhouse this morning. He never reached the cookshack."

"Couldn't he have ridden out . . . to check on something?"

"His horse is in the corral, and best we can tell, none are missing. Even his saddle is still here."

Mary Catheryn pursed her lips and scanned the far meadows where they met the tall stands of ponderosa pine and groves of quaking aspen. She had forgotten just how beautiful the valley was, just as she had forgotten how dangerous it could also be, a fact borne out by the strange disappearance of her foreman.

Rawlings laid his hand on her shoulder. "This is uncertain country, Mary Catheryn. Anything could have happened to P.H. That's another reason for you to set the date. You've been promising you would. Let me protect you. Let me help run the Slash Bar. You need a man to lean on, and I want to be that man."

She smiled up at him, her green eyes warm and trusting. Zebron had always been such a gentleman. In Baltimore, he catered to her every whim. His manners were impeccable, his knowledge of the arts impressive, and his self-confidence reassuring.

And Mary Catheryn wanted to marry, to have children, raise a family, and to her own surprise, realized she wanted to build the Slash Bar into the ranch of which her father had always dreamed. But, as much as she cared for Zebron, she never felt that little tingle, that rush of emotion when he appeared.

She shook her head. Maybe she was too particular. Maybe that little tingle, that rush of emotion was just the silly talk of giggling girls. Maybe Zebron Rawlings was the perfect match for her.

"Well?"

His question pulled her back to the present. Her smile flickered, then steadied on her lips. "Tomorrow night. At the cotillion. Like I told you. I'll set the date in front of everyone. Now, let's send some boys out to look for P.H."

"I already have," Rawlings replied.

Her eyes twinkled. She arched an eyebrow questioningly.

Rawlings laughed. "I told you. You need me to do all of this for you."

Mary Catheryn studied him a moment, amusement crinkling her eyes. "Maybe so," she replied, turning back into the main house.

* * *

Zebron Rawlings hesitated before following her, casting his gaze toward the Triple B. Somehow, he needed to get word to Albert Barnett about the disappearance of the old foreman.

P. H. Hall stared in fear at the grinning Apaches. He struggled futilely against the ropes about his wrists. He looked at Ben Elliott, wanting to cry out, but the words stuck in his throat.

Ben nodded to the Apaches. "They're the reason you'll talk to the marshal, P.H. I've got a heap of moving around to do, and I can't keep an eye on you, so my brother here, White Eye, will be mighty pleased to show you the hospitality of his *rancheria* until I'm ready for you."

White Eye stepped forward, his white teeth a brilliant grin against his sun-blackened face. "This is why you called, Little Tin Man?"

Pouring a cup of coffee and offering it to White Eye, Ben replied, "I need help. This man and other whites are against me. He has information for the law. Take him to your *rancheria*. He must be kept safe until I send for him."

With an amused gleam in his eyes, White Eye leered at P.H. and stroked the smooth handle of his knife. "That is not what I wished to hear, my brother. We are soon at the Moon of the Corn. A sacrifice would insure plentiful crops."

P.H.'s eyes grew wider, and he took a step back. "Ben . . . don't let them get me. Please, I promise to do whatever you say. Just don't let them get me."

Ben laid his hand on White Eye's shoulder. "I am ashamed I must ask you for help, but there is no one for me to trust except my brothers."

The three Apaches behind White Eye grunted and nodded to each other, proud of the faith and trust Little Tin Man placed in his brothers.

"Do not fear," said White Eye, his dark eyes twinkling in merriment. "We will keep him safe for you. Of course," he added, grinning wickedly at the frightened foreman, "one or two missing fingers would hurt nothing. Is that not true?"

Suppressing his own laughter at P.H.'s discomfort, Ben joined in the game, his voice grave and serious. "Just as long as you don't do anything, my brother, to prevent him from talking to the marshal."

P. H. Hall sat heavily on the floor of the cave and began to cry.

Before sundown, Ben saddled the dun and headed for the Slash Bar, reaching the edge of the forest nearest the main house long after dark. The windbreak row of pines leading from the forest to the ranch buildings stood like dark sentries in the night.

He had not decided exactly what he would say to Mary Catheryn. P.H. had admitted Borke killed her father. A jasper didn't have to be as smart as a bunkhouse rat to know the foreman acted on Barnett's orders. On top of that, Barnett had known Rawlings during the war. There was a thread there, one strong enough to convince Ben that the three were working together.

Of course, the only way Mary Catheryn would believe Ben was if she heard the words from P.H.'s own lips.

At least Ben could warn her, put her on guard.

But, what if she told Rawlings? He would then certainly relay the information to Albert Barnett.

Ben shrugged. What if she did tell Rawlings, and what if he did pass word on to Barnett? What would that change? Nothing—except, perhaps rattle Barnett and Rawlings more.

Ben dismounted and tied the dun to a pine. He peered across the meadow.

Behind the corrals, a large fire burned. A couple shadows walked in front of it.

Ten minutes later, Ben dropped into the tall grass near the hardpan and frowned at the half dozen wagons parked near the corrals. Three surreys, two buggies, and one buckboard, all fancy rigs, not for working ranch hands.

He cut his eyes toward the slumbering ranch house and then to the blazing fire behind the corrals. The two cowpokes squatted by the fire with their backs to him. The succulent aroma of broiling beef filled the night air. Obviously, Mary Catheryn had overnight guests and big plans for the coming day. He studied the dark windows, reconsidering his plan to see her. Finally, he decided to barge ahead.

Mary Catheryn peered around the edge of the curtain. Ben struck a match so she could see his face. She stared at him so long without moving that Ben began to think she would not open the window.

The starlight etched shadows across her forehead as she scowled and opened the window. "I told you not to come back here," she said, her voice a harsh whisper.

"Just listen. Two minutes. That's all I ask. Then you can do whatever you want."

Tugging her house robe around her slender body tightly, she nodded and stepped back into the dark bedroom. Ben followed.

"Don't light the lamp," he whispered, squatting by the window so he could watch outside. He heard the rustle of the feather mattress as she sat on the edge of the bed. The mixed aroma of talc and perfume filled the darkness.

"All right. Two minutes."

"Last time I was here, I told you I'd be back with proof of what I said about Barnett. Now, I have it, proof you can't ignore because it comes from your own foreman."

He heard a gasp of surprise. "P.H.? You know where he is?"

"I have him in a safe place."

"Where?"

Ben squinted into the darkness, but Mary Catheryn was only a vague shadow on the edge of the bed. "That isn't important. The important thing is that P.H. admitted that Rafe Borke is the man responsible for the death of your father. And Borke had to be acting on orders from Albert Barnett."

The shadow on the bed stiffened, and a sharp intake of breath was followed by several tense moments of silence. When Mary Catheryn spoke, her voice was choked with emotion. "What did you say?"

Ben spoke gently, hating the pain he was inflicting on her. "P.H. admitted it. He also said that Barnett and Rawlings knew each other during the war, that they knew each other before you introduced them that day on your front porch."

Mary Catheryn said nothing. In the darkness, Ben had no way of telling how she was reacting to the stunning news. He continued, "I don't completely understand what Rawlings and Barnett are to each other, but I figure that since Barnett is after this valley, he sent—"

"Stop it! You hear me, stop it!" Her cry slashed through the dark bedroom. "You're lying." Her voice trembled, on the verge of tears. "I don't know why, but you're lying."

"No. I . . ."

Mary Catheryn screamed, a shrill, piercing cry that echoed across the meadow.

Ben started to go to her, but the thump of running feet froze him. He stared at the door, then leaped out the window and raced to the windbreak to lose himself in its shadows. A feeding rabbit scurried from under his feet.

Behind him, the windows of the main house and the bunkhouse lit up with a soft glow. Sharp voices split the air. Shouts rolled across the meadow.

Ben ducked into the forest and swung into his saddle. He sat silently for a few seconds, ears strained for any pursuit. Satisfied there was none, he turned back to his valley, disappointed with his visit to Mary Catheryn.

Yet, what could he have expected? Hell, he as much as told her that Rawlings courted her so he could gain ownership of the Slash Bar. How would that make anyone feel, especially a vulnerable young woman?

He studied the ranch, regretting the pain he had caused her, yet fully aware there had been no other way.

Ben rose with the sun the next morning. With a steaming cup of coffee in his hand, he laid plans for the coming night. The only explanation for the number of houseguests indicated by the fancy buggies and the side of beef on the spit was that Mary Catheryn was throwing some kind of shindig. Probably a square dance with barbecue and all the trimmings.

Albert Barnett was a certain guest, and as always at these big fandangos, the ranch hands accompanied their boss and put on a celebration of their own with the other ranch hands. With luck, the Triple B would be deserted save for one or two solitary cowpokes left behind, a perfect opportunity for Ben to prowl through the main house. Maybe even the land titles in Barnett's office. If P.H. had told the truth, and if Barnett had not moved them.

Ben shook his head. Two mighty big *ifs*.

Chapter Thirty-seven

Perched on the rim of the Mogollon Plateau overlooking the Triple B, Ben watched as Albert Barnett climbed on the spring-supported seat of his buckboard and popped the reins against the croup of a clean-looking sorrel.

Tagging after the buckboard were fifteen riders. A cloud of dust billowed up behind them and slowly spread over the meadows on either side of the road. Two miles up the road, the party disappeared into the forest.

Ben waited, his eyes on the Triple B. Soon, two cowpokes came out of the bunkhouse and headed for the chuck house. A few minutes later, the smoke drifting from the stovepipe on top of the chuck house grew thicker. The ranch hands were probably boiling a new pot of coffee for dinner, planning on enjoying the luxury of a free afternoon.

Much later, the two went back to the bunkhouse, one carrying a coffeepot, and the other, a bottle of whiskey and two cups. An hour passed. They had not shown themselves again.

Patiently, Ben waited.

Slowly, the sun slipped toward the mountains.

Pressing his knees lightly against the dun's ribs, Ben eased down a tortuous trail to the valley, reaching the edge of the forest just after sundown. A pale light shone in the bunkhouse window.

He knew he was taking a risk, but the chance of finding copies of the original titles was worth it.

Ben guessed it was about ten o'clock when the lamp in the bunkhouse went out. He waited another hour before making a move, figuring he had about three hours before Barnett and his men returned from the party at the Slash Bar.

At the Slash Bar, the cotillion was in full swing. Furniture had been moved from the large dining room, baring the puncheon floor for the square dancers, two circles of whom were swirling to the singing calls of "Red River Valley." On a riser along one wall, the caller clapped his hands and chanted the prompts, ad-libbing in between. Behind him, a single fiddler stomped his feet and flapped his elbows as his rosined bow flew over the fiddle strings while two more fiddlers awaited their turn.

A long table with a lace tablecloth extended along the opposite wall, a bowl of pink punch on either end and platters heaped with barbecued beef; roast chicken with tart apples; smokehouse-almond fish; ornate bowls filled with potatoes, boiled, fried, mashed, and caked; corn, both creamed and boiled; baked beans; peeled tomatoes; succotash; baked Hubbard squash; a salad of tender greens with blackberries; fresh sourdough biscuits; and for dessert, if anyone had room left, tubs of doughnuts and gallons of plum duff.

Zebron Rawlings caught Barnett's eye as the cattle baron danced with his hostess. The lanky man strolled out on the porch with a cup of punch in his hand. A few minutes later, Barnett came out to stand by him. He extracted a cigar from his inside coat pocket. He touched a match to the tip.

"We got trouble," Rawlings whispered. "Bad trouble."

Barnett smiled and nodded at a couple strolling past, enjoying the crisp night air. Keeping his eyes on the giggling young couple, he muttered, "What kind?"

"Elliott was here last night. He found out about John Wills, and he suspects that you sent me to Baltimore to court Mary Catheryn."

Albert Barnett forced a gay laugh for the benefit of another couple who had strolled out on the porch, but under his breath, he said, "But, he can't prove anything. It's all supposition."

"He's got P. H. Hall hidden away somewhere. The old man spilled everything about John Wills's death."

The statement stunned Barnett momentarily, but he quickly recovered. "It's the old man's word against ours." He pulled his timepiece.

Rawlings studied the big rancher through narrowed eyes. A wry grin twisted his lips. "You still got Elliott to worry about."

Barnett studied the growing ash on the end of his cigar. He looked back to Zebron Rawlings and very deliberately extended his arm and flicked the ash to the ground. "We'll take care of him."

"We?" Rawlings arched his eyebrows.

Shaking his head slowly, Barnett grinned. "We."

For several seconds, the two men stared at each other, testing the other's resolve. Albert Barnett broke the strained silence. "It's time you earned your keep, Zebron. Any of us see Elliott, we don't wait. Kill him on sight."

Rawlings couldn't resist smiling. "On sight? Hell, Albert, just about every jasper that's seen him so far is buried out there," he said, nodding in the direction of the Triple B.

Albert Barnett allowed a faint smile to play over his lips. "Maybe so, but it looks like it's going to be up to you and me. Don't forget. In the next few years, we're going to have enough money that you can use double eagles for target practice." He hesitated and glanced briefly over his shoulder. "What about her? You got a date for the marriage?"

"She announces it tonight."

"Good."

"Come over to my place in the morning. Let's talk more about this marriage."

Finally, after eight years, Albert Barnett would own the entire valley. Of course, he reminded himself, there was still the girl. As long as she lived, a piece of the valley remained beyond his grasp.

But that would be remedied.

Back inside the caller cried out, "Grab your partners. We're about to 'chase the rabbit.'"

At the Triple B, Ben floated like a wraith through the darkness, reaching the ranch house just as the waning moon rose over the rim of the Mogollon. The pale light allowed him to move through the ranch house to Barnett's office, the logical repository for the rancher's valuable papers.

The window in Barnett's office faced the bunkhouse. Ben eased across the room and closed the heavy drapes, enshrouding the room in total darkness. He struck a match and held it at arm's length so he could study the room. Against one wall was an open rolltop desk.

Striking a second match, Ben quickly rummaged without success through the pigeonholes above the desktop. He struck a third match and searched the desk drawers. Still nothing.

The match burned down to his fingers. He dropped it. "Damn," he muttered, touching his scorched fingers to his tongue before lighting another match.

At the bunkhouse, one of the cowpokes had stepped outside to relieve himself. Through Barnett's office window, he glimpsed a brief flare of light, which quickly disappeared. He frowned, then awakened his compadre. Barefoot, they slipped over to the main house.

In the office, Ben studied a heavy wooden highboy with a lock built into the door. Using his knife, Ben jimmied the lock.

Lighting another match, Ben opened the door. Inside were several drawers on one side and a supply of liquor on the other. The first few drawers contained various documents. His heart thudded against his chest when he opened the fifth drawer and saw a folded document with his name on it. Quickly, he shook the document open with one hand and held the match close so he could read it. It was the original title, the one he filed in 1865.

Without bothering to check the names on the other documents, Ben stuffed them inside his shirt and turned to go, but suddenly he froze, his eyes fixed on a small piece of black cloth in the rear of the drawer.

His mouth was suddenly dry, his hand shaking as he reached for the cloth. He held it in the flickering light cast by the match. A lump rose in his throat. His ears pounded.

The flimsy remnant of cloth was an eye patch!

A wave of dizziness swept over Ben as he stared at the thin strings sewn to a half-moon patch of cloth. Slowly, his brain began to function. Pieces fell into place. The giant Yankee that day in the Mohawk Mountains. His speed with a six-gun. Barnett beating Charlie Little to the draw. The gold shipment from Yuma to Tucson.

Ben stood frozen, staring in disbelief. Now, things made sense. The ranch, the Triple B—bought with the gold stolen that day the entire patrol of soldiers had been murdered.

The match burning his fingers jerked him from his daze. Quickly, he stuffed the eye patch in his vest pocket and in the darkness, closed the highboy door. Easing across the room, he headed for the front door.

When he stepped on the front porch, a voice halted him in his tracks. "Don't move, cowboy."

For a moment, he froze; then he spun to face the voice. He glimpsed a shadowy figure before his head exploded like the Fourth of July.

Chapter Thirty-eight

Darkness swirled about Ben, pushing him ever upward toward a faint glow no larger than a speck of sand. The glow grew larger, then smaller. Unintelligible voices tumbled down the dark well about him, garbled and distorted, wavering in intensity. A throbbing pain filled his head. He squeezed his lids tightly, trying to close out the pounding.

Slowly, the pulsating pain faded, and the voices became intelligible. He opened his eyes.

Two cowpokes sat at a table playing poker.

Ben groaned.

They looked around at him and laughed.

After the square dance was over, after all the fiddle music had died away, after each worn-out dancer had retired to his and her room, Mary Catheryn stood on the porch gazing at the waning moon, a brilliant white ellipse in the star-filled sky. Zebron Rawlings came out to stand by her side.

She looked around. "It's beautiful tonight, isn't it?"

Rawlings was testy, upset. He ignored her question.

"You promised to announce the date for the wedding tonight." His tone was accusing.

She looked up into his face, which was lost in the shadow cast by the moon. She sensed his anger. "I know, Zebron. I'm sorry, but I . . . I just couldn't. I need some more time. Please, don't be angry with me."

"Why shouldn't I? You made me look like a fool in front of my friends. Maybe I shouldn't have told them, but I was so excited, I couldn't help myself. They were all expecting the announcement."

Mary Catheryn had truly planned on setting a date, but, although she did not believe Ben Elliott's story, it had raised questions of which she had not been aware, questions that took on a different perspective when Zebron Rawlings and Albert Barnett had disappeared out on the porch earlier.

She knew their conversation was nothing more than a friendly discussion of range conditions and the weather, typical conversation between all ranchers, but still—

A long sigh escaped her lips. "I know they were expecting it, but I just need a little more time." She reached out her hand to lay it on his arm.

He jerked his arm away. "You're going to have to make up your mind, Mary Catheryn."

Startled by his sudden move, she tried to placate him. "I told you, I will."

"When?" His tone had grown demanding. "I might get tired of waiting." He bit his tongue as soon as the words were uttered.

Her ears burned. Blood rushed to her cheeks. She tilted her chin. "If that's how you feel, Zebron Rawlings, then you can just forget all about it. As far as I'm concerned, the marriage is off." With those last words, she spun on her heel and stormed into the house.

Rawlings glared after her. "You damned idiot," he muttered to himself. "When are you going to learn to control your temper?"

He stood on the porch several minutes, staring at the now dark house. With a shake of his head, he turned to the bunkhouse. In the morning when he returned from the Triple B, he'd apologize. All this quarrel meant was a short delay. He had her wrapped around his little finger.

The next thing Ben knew, a sharp pain in his side jarred him awake. He struggled to open his eyes, but all he could see was the fuzzy outline of Albert Barnett. The large man's face was a blur. Behind him was a face with a thick beard. Borke.

"Wake up, Elliott." Barnett leaned down and slapped Ben in the face with the sheath of land titles he had pulled from the unconscious cowpoke's shirt.

Ben remained motionless, and then another sharp kick caught him in the ribs. He rolled over and moaned. Then came a third kick, and a fourth. Ben lay motionless as waves of pain washed over him.

One of the ranch hands laughed. "He's out cold, Mr. Barnett."

Albert grunted. "No matter." He looked at the two cowpokes. "Take him out and get rid of him."

Rafe Borke interrupted. He caressed the handle of his six-gun. "Let me, boss. I owe him."

Barnett eyed his foreman coldly. "All right, but make damned certain you do the job right." He moved to the fireplace and held up the land titles. "I'm burning these now. You take care of him."

The two cowhands tied Ben's hands in front and threw him over the saddle. They tied his hands to his feet under the horse's belly. Rafe Borke grabbed the lead rope and swung aboard his own pony. He knew exactly where to take Ben Elliott.

At the Slash Bar, Mary Catheryn slammed the door to her bedroom and threw herself across the bed. She buried her face in her arms and sobbed, unable to believe the sudden explosion of anger from Zebron Rawlings.

The jolting ride jarred Ben awake. His head throbbed, and he felt the blood pounding in his ears.

Borke rode up a seldom-used trail leading to the Mogollon Plateau. Halfway to the rim, the trail widened and pulled away from the wall of the escarpment. On one side was a sheer drop to the valley below. On the other, a bottomless crevice that sloped steeply into the bowels of the plateau.

The burly foreman had used the crevice a few times. He had no idea its depth, but it was sufficient so that not even the odor of decay reached the top. Borke reined around and pulled up beside Ben. He laughed, a harsh snarl. "This is your last night, Elliott. You messed with the wrong fellers."

Slumped over the neck of his pony, Ben craned his neck to look up at the grinning foreman. He struggled against his bonds. The moonlight flashed on the barrel of a .44 and a blinding pain exploded in his head.

Half conscious, Ben felt the rope binding his feet together under the belly of the pony go limp. Rough hands yanked him headfirst to the ground. His skull cracked against the rocky trail.

A boot kicked him in the ribs. Ben groaned.

"Good-bye, Mr. Elliott." Another kick knocked Ben over the edge of the crevice, and he plunged downward, scraping against the jagged slope of the chasm.

Borke stared into the darkness, straining to hear, but the sound of the body striking the bottom never reached his ears. He struck a match and tried to peer into the darkness, but he could only see a foot or so beyond the pale glow of the burning match. After a few moments, he shrugged and mounted his pony. He had nothing to worry about. He'd never heard the other bodies strike bottom either. With a cruel laugh, he climbed on his pony and headed back to the Triple B.

Chapter Thirty-nine

Mary Catheryn awakened before sunrise from a restless sleep. Her argument with Zebron Rawlings had nagged at her all night until she finally convinced herself that Ben's accusations were unfounded. Just before she dropped into a troubled slumber a few hours earlier, she decided to apologize. After all, she had indeed promised to announce the date for their marriage last night. Zebron had a right to become angry. Well, she would set that straight. If Zebron had no objections and since today was already Thursday, they would get married a week from Sunday.

She hesitated, glad she had made up her mind, but vaguely disquieted as to why she did not feel happy over her decision. Mary Catheryn pushed her concern aside, and slipping from under the down comforter, dressed quickly and hurried to the bunkhouse, but Zebron had already ridden out.

"Over to the Triple B, Ms. Mary," said the cook. "Him and Mr. Albert had some business to discuss."

Mary turned back to the main house, strangely relieved that Zebron was not around to accept her apology. She frowned, chiding herself for being too proud. By the time she reached the main house, she had decided to ride over to the Triple B.

In fact, she'd have Teresa prepare a picnic, and on the way back to the Slash Bar, she and Zebron could spread a blanket by the cold stream that divided the two properties and enjoy the sunny afternoon. And then, in such a romantic setting, she would give him the good news.

Ben stared up at the moon-silhouetted slab of saw-tooth granite over which his tied wrists had snagged in his fall. Twisting his head to look over his shoulder, all he could see below was an obsidian blackness. Cool air rushed over him from the depths of the crevice.

He flexed his fingers, trying to work circulation into them as he studied his predicament. He had been mighty lucky. The sloping wall of the crevice had numerous outcroppings of granite, none so large as to stop a falling body, but in his case, large enough for the rope binding his wrists to loop over.

The slope above was too steep to crawl, but if his hands were free, he could use the outcroppings as hand-holds and drag himself to the top some twenty feet above.

Grateful that he was wearing his moccasins, he felt along the wall with his feet, searching for a niche for his toes. He touched a single knob of granite, extending less than three inches from the wall. While the protrusion was not large enough for both feet, it did provide a delicate balance while he sawed the ropes binding his hands against the jagged edge of the granite shard.

Sweat beaded on his forehead despite the cool air sweeping up from below. The beads pooled, then ran down into his eyes. He blinked against the sting, but he continued sawing.

As each strand parted, Ben felt the ropes loosen. When he guessed the rope was almost in two, he grasped the outcropping with his right hand and continued sawing with his left.

Suddenly, the rope separated, and Ben lurched to his right. His fingers clawed into the granite outcropping, halting his fall. For hour-long seconds, he hung precariously, his body sagging toward the bottomless pit, his toes digging into the granite knob as he clutched the outcropping with his other hand.

His grip began to weaken. Clenching his teeth, he struggled to stop the inexorable straightening of his fingers, but he was exhausted. Then he remembered the eye patch, and the big man who had worn it in the canyon so many years ago. Anger flooded his veins. His fingers tightened their grip, and slowly, he pulled himself erect.

Both hands now grasped the outcropping. He leaned his forehead against the cool granite until the pounding in his chest subsided.

By the light of false dawn, he studied the rocky slope above him, noting the position of the jutting shards of granite. Taking a deep breath, he reached for the first one and grunting with exertion, pulled himself upward, stretching then for the next handhold.

Five minutes later, he gained the top and rolled over onto the trail, gasping for breath. As the rush of adrenaline slowed in his veins, Ben sat up, dragging his tongue across his dry lips. The valley below was slowly awakening. Far to the north, smoke rose from the Triple B. Back to the south some eight or ten miles was the Slash Bar.

His stomach growled. He climbed to his feet and headed up the trail to the rim, chiding himself for being so careless the night before. At the same time, he reminded himself that had it not been for a stroke of luck in the ropes snagging on the outcropping, he could be sprawled dead at the bottom of that crevice.

"That kind of luck happens only once," he muttered as he reached the rim and headed for his hidden valley. He didn't have any time to waste. Once he outfitted himself, he was going after Albert Barnett, or Jake Barnes as the big rancher once called himself.

Ben had not been able to force Barnett into a foolish mistake, and now, he was tired of the effort. Now, he was going to take the first step. Now, he was going to kill Albert Barnett, and anyone who interfered, even if he had to run from the law for the rest of his life.

Mary Catheryn pulled up in front of the Triple B at midmorning. Zebron's gray gelding was tied at the rail in front of the house. By the corral was parked a weather-beaten army ambulance with a shabby Saltillo blanket for a top. Four long-haired, spavined nags stood in the corral, heads drooped between their legs.

The rest of the ranch appeared deserted. The wranglers were out working stock, she figured.

Mary Catheryn knocked on the door. There was no answer. She removed her flat-crowned hat and fanned herself as she looked around the ranch. She saw no sign of Zebron or Albert. They must be inside. She knocked again. Still no answer.

Slowly she opened the door and stuck her head inside. "Hello? Mr. Barnett? Zebron?" Voices drifted from behind a closed door beyond the parlor.

She felt like an intruder despite calling out for them.

She eased across the room to the door. Just as she raised her fist to knock, a loud voice echoed from inside. "Dammit, I told you to get her to set a date. What in the hell did you do to botch it this time?"

Mary Catheryn's fist froze in midair. The voice on the other side of the door belonged to Albert Barnett. She leaned forward, straining to hear.

Zebron defended himself. "I told you, I'll take care of it. Hell, all I got to do is apologize, sweet-talk her a little, and then she'll go along with me. I know the woman. I should. I've been courting her for the last two years." He paused, then added, "And it sure as hell hasn't been easy. She's spoiled rotten . . . Daddy's spoiled little girl."

The words slapped Mary Catheryn across the face. She gasped and stepped back, stumbled over an ottoman and fell against a piecrust table, sending a parlor lamp crashing to the floor.

Startled exclamations from behind the door sent her scrambling to her feet. She rushed from the house and jumped onto the buckboard just as Barnett and Rawlings ran onto the porch.

"Mary Catheryn! Wait!"

She ignored Rawlings. She cracked the horsewhip over the blue roan's head. She glanced over her shoulder and stiffened. Rawlings had swung into his saddle and was coming after her. She sobbed. There was no way she could escape.

Moments later, he pulled up beside her and motioned her to stop, but she lashed out at him with her whip, catching him across his sallow face. He jerked away, then goaded his pony ahead and leaned over and grabbed the bridle of her horse. Without slowing, he led the wagon in a wide circle back to the ranch house.

"No. Let me go. You hear me. Turn that horse loose."
Mary Catheryn jerked on the reins, but Rawlings held
tight. She struck out at him with the whip, but he was
beyond reach.

Wearing a grim expression, Barnett stood on the
porch.

Mary Catheryn decided to bluff her way when Rawlings halted the wagon. She remained in her seat, her
back stiff, her eyes forward, her jaw set. Both men approached. She did not look at them. "I insist you re-
lease me."

Rawlings grunted. "See what I'm talking about," he
said to the big rancher. "She's a spoiled brat."

"Not too smart either," Barnett added.

Eyes blazing, Mary Catheryn said, "You let me go,
or I'll . . ."

Barnett's big hand shot out and yanked her off the
buckboard into the dust at his feet. It billowed into her
eyes and mouth.

"You won't do a thing, missy."

She struggled to sit up, rubbing her eyes and gag-
ging.

"Put her in the pantry," Barnett ordered.

Rawlings grabbed her arm and jerked her to her
feet, dragging her after him into the house. Mary Catheryn slapped at him. "Don't you touch me. You . . .
You . . ." She dug her nails into his face.

He yelped and cursed. "You spoiled little . . ." His
hand flashed through the air and struck her cheek,
knocking her to the ground. "Now, you behave yourself." He half dragged, half carried her into the house
and shoved her into the dark pantry. She fell to the
floor and sobbed.

Rawlings locked the door. "Now what?"

Barnett shrugged. "Simple. We'll say you two eloped. You disappear and come back in a month with the marriage certificate and with the sad news that she met with a terrible accident. Who's to question you?"

Rawlings glanced back at the pantry. "You really going to kill her?"

A cruel grin twisted Barnett's lips. "She'll wish she was dead. Torres came in last night. He's sleeping over in the bunkhouse. That's his rig over by the corral." Barnett nodded to the ambulance.

"Torres? The Comanchero? You're giving her to the Comancheros?"

"Giving? Hell, I'm selling." He looked squarely into Zebron Rawlings's eyes. "You got a problem with that?"

The lean gunfighter returned the hard look, and then a faint smile appeared on his face. "Get a good price."

Chapter Forty

Ben eased the sorrel into a thicket of laurel near the edge of the forest overlooking the Triple B. The ranch appeared deserted except for a blue roan standing hip-shot in the traces of a buckboard by the main house. As he watched, Rawlings emerged from the house and led the horse and buckboard to the barn where he un-hitched the animal and turned it into the corral.

Minutes later, two Mexicans wearing broad sombreros came out of the bunkhouse and proceeded to hitch the team of spavined horses to the battered ambulance by the corral.

Ben frowned. He knew Comancheros when he saw them.

They climbed onto the seat and drove over to the main house. While one remained in the ambulance, the other disappeared into the main house without knocking. Moments later, he reappeared, dragging a struggling woman with him. Barnett and Rawlings followed.

Ben leaned forward, trying to discern the identity of the woman. In her struggles, her hat flew from her head, revealing a flash of red hair. It was Mary Catheryn!

She jerked away from the Comanchero and when he

turned to grab her, she slapped him. He retaliated, striking her on the point of her chin with his fist. Mary Catheryn collapsed.

The Comanchero threw her in the wagon and climbed on the seat beside a second Comanchero. Barnett and Rawlings approached, and for several moments, they spoke. After gesturing to the south, Barnett took a step backward and the leering driver laid a whip across the backs of his rail-thin horses and headed south for the border.

Ben hurried back to the sorrel. There was only one trail out of the valley that a wagon could travel easily. He knew exactly where he would wait for the Comancheros.

Cutting through the sentinel pines, Ben reached his destination an hour later, a head-high ledge on the backside of one of the bends in the series of switchbacks that ascended the mountain.

He tied the sorrel in a thick copse of pinyon some distance from the trail and squatted beside a boulder on the ledge. He could hear the clatter of hooves striking the rocky trail long before the Comancheros reached the ambush. Ben reached for the Durham, then decided against it. No telling where the currents drifting up and down the mountain would carry the odor.

Fifteen minutes later, he heard hoofbeats, but not from the direction of the valley. These came from above. Ben slipped behind the boulder. He did not have long to wait. Five minutes later, Marshal Ike Hazlett followed by Sheriff Jess Lowry and ten hardcases rode past, heading for the valley.

Ben grimaced. He had enough to worry about without another posse on his tail.

At least, they would save him the task of rescuing

Mary Catheryn, for in less than ten minutes, the posse should meet up with the Comancheros on the trail. Still, Ben decided to make certain.

Leaving his pony behind, Ben ghosted through the pines some distance from the trail, keeping the riders in sight. He skirted a windfall and froze. Fifty yards ahead, the Comanchero ambulance was parked in a cluster of pinyon off the road.

Ben dropped to his belly and quickly scanned the area for the Comancheros. To his right, behind boulders along the trail, crouched one of the Mexicans. The other one, Ben decided, must be with Mary Catheryn in the ambulance.

Angling to his left, the wiry rancher took advantage of spindly undergrowth to circle the wagon. Sure enough, the second Comanchero stood beside the wagon, his six-gun trained on Mary Catheryn. Both were concentrating on the posse.

Silent as a mountain lion, Ben came up behind the Comanchero. Mary Catheryn glanced around, but Ben held his finger to his lips. He shucked his six-gun. He took another step and laid the muzzle alongside the Comanchero's temple. The man dropped like a pole-axed steer.

The first Comanchero still crouched by the trail.

Quickly Ben propped the unconscious Mexican against a wheel and wrapped his limp fingers around a handgun. "Over there. Next to the pine," Ben whispered to Mary Catheryn.

Seeing what Ben had in mind, she nodded and did as he said.

Removing his hat, Ben disappeared into the briars, a thin tangle that it seemed could not hide even a rabbit, but during the years Ben had lived with the Coyoteros, he learned their ways well. Every Apache brave possessed the skill and knowledge to hide in plain sight.

As the clatter of hoofbeats died away, the remaining Comanchero hurried back to the ambulance. "*Han ido.* They have gone. *Esperaremos antes continuamos.* We will wait before we continue," he said to the back of his compadre.

There was no answer, no movement.

He gaze flicked to Mary Catheryn. Her eyes grew wide.

"*Me oyes*? You hear me?" He nudged his friend, who rolled over on his side.

A twig snapped behind the Comanchero. He spun, and Ben smashed a knotted fist between the surprised Comanchero's eyes. He fell like a sack of oats.

Ben stripped the Comancheros of their weapons, which he then hurled deep into the forest behind them.

Mary Catheryn jumped to her feet, her eyes filled with relief. Before she could speak, Ben took her arm and rushed her through the forest to the sorrel a few hundred yards up the mountain.

He swung into the saddle and pulled her up behind him. She asked, "Where are we going?"

"To a hidden valley where you'll be safe."

She didn't reply. A few minutes later, she asked, "Until when?"

"Until it's all over," he said, his voice cold and hard.

"I . . . I . . ." Mary Catheryn became silent.

Ben understood. "Just hold on."

The ride to the valley was long and hard, but not one word of complaint escaped Mary Catheryn's lips.

When they entered the lush little valley, and Ben helped her dismount, Mary Catheryn stared in awe.

"It's beautiful." In the distance, several fat ponies stared at them. After a moment, they went back to grazing.

In the cave, he pointed to a couple wooden boxes. "You get hungry, grub's in there. Back yonder is meat," he said, nodding to a haunch of venison hanging from a wooden stake driven into a crack in the granite ceiling. He showed her the blankets, the Winchesters, and last, the trout pond.

Mary Catheryn looked around the valley once again. "I'm impressed. Looks like a person could live in here quite a spell."

Ben grinned. "If a man had to." For a moment, he looked at her, a faint smile on his lips. The smile faded. "You be okay here by yourself?"

She grew serious. "Don't worry about me. I'll be just fine." She hesitated; her brows furrowed. "You're going after Zebron and Albert Barnett." It was not a question, but a reluctant acceptance of the inevitable.

"Yes."

"I . . ." She glanced at the ground, then lifted her head and looked him straight in the eyes. "I'm sorry I didn't believe you. I know now that you only wanted to help me. I apologize."

She was truly contrite. Ben tried to make her feel better. "Those two could have fooled anyone. Don't feel so bad."

"Barnett didn't fool Pa. "

Ben grinned at the memory of hardheaded John Wills. "Nobody ever fooled your pa." His grin faded. "You know your life's in danger?"

"Yes," she replied simply, her jaw set, her green eyes cold with determination.

"If I'm not back this time tomorrow, build a fire and send up a steady stream of smoke for just a few minutes."

She frowned, but Ben continued. "Within an hour or two, you'll be visited by Coyotero Apaches. Tell them that Little Tin Man wants them to take you to Prescott. Load up a couple of those ponies with grub and ammunition. In Prescott, ask around for my ranch hands if any of them are there. Get them to go with you down to the territorial governor in Tucson. Camp on his doorstep until he listens."

Mary Catheryn nodded. "Don't worry. I have a feeling you'll be back."

Ben swung into the saddle. "I'd like to," he replied, smiling down at her.

"By the way. How'd you get the name Little Tin Man?"

"It's a long story."

Mary Catheryn stepped back from the dun. "I want to hear it sometime."

Chapter Forty-one

Three of the posse spotted Ben riding through the forest along the base of the Mogollon Rim. They gave a shout and spurred their horses after Ben, who calmly unbooted his Winchester and knocked the one posse member from his saddle with a well-placed slug in the hardcase's shoulder. The other two reined up.

"That oughta make them stop and think," he muttered to his pony. Nevertheless, Ben extended his circle around the Triple B, moving slowly, hoping to avoid any more confrontations until he had Barnett in front of him.

Of course, Ben didn't fool himself into believing he could just walk up on J. Albert Barnett or Jake Barnes, or whatever name the murdering owlhoot went by. No, he was going to have to go through Rafe Borke and Zebron Rawlings first. And then, he still had the posse to worry about. Though he did not know Ike Hazlett well, he surmised from their brief encounter that the lawman was a bulldog when he was convinced he was in the right. For him to have returned meant he either had decided this entire situation had gone far enough, or he had been ordered by his superior.

Ben looked over the glorious, sprawling valley through which he rode. He clicked his tongue and shook his head. A sense of loss washed over him. Either way, his days here were over.

He drew up and stared at the herd of cows in a distant meadow, a couple thousand, at least. He rode closer, noticing a mixture of brands, his own, the Key, as well as the Slash Bar, Ches Lewis's Circle O, Colly Weems's Rocking T, and Leland Pickett's Smoking P. "Albert sure as hell didn't waste much time," Ben muttered.

He pulled up on the crest of an aspen-covered ridge that overlooked the Triple B. There was no activity at the ranch. To the west, the sun balanced gingerly on the black, jagged silhouette of the Juniper Mountains. It dropped behind the slopes, quickly rolling its shadows across the valley.

A light came on in the chuck house. Ben studied the ranch again. He needed a distraction.

Albert Barnett unbuttoned his vest and held up a glass of bourbon in toast. "To us," he said.

Along with his tie, Zebron Rawlings had shed his drab coat and vest. He honored the toast. "To the whole damned valley."

They downed their drinks, but neither reached for the decanter to refill the glasses. Both men were well aware of the game, of how life takes uncanny twists and turns. At the moment of a man's greatest success, his world could be pulled down about him unless he remain watchful.

That would not happen to Albert Barnett or Zebron Rawlings. They had spent years cheating and conniving to reach this point, and they were not about to lose it because of some foolish human frailty.

Barnett sat his empty glass on the table and stared out the window at the setting sun. "No sense in you going back to the Slash Bar. We'll tell everyone that you and the Wills girl eloped from here. Head over to New Mexico Territory. Come back in about a month. I'll have all the papers, the marriage certificate, a letter from a priest swearing the marriage is valid, a will leaving everything to you, and a certificate of death for the girl. We'll wait a few days, then transfer the title into your name." He turned back to Rawlings. "Then we'll celebrate."

Sometime later, Rafe Borke jerked to a halt in the bunkhouse doorway and stared down the valley. A sudden grimace carved deep wrinkles in his forehead when he saw the glow lighting the southern horizon across the entire valley. There was only one thing it could be. "Damn! Wildfire," he said, the word a harsh explosion. Then he felt the ground vibrating under his feet.

He yelled over his shoulder and sprinted for the barn. "Stampede!"

Sleepy cowpokes stumbled from their bunks, rubbing the sleep from their eyes and staring in disbelief at the flames leaping high into the dark sky. The ground under their feet shook, and an ominous rumble filled the air.

Two thousand head of frightened beeves were bearing down on them.

After setting the blaze, Ben rode hard to reach the forest behind the Triple B. In the midst of the confusion created by the stampede, he planned to slip into the main house.

He watched Rafe Borke run to the corral. Half-dressed cowpokes stumbled from the bunkhouse.

Lamps came on in the main house. Within minutes, every hand on the Triple B was headed south, hoping to turn the oncoming surge of frightened cattle.

The flames leaped higher, stretching their yellow fingers into the dark night, painting an eerie glow across the sky. Ben rode in unseen. He dismounted behind the barn, looped his reins around the saddle horn, and slapped the nervous sorrel on the croup, sending it into the night away from the approaching flames.

Palming his .44, Ben remained in the shadows. Peering around the corner, he spotted two dim figures on the dynamite-shattered porch of the main house. There was no mistaking Albert Barnett's massive body. The other was thin, not quite as tall. Zebron Rawlings.

Ben glanced around, wary of the missing Rafe Borke. He guessed the foreman rode to head off the stampede, but he couldn't be positive. He had to be careful. Watch his back every second.

The two shadows remained on the porch, both postured to watch the approaching fire. Ben disappeared into the shadows and circled behind the main house. He sprinted the last hundred yards to the house across the hardpan. The breeze carried the stinging odor of smoke, burning his nostrils, watering his eyes.

The vibration under his feet grew more intense. Faint yells and gunshots echoed through the night, cut through the rumble of the panicked cattle. Ben pressed his back against the corner of the main house. He gasped for breath and steadied his shaking hands.

He strained his ears, trying to pick up the conversation of the two men, but all he heard was bits and pieces, garbled by their whispers and the ever-increasing roar of the stampede.

Ben peered around the corner. The two men were

less than twenty feet from him. He could drop both before they knew what hit them. Neither would hesitate to do the same to him, but Ben couldn't. He was no back-shooter.

Holstering his six-gun, Ben took a deep breath, and stepped around the corner, his hand inches from the walnut handle of his .44. "Barnes!"

The two men froze.

Ben had to yell to be heard above the roar of the stampede. "It's me, Barnes. It's payback time."

Abruptly, Albert Barnett dived for the front door while Rawlings spun and fired. In the same instant, Ben shucked his six-gun and blasted away. Orange flames leaped from the two muzzles, lighting the darkness.

A stab of pain in his side knocked Ben around, but he dropped to a knee and fired two more times. The shadow on the porch screamed and sprawled on the ground beside the front steps. Suddenly, the firing was over. Ben dropped to the hardpan and rolled behind the corner of the house, his fingers grabbing for the cartridges in his belt. Quickly, he reloaded, trying to ignore the pain in his side.

The back door slammed. Clenching his teeth, Ben hurried to the rear of the ranch house in time to see a shadowy figure disappear into the inky darkness of the barn.

By now, the frightened wall of bellowing cattle had reached the ranch. Dust rose in great clouds. Men shouted. Cattle bawled. For long minutes, the cattle swept past, crushing the corrals, scraping against the front porch, tearing away what little remained, and grinding Zebron Rawlings into the hardpan.

Ben remained pressed against the side of the house, grateful the debris of the porch was forcing the herd

•

wide. As suddenly as they arrived, the herd was gone, still pursued by the cowhands in an effort to halt their mad, headlong dash.

Under cover of the settling dust, Ben raced to the barn and threw himself into the shadows just inside the open doors. He grimaced against the pain in his side. He scooted against the stack of feed sacks and explored his wound in the dark. A clean one. The slug had passed through without hitting a vital organ. More pain than anything.

He waited, straining his ears. Through the rear door of the barn, Ben saw the approaching flames leap high into the night sky, still half a mile distant, but lighting the interior of the barn with a macabre relief of eerie light and bottomless shadows.

Suddenly, a shadow bolted from the darkness and raced for the rear door. Ben threw a wild shot, but Albert Barnett ducked around the corner of the door and snapped off two slugs at Ben. The first missed, but the second ripped the .44 from his hand.

Ben dropped to his knees, squeezing his stinging hand to his chest. He flexed his fingers. At least, nothing was broken. He reached for his knife. Now, it was Apache time.

Deep in the shadows, Ben pulled a cartridge from his belt and tossed it across the barn. No sooner did it clatter against the wall than a belch of yellow and orange flame lit the darkness. Barnett was outside the barn, next to the open door.

Ben tossed another cartridge and quickly slipped outside. By now, the flames illumined the entire ranch in a flickering yellow glow. Back to the north, the sound of the stampede faded. Soon, Barnett's hands would be returning, and with them, Rafe Borke.

Chapter Forty-two

Staying in a crouch, Ben slipped around the barn, a wispy shadow in the light of the racing flames. He paused at the corner, his back against the clapboard, his breath coming in labored gasps. He grimaced against the pain in his side. Sweat and dirt stung his eyes. He dragged his arm across his forehead.

Flexing his fingers around the bone handle of his knife, Ben took a deep breath and peered around the corner. The grinning face of Albert Barnett leered at him. Instinctively, Ben jerked back. At the same time, Barnett's .44 roared and splinters from the corner of the barn stung Ben's face.

Grabbing at his stinging face with his free hand, Ben staggered back. Suddenly, a numbing blow smashed his other hand and sent the knife spinning. A second blow knocked Ben into the barn. He bounced off the wall and fell to his knees.

An alarm screamed in his brain. He shook his throbbing head, clearing his vision only to stare up into the sneering face of Albert Barnett, illumined by the flames as they swept past the barn.

The broad-shouldered man set his square jaw. His

eyes were cold and unfeeling, like the blank eyes of a rattlesnake. "I knew I should have come after you myself." He tilted the muzzle of his .44 at Ben's forehead. His sneer grew broader. "You got no idea how much trouble you've caused me, or how much pleasure this is going to give me."

Ben staggered to his feet, but the wound in his side forced him to lean against the barn. His brain raced, trying to buy time. "The same kind of pleasure you took when you slaughtered that entire company of Confederate soldiers in the Mohawks?" Ben's voice was filled with scorn. "What was your handle then, Jake Barnes?"

A frown knit Barnett's forehead. Then his eyes grew wide as he remembered. "I'll be damned. I swore then we missed one of you Johnny Rebs."

"Two. You missed two of us."

Barnett shook his head. "I don't think so. Just you."

Ben glanced past Barnett, his eyes searching desperately for a weapon, any kind of weapon. There was nothing within reach. His knife was too far. "You missed Charlie Little."

The cattle baron grunted. "The freckle-faced kid." He cocked his .44. "Well, he's just as dead now as he would have been back in the mountains. Like you're fixing to be."

Just as the big man squeezed the trigger, Ben dropped to his knees and scooped a handful of dirt into Barnett's eyes.

The hammer snapped on a spent cartridge.

Ben drove his shoulders into the wealthy rancher's knees, knocking Barnett's legs from under him, sending him sprawling into the dirt with a cry of alarm. He hit the ground and rolled, his hand scrabbling for the knife Ben had dropped.

Clutching the knife, Barnett jumped to his feet and fell into an attack posture, legs bent, arms extended. He taunted Ben with the knife, waving the tip in a small circle. The dancing light from the fire gave an eerie cast to his twisted face. His brows knit, and he charged Ben, wielding the deadly knife in broad, slashing strokes.

Ben leaped back to avoid the swooping blade. He stumbled and fell against the corral. Barnett sneered. "No place to run now, Elliott." He lunged, and Ben sidestepped and shoved the larger man into the rails.

Barnett bounced off the green pine logs and sat back abruptly on the ground, stunned. Ben kicked the knife from his hand, and as the big rancher pushed himself to his feet, Ben swung from the ground and slammed a knotted fist into the big man's chin.

With a grunt, Barnett shook his head and threw a straight right. Ben ducked and slammed half a dozen hammering blows into the big man's stomach. It was like hitting a tree stump.

Swinging a massive arm, Albert Barnett struck Ben in the temple, spinning him to the ground. He aimed a kick at Ben's head, but the agile man rolled aside and kicked Barnett's other foot from under him. The big man slammed to the ground.

His ears still ringing from the last blow, Ben leaped at the rancher, but Barnett merely grabbed Ben in mid-air and slung him over his head, slamming the lighter man into the side of the barn.

Stars exploded in Ben's head. Vaguely, he felt the blows Barnett was raining down on him. He felt himself picked up and bodily hurled through the air. He bounced off another wall and hit the ground.

He struggled to his feet and swung wildly, but a smashing blow caught him on the forehead and sent him spinning into the barn where he grabbed a support post to keep himself on his feet. Through the fog clouding his brain, he heard Albert Barnett laugh. "I'm gonna stomp your head clean flat, Elliott."

Ben gasped for breath, knowing the rancher would do exactly what he said. From deep inside, he pulled up enough strength for one last stand.

Outside, the flames had moved past, lighting the interior of the barn faintly. With a leering grin on his face, Barnett took a step forward, and Ben busted him on the jaw with a left uppercut, snapping the big man's head up. Instantly, Ben threw a right, connecting with Barnett's Adam's apple.

Barnett gagged and grabbed his throat. Ben sucked in a lungful of fresh oxygen and redoubled his efforts, pumping his arms, driving his bleeding fists into the big man's midsection.

Suddenly, the giant rancher erupted in a shout of anger. He backhanded Ben, sending him sprawling into a support post and bouncing to the ground. Dazed, Ben shook his head and tried to clamber to his feet, but Barnett kicked him in the ribs, lifting him off the ground and spinning him into a stack of hay.

Ben lay spread-eagled, legs splayed, arms outstretched. His blood tasted like warm copper. Through swollen eyes, he saw the gloating expression on Barnett's face as the big man picked up a singletree and raised it over his head, a macabre figure struck in relief by the prairie fire.

Digging his heels into the ground in a frantic effort

to scoot away from the big man, Ben felt an excruciating pain in his shoulder as he impaled himself on a sharp object. He grabbed at his shoulder, and his fingers touched the cold steel of a pitchfork.

Barnett took a step forward, lifting the singletree higher. "Say your prayers, cowboy." He grunted and a cruel grin cut a black gash in his face.

Ben slid the pitchfork over his shoulder and grabbed the handle. With every muscle in his arms, he thrust the pitchfork at the big rancher, driving the tines into Albert Barnett's belly.

The big man froze. His face was lost in the shadows, but Ben saw his large frame quiver. The singletree slipped from his fingers and fell to the ground. After a few tense seconds, Albert Barnett moaned and dropped to his knees, his hands grasping for the tines, fumbling to withdraw them.

Ben rolled aside and stumbled to his feet. For a moment, he stood staring down at the fallen man who slowly tumbled over on his side, his fingers intertwined with the pitchfork tines. A soft groan escaped his lips, and he rolled onto his back.

The distant flames threw a cold yellow glow about the dying man. Blood trickled down the side of his mouth and dripped into the darkness beneath him.

Chapter Forty-three

To the south, hoofbeats sounded above the roar of the fire. Ben staggered outside for Barnett's handgun. Quickly, he reloaded and turned back to the barn.

Just as he stepped through the door, a terrifying scream froze him. Albert Barnett, his expensive vest soaked with blood, and his face twisted with hate, charged Ben with the pitchfork.

Ben's hand flashed to the six-gun and two shots boomed, one report on top of the other. Albert Barnett's feet shot up in the air as the 250-grain slugs slammed his head backward. He struck the ground and lay motionless.

Ben stared down at the man, finally daring to breathe.

Behind him, a voice called out, "Elliott!"

Without hesitation, Ben leaped into the shadows of the barn, expecting gunfire, but there was nothing but silence.

The voice spoke again, raw, guttural. "I know you're in there, Elliott. Come on out. We got you surrounded." It was Rafe Borke.

Drawing deeper into the shadows, Ben remained silent. He ejected the two spent shells and replaced them with heavy slugs powered by thirty grains of black powder.

"Barnett? You in there?"

Ben remained silent. Borke didn't know who, if anyone, was in the barn.

"Barnett! You hear me? Answer if you're in there."

The eerie yellow light from the fire no longer poured through the open door for the racing flames were now far to the north.

There came a scuffling of feet outside the barn. Ben rose in the shadows so he could see the door. Voices came through the darkness. "You can't burn it down. Barnett might be in there, unconscious or something."

Borke guffawed. "Tough. He shoulda answered."

"Maybe he's unconscious," said a third voice.

"That's his bad luck. I don't need him. He showed me what he was up to. I can do the same thing he done."

A dark object flew through the open door and clanged against a post. Suddenly, the acrid stench of coal oil filled the barn. A lit match looped through the darkness to the floor. For a brief moment when the match struck, it flickered, then the coal oil caught, and a blue and yellow flame raced into the barn.

"Watch for him on that side," Borke yelled.

"We got 'em," came the reply. "He'll never get out on this side."

The flames leaped high, fueled by the dried hay piled in a corner. Ben had to move fast. In seconds, the barn would be a funeral pyre. Staying in the shadows, he aimed several kicks at the side of the clapboard barn, then raced back to the door.

His ploy worked. Several shouts came from outside. "Around the side. He's breaking out the side of the barn."

Shadows flew past the open door. Taking a deep breath, Ben broke from the barn and raced across the hardpan to the main house. The distant flames silhouetted him, and with each step, he expected to hear shouts of discovery.

He jumped on the porch and leaped for the door, slinging it open. He took one step inside, and his head exploded.

Ben opened his eyes to the sun streaming through the window, framing him where he lay on the floor.

A rough voiced chortled, "Look who's woke up. Just in time for his own hanging."

Jess Lowry laughed, a cruel braying. "Yep. No sense in hanging a man unconscious. He don't get the full effect of his punishment that way."

Rough hands jerked Ben to his feet. Still groggy, he struggled weakly against the steel claws holding him. "You'll never get away with this, Lowry. Hazlett's around. He'll run you down."

"Don't bet on it," the sheriff shot back. "Them federal boys got no jurisdiction over Prescott. That's me."

"Stop the palavering," Rafe Borke grunted. "Let's get on with it. Shoulda done it last night."

Jess Lowry shook his head. "Wouldn't have been legal, not with me not here. This way, nobody can say nothing."

Borke opened the door, shoved Ben on the porch ahead of him, and froze.

In a semicircle around the porch sat thirty war-painted Apaches forking wiry ponies. Each brave held a cocked Winchester trained on the front door. In the middle of the Apaches astride their ponies sat Mary Catheryn Wills, P. H. Hall, and Ike Hazlett.

Hazlett spoke up. "Just drop them handguns, boys. Else, you're gonna be host to a heap of lead."

Handguns clattered to the plank floor.

"Not me," shouted Rafe Borke, giving Ben a shove and leaping back into the house and slamming the door.

Ben jumped to his feet and started for the door, but a chilling scream from inside stopped him. Moments later, White Eye emerged from the house, wiped his bloody knife on his bare thigh, and nodded to Ben. "Little Tin Man not worry about this one."

Ben and Mary Catheryn forked two ponies facing Ike Hazlett and his prisoner, P. H. Hall. Behind the marshal, eight frightened cowpokes sat in their saddles, wrists bound to saddle horns. And behind the owlhoots was Marshal Hazlett's posse, thirty savage Apaches.

"With what I know and Hall's testimony about the land titles, you got nothing to worry about, Ben. From the first, I didn't reckon you'd done any of them things, but Barnett had a lot of friends in powerful places."

Mary Catheryn looked up at Ben, her eyes beaming with happiness. "I'm just glad it's all over, Marshal. I want to thank you for your help."

Hazlett laughed. "You're the one who did it, miss. I'd never had the nerve to call them Apaches in like you did."

White Eye pulled up beside Ben. He looked at Mary Catheryn. "Little Tin Man and his woman will always be welcome in the wickiup of White Eye."

Mary Catheryn blushed. Ben laid his hand on hers. "We'd be right happy to take you up on that offer." He hesitated and grinned at Mary Catheryn. "Wouldn't we?"

Her blush deepened. She nodded. "Yes," was all she said.

BARJACK AND THE UNWELCOME GHOST

Marshal Barjack likes to keep peace and quiet in the tiny town of Asininity. It's better for business at the Hooch House, the saloon that Barjack owns. But peace and quiet got mighty hard to come by once Harm Cody came to town. Cody's made a lot of enemies over the years and some of them are hot on his trail, aiming to kill him—including a Cherokee named Miller and a pretty little sharpshooter named Polly Pistol. And when the Asininity bank gets robbed, well, now Cody has a whole new bunch of enemies . . . including Barjack.

Robert J. Conley

ISBN 13: 978-0-8439-6225-3

The Classic Film Collection

The Searchers by Alan LeMay

Hailed as one of the greatest American films, *The Searchers*, directed by John Ford and starring John Wayne, has had a direct influence on the works of Martin Scorsese, Steven Spielberg, and many others. Its gorgeous cinematic scope and deeply nuanced characters have proven timeless. And now available for the first time in decades is the powerful novel that inspired this iconic movie.

Destry Rides Again by Max Brand

Made in 1939, the Golden Year of Hollywood, *Destry Rides Again* helped launch Jimmy Stewart's career and made Marlene Dietrich an American icon. Now available for the first time in decades is the novel that inspired this much-loved movie.

The Man from Laramie by T. T. Flynn

In its original publication, *The Man from Laramie* had more than half a million copies in print. Shortly thereafter, it became one of the most recognized of the Anthony Mann/Jimmy Stewart collaborations, known for darker films with morally complex characters. Now the novel upon which this classic movie was based is once again available—for the first time in more than fifty years.

The Unforgiven by Alan LeMay

In this epic American novel, which served as the basis for the classic film directed by John Huston and starring Burt Lancaster and Audrey Hepburn, a family is torn apart when an old enemy starts a vicious rumor that sets the range aflame. Don't miss the powerful novel that inspired the film the *Motion Picture Herald* calls "an absorbing and compelling drama of epic proportions."

To order a book or to request a catalog call:
1-800-481-9191
Books are also available at your local bookstore, or you can check out our Web site **www.dorchesterpub.com**.

Cotton Smith

"Cotton Smith turns in a terrific story every time."
—*Roundup Magazine*

Tanneman Rose was a Texas Ranger turned bad. When he and his gang robbed a bank, he brought shame to the badge. A jury found him guilty, a judge sentenced him, but Rose swore he wouldn't die in prison. Instead he died while trying to escape. Time Carlow helped to capture his fellow Ranger that day at the bank, and now he's investigating a very odd series of murders. Each victim was involved in sending Tanneman Rose to jail. Could it be a coincidence? Or is Rose's gang out for revenge? Or Rose, himself? Time doesn't believe in ghosts—or coincidences. He's got to find the answers and stop the murders...before he becomes the latest victim.

Death Mask

ISBN 13: 978-0-8439-6200-0

Based on the immortal hero from the bestselling
Riders of the Purple Sage!

ZANE GREY'S™ LASSITER

BROTHER GUN

JACK SLADE

Lassiter, the solitary hero from Zane Grey's *Riders of the Purple Sage*, became one of the greatest Western legends of all time. Now America's favorite roughrider is back in further adventures filled with gun-slinging action and rawhide-tough characters.

BLOOD BROTHER

Lassiter owed Miguel Aleman for saving his life. To repay the favor, he swears to protect Miguel's troublesome son Juanito. He never thought he'd have to make good on his oath so soon, though. When Juanito kills a horse trader in a drunken brawl, he faces the gallows—unless Lassiter can save him. But the only option Lassiter has is to break the law himself...which might very well leave him swinging right along with his blood brother.

ISBN 13: 978-0-8439-6238-3

□ **YES!**

Sign me up for the Leisure Western Book Club and send my FREE BOOKS! If I choose to stay in the club, I will pay only $14.00* each month, a savings of $9.96!

NAME: _____

ADDRESS: _____

TELEPHONE: _____

EMAIL: _____

□ I want to pay by credit card.

□ **VISA**   □ **MasterCard**   □ **DISCOVER**

ACCOUNT #: _____

EXPIRATION DATE: _____

SIGNATURE: _____

Mail this page along with $2.00 shipping and handling to:
Leisure Western Book Club
PO Box 6640
Wayne, PA 19087
Or fax (must include credit card information) to:
610-995-9274

You can also sign up online at **www.dorchesterpub.com**.

*Plus $2.00 for shipping. Offer open to residents of the U.S. and Canada only. Canadian residents please call 1-800-481-9191 for pricing information. under 18, a parent or guardian must sign. Terms, prices and conditions subject to ange. Subscription subject to acceptance. Dorchester Publishing reserves the right to reject any order or cancel any subscription.

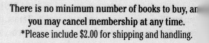